ASCENDING SPECIES

ASCENDING SPECIES

RAND PAULSEN

BROWN BOOKS
PUBLISHING GROUP

Ascending Species: A Novel

Brown Books Publishing Group
Dallas, TX/New York, NY
www.BrownBooks.com
(972) 381-0009

A New Era in Publishing®

Publisher's Cataloging-In-Publication Data

Names: Paulsen, Rand, author.
Title: Ascending species / Rand Paulsen.
Description: Dallas, TX ; New York, NY : Brown Books Publishing Group, [2025]
Identifiers: ISBN: 978-1-61254-713-8
Subjects: LCSH: Extraterrestrial beings--Fiction. | Outer space--Fiction. | Civilization--Fiction. | Animal species--Fiction. | Planets--Fiction. | LCGFT: Science fiction. | Action and adventure fiction. | BISAC: FICTION / Science Fiction / Space Exploration. | FICTION / Science Fiction / Action & Adventure.
Classification: LCC: PS3616.A9536 A83 2025 | DDC: 813/.6--dc23

ISBN 978-1-61254-713-8
LCCN 2024951090

Printed in the United States
10 9 8 7 6 5 4 3 2 1

For more information or to contact the author, please go to www.AscendingSpecies.com.

CONTENTS

FOREWORD

This text chronicles four nonhuman Species. Good faith has been applied in translating the information into the human language in which you are reading this, as well as adaptation to include the cultural concepts, expressions, and perspectives relevant to the time and place of publication. Inaccuracies are possible and probable due to errors in translation.

Allow for difficulties with translation.

Read slow. Pause to contemplate.

Engage your imagination and enjoy the images in your mind.

Be aware that everything depicted here is, in reality, much stranger than you think.

—Dnar

PROLOGUE

The day starts as usual, except for the meteor streaking a red line high in the sky.

The other primates are jumping down from the trees. She jumps down from the tree.

The others are moving toward the river. She follows.

She hears a loud, sharp cry behind her.

Everyone looks. Someone is trying to stand, favoring a leg. She can see that the leg is broken.

The one with the broken leg cries again. Everyone else scatters for cover in the tall grass or the trees.

Injuries attract predators.

She goes to the grass. There are roots and possibly other food there.

As she's chewing a tasty root, a shrill scream comes from the one with the broken leg. A predator has arrived.

She carefully peers through the tall grass until she's sure that only *one* predator has come.

The screaming stops.

It should be safe to move on.

A pod of the two-tentacle Species notices a large school of their favorite food.

The food is a small, fast-moving fish with poor eyesight.

These fish can quickly change color to blend in with their background or with the rest of the school. The small fish are easily influenced by passing vegetation, rock formations, or anything else that catches an eye.

When one of the fish changes colors, others quickly change to the same color. This creates a flashing effect across the entire large school.

The small fish also try to follow the others in their school. This causes the fish to dart back and forth as they try to follow each other. Schools often split up but usually merge back together.

The frequent color changes and rapid movements make the fish stand out. The feeder fish are easy to spot by larger fish and the two-tentacle Species.

The feeder fish tend to stay grouped together in large numbers, though small schools occasionally end up trapped in shallow water or the cliff caves.

The pod of the two-tentacle Species patrols the shallows for their meals.

The large reptiles are aware of the things in the sky. However, the meteors passing overhead don't seem to be important.

The large reptiles ignore the sky. They continue their normal daily lives of napping in the tall grass, crawling through the trees, hunting food, and avoiding danger.

The red streaks in the sky increase in number and run from horizon to horizon.

The four-legged, burrowing Species is concerned about the strange sky.

They spend most of their time collecting vegetables, nuts, and fruits. What happens in the sky could affect their scavenging.

They hoard food in their underground burrows and can usually stay underground for ten to fifteen days at a time.

On this day, the burrowing animals do not venture out for more food. They instinctively sense a storm and remain in their shelters to wait it out.

She and the others in her group of primates have seen streaks in the sky before. Although before, the streaks were white or black.

This time, the streaks in the sky are red.

The daylight is getting dimmer. Something is not right.

The group grows increasingly agitated.

Over the course of many days, the two-tentacle Species notices that the shallow water is getting darker.

By instinct, they believe a storm must be coming. By habit, they retreat into deeper water to avoid any possible danger near the surface.

She and her group watch as the red streaks turn into red clouds that fill the entire sky. Days of diminishing sunlight continue.

The air hangs heavy, and it's becoming more difficult to breathe. The group *should* be very agitated, but instead, they are listless.

Many begin to get sick.

At first, the reptiles are pleased with the easy meals of dead and dying prey. Then they notice the dying plants, which concerns the reptiles on an instinctive level.

Other reptiles of their kind are also found dead or dying. The large reptiles would normally consider them to be additional easy food, but the reptiles find they have little or no appetite.

They just want to sleep.

The burrowing Species waits through many days of very little sunlight. Their stores of hoarded food dwindle.

They ration their food, but soon it is completely gone. They're getting hungry. They must find more food soon.

The air in their burrows is smelling bad, too.

The surface of the water becomes pinkish. Then it turns bright red.

The two-tentacle Species retreats to deeper water, but they can only go so deep. The disturbing red water continues to descend into the depths.

The redness seems to kill everything in its path, and the foul red water is inescapable.

QUEUE

The large reptile crawls through the dead underbrush, searching for something to eat. Food has been difficult to find. Also, he is too weak to do much of a hunt.

He comes across a small clearing among some dead trees. He gets a bit of luck. There are several egg-nest mounds here. The reptile recognizes the nests as those of his own kind—shallow pits covered with a thin layer of loose dirt.

The first mound is disturbed. All the eggs are broken. Aside from the eggs being larger than usual, it seems like a typical hatch. The first one or two hatchlings often eat the remaining unhatched eggs.

The second mound is only partially disturbed. There are some empty eggshells, but he should find some unhatched eggs. He draws a front claw slowly through the soft dirt.

He finds it difficult to stand on only three weary legs.

The reptile notices a disturbance in another mound. The dirt is moving. It's the sign of an emerging hatchling.

The reptile works his way over to the disturbance. A hatchling pushes its head and the top of its eggshell through the dirt. Moving as quickly as he can manage, he gets to the hatchling while it's still trembling in the bottom of its shell.

The reptile pauses briefly at the sight of the hatchling.

Maybe these are not of his kind. Yes, the hatchling looks like one of his kind, but its head is too big, and its eyes are closer together.

A few quick chews and he gulps it down.

The reptile finds an unhatched egg. Using a technique learned from much practice, he sticks the tips of his two front claws and back pincer claw carefully into the eggshell and pries it open. A third of the shell is removed.

A body falls out of the egg. The tiny reptile was close to hatching. This one also looks strange with the large head and short tail.

A few quick chews and he gulps it down.

The reptile rakes the mound, searching for another egg. He hears a rustling in the brush near the edge of the clearing. He looks—but sees nothing.

He checks his surroundings. He returns to clawing through the mound.

More brush rustling. The sound is coming from the end of the clearing. A hatchling emerges from the brush and stops at the edge of the clearing.

This hatchling is big. It might not be worth trying to catch.

The large reptile sees movement on the side where there are more trees. Three hatchlings emerge and scamper around.

Soon after, there's movement on the side with fewer trees. Two more hatchlings appear on that side.

The reptile watches the hatchlings scurry around, in and out of the mostly dead brush, on both sides.

At the end of the clearing, the larger hatchling remains motionless. The larger hatchling stares back at him. Its eyes are too close together.

Then, the larger hatchling *stands up on only its back two legs!* The large reptile is surprised and disturbed.

The reptile notices that the larger hatchling was bleeding from several places.

The larger hatchling appears to have deep wounds on its front leg and shoulder, likely from a fight in the nest after hatching. Some of the smaller cuts could have been from the sharp edges of eggshells.

Not many leave the nest without some lifelong scars.

The large reptile looks to one side of the clearing. Those two hatchlings are now standing on their back legs.

His anxiety increases. They should not be standing on two legs.

On the other side, one of the three hatchlings is staring at him. This hatchling slowly circles behind the large reptile.

At least this hatchling is on all four legs.

He glances back at the larger hatchling. It's still standing on two legs at the end of the clearing. It's staring at him, calmly.

The reptile doesn't like this. There are too many of them and they're behaving strangely. He starts to back off.

As the reptile backs away, the larger hatchling begins slowly moving toward him. The larger hatchling is *walking*—on only two legs!

The reptile recoils. This is extremely disturbing.

The reptile turns away.

One of the three hatchlings suddenly rushes toward him. By reflex, the reptile flinches and backs away.

The large reptile moves to leave the clearing.

The hatchling runs ahead of him a short distance. It stops and turns back. It stands up on its back two legs and looks at him.

Something is very wrong here. The reptile hurries to leave.

The hatchling darts toward him again, but it veers off. The hatchling circles ahead and stops.

The reptile slows his pace as he tracks the strange hatchling.

Suddenly, he feels sharp stabbing pains in both of his lower back legs. He stumbles. He looks back.

Two hatchlings scurry away from him.

The large reptile stops to inspect the areas of the pain. He's bleeding. He's been bitten, on both legs!

This is bad.

The injuries will make it difficult to walk.

What kind of creatures are these? Yet somehow, he believes that they are his own kind, even though they are different.

The thought is terrifying.

There's movement all around him. In a quick glance, he takes in the scene.

Hatchlings are charging at him from all sides. All of them, except for the larger hatchling. It's at the end of the clearing, on two legs, *walking* toward him.

The reptile locks eyes with the larger hatchling and shivers.

That calm stare is the last thing the reptile sees before another hatchling lands on his face and slashes out his eyes.

She rests in her burrow and waits. She remembers when the sky turned red, and almost everything died. Food has been difficult to find since then. She is one of a small number of her pack to still be alive.

It's the birthing season now. This will be her third litter. This litter has been difficult and painful. She's been feeling sick for most of this pregnancy.

Something doesn't feel right inside her.

Things should be better soon. The water is clear again. The plants are coming back. Nuts are appearing on the surviving trees.

Ow! The pain keeps getting worse. Her belly is very big. This is going to be a large litter. She's eager for them to be out of her.

She nibbles on one of the remaining roots. She hasn't been able to gather food for many days. She's unable to move much, and her stomach is too big to fit through the tunnel.

For now, she's trapped in the burrow.

Oww! The large litter shifts inside her. Excruciating pains stab down her back legs. At these moments, all she can do is squirm and withstand the pain until it passes.

The litter is finally starting to come! She already feels so weak. Something is wrong. The first one isn't coming out. Something inside her is blocking it.

She squirms and shivers. She has to push out the blockage. Waves of stabbing pain consume her.

Through the pain, she senses a change. It moved! The blockage is moving out.

She gasps and breathes heavily. She looks down through tear-filled eyes.

To her horror, she sees that the blockage is a large wriggling head.

It's too big! She lets out a long, quivering squeal and passes out.

Unconsciousness fades, but complete awareness does not come before she passes out again.

She slowly begins to wake. After a groggy moment, she realizes that her litter is nursing. She looks down.

She is confused by what she's seeing. There is no litter. There is just one very large baby, and it's *purple*, not tan. She passes out again.

She wakes in a panic, feeling unsteady. She looks around the burrow. There is the baby—the one, strange-looking, very large, purple baby.

It's sleeping.

She knows that she must eat. She looks for a root. They're all gone. There's not even a leaf or twig.

Her nipples are sore, and her mammary feels empty. The baby must have eaten everything it could find.

She tries to get on her feet. She hurts everywhere. Her back legs are not working right. She crawls, dragging herself with her front legs, across the burrow chamber.

She clambers up to the exit and pulls herself into the tunnel.

She manages to slide down the sloping part of the passage. She must stop several times to let the pain subside and catch her breath.

The last part of the tunnel goes upward before opening to the outside. She needs to rest for a moment. The brighter light and fresh air are rejuvenating.

She notices that the air lacks the pungent scent of vegetation.

Strange. The wind must be blowing in an unusual direction.

Finally, she reaches the opening. She struggles through the opening. Her front legs burn from the exertion.

With her back legs still hanging inside the tunnel, she eagerly chews on a tuft of grass. Instead of just eating the tips, she eats all of it, down to the dirt.

She rests her head on the ground for a moment. She feels sick to her stomach.

She begins to crawl toward the top of the hill. She needs to get over the hill and into the meadow to find good roots.

Near the top of the hill, she realizes that she still doesn't smell the meadow. She takes a strong whiff. There's barely a scent of it.

Panic builds!

She hurries to the top of the hill and looks down. She is shocked by what she sees!

Something bad has happened to the meadow. Large areas of it are bare ground. About a quarter of the meadow is just . . . gone!

She sees movement in the tall grass nearby. If it's a predator, she will not be able to run away. Something rises out of the grass.

To her astonishment, it looks like her baby, except that it is much larger.

The, uh, "baby" is bigger than her. It's standing on only its hind legs. The baby is chewing and looking around.

It sees her. It begins to move toward her.

She is amazed to see the strange baby *walk* on only two legs!

The baby approaches her. It's still chewing. It tilts its head sideways and looks at her. It extends a front leg toward her.

The baby is holding a half-eaten bulbous root in its extended paw. In its other front paw, it's holding a bunch of other bulbous roots.

The giant baby takes another bite of the root and looks at her while it chews.

She doesn't know what to do or even what to think. She just stares up at it with her mouth hanging open.

The strange baby puts the last bite of the root in its mouth.

It takes a few more steps toward her. The giant baby sways side to side as it walks on only its back legs.

While still chewing, the giant baby selects another root and drops the rest on the ground in front of her.

She kinks her neck to look up at the baby's strange, yet familiar face.

She watches, astounded, as the giant purple baby wobbles away on only two legs.

She sits in the trees with the others of her group of primates. She nibbles on a fruit and rubs her extended belly.

She is among the pregnant females for the first time this season. As usual, the older, dominant female was the first to be pregnant. The older, dominant female has been the first to have a baby for the last four seasons.

The older, dominant female is usually the first at everything: the first to drink when they find a river, the first to eat when the males bring back food.

That is the way the group thinks of her: "the First."

Most in the group are wary of the First. The First is often angry and quick to lash out at someone in the group.

The First is angry now. One of the other females is having a baby before the First has had her baby. The First walks among the group, hissing at some, hitting others.

The other female is taking much longer than usual to have the baby.

The other female suddenly screams. The other female wails the howl of fear. Then the other female wails the howl of loss.

Something is wrong.

A circle of people quickly forms around the other female.

Many in the group become agitated. Some leave the circle with a look of disgust. Some, particularly the pregnant females, leave with looks of concern and fear.

She moves closer.

The First is standing over the other female. The First is happy about something.

She works her way closer to look at the baby. The group continues to behave strangely, and she sees why.

The baby is all wrong.

Its head is too big. It has no hair. Its face is weird. The baby appears to be dead.

The sight of the stillborn, malformed baby sends shockwaves through the group.

The situation grows worse when another pregnant female has the same thing happen. That baby also comes out dead and malformed.

All the pregnant females are afraid, even the First.

Everyone is agitated.

Tension mounts within the group. There are fights among the males. The females are suspicious of each other. The situation is dangerous.

The time comes for the First to have her baby. The First goes off to be alone.

The cry of a baby comes from the grass near the river.

In anticipation, all heads turn to look in that direction. Everyone seems to be anxiously holding their breath.

A scream comes from the First. Then the First wails the howl of fear.

Even though it's known that the First does not like anyone to watch her having her babies, everyone rushes over to see what has happened.

Instead of walking over and standing at the back of the crowd like before, and because it *is* the First, she climbs up a nearby tree to get a look.

The baby is sprawled in the grass, crying. Even from the tree, she can see that the baby is pale and has no hair.

The group is not happy. The baby is malformed like the others.

The First is moaning and hissing at the group that has surrounded her. The First beats her fist on the ground.

The First avoids the baby.

The First must be weak from the birth, but she pulls herself to her feet. She hisses at some of those surrounding her. The First attacks a pregnant female who is standing at the front of the group.

The pregnant female waddles away quickly.

The whimpering baby is struck by some dirt kicked up by the First. The baby screams and cries.

In an angry frenzy, the First picks up a rock and lunges over to the crying baby. The First slams the rock down on the baby's head.

The baby stops crying.

The group stands there for a moment, stiff and silent. Then they begin to move away. The First drifts toward the river with her head down.

The motionless baby is left behind.

The light in the sky is fading.

She carefully climbs down from the tree. She decides to hide from the group. She's not sure what will happen now, and she's scared.

Her time is growing near. She is very agitated. Another baby has come out dead and malformed.

Another young female is now making the sounds of *her* first baby coming.

She must see what happens with this baby. She climbs a nearby tree to watch.

A group gathers around the young female. The First is there.

It seems like this is taking a very long time. She shifts around in the tree many times to find comfortable spots.

Finally, there is a commotion below.

She hears the cry of the baby, followed by the young female wailing the howl of fear. She sees the hairless baby between the young female's legs.

The young female sits silently, staring at the baby. The baby cries softly.

The First comes into view. The First tries to give a rock to the young female, who continues to just sit there.

The First becomes agitated, screeching and jumping around. The First charges and hits the young female several times.

The First puts the rock in the young female's hand. The young female drops the rock and tries to crawl away.

The First grabs her by the hair and yanks her back to the baby. The First puts the rock back in the young female's hand.

Breathing heavily, the young female sluggishly lifts the rock over her head. The young female sits there for a long moment, just holding the rock above the malformed baby.

The First is not happy.

The First screeches and jumps around. She pounds her fists on the ground.

The young female continues to hold the rock over the baby.

The First rushes in at the young female, stepping on the baby.

The baby lets out a loud wail. The baby screams and cries while the First hits the young female many times.

The shaking young female tries to crawl away again.

The First pushes and pulls the moaning young female back to the baby. Again, the First puts the rock in the young female's hand.

The First screeches at the young female.

The young female slumps to the ground, breathing heavily and bleeding a lot.

The baby cries loud, long wails.

The First moves up behind the prone young female and bashes her on the head with a large rock, many times. The young female doesn't move again.

The First jumps over to the crying baby, still holding the bloody rock.

The dismayed group begins to back away. Some turn and leave quickly.

The First repeatedly smashes the baby with the rock. The baby stops making noise.

The First looks up at a few of the group who are still watching her. The First hits the baby a couple more times with the rock. The First looks at them again.

The stragglers avert their eyes and move away, following the others.

She tries to avoid the group, but it's very risky to be alone. There are dangers, like predators and bugs.

She must go among the group occasionally. She doesn't like to, but someone is always near the food and water.

The others of the group look at her badly.

They look at all the pregnant females this way.

Soon, another female is having her baby. She watches from a distance this time.

She knows what has happened from the wails and how the group moves away. It's another stillborn, malformed baby.

The daylight will be fading soon. Most of the group has left the river in search of food or a place to sleep. She is very thirsty and must get water.

She takes a good, long drink from the river.

In the still water, she stares at her reflection and the patch of lighter gray skin above her right eye. She never thought about the unique marking before.

Now, she covers her hand over the blemish.

A sharp pain jolts her, and she lets out a brief cry. She instantly wishes that she hadn't made a sound.

Someone downstream is watching her.

Her baby is starting to come. She hurries into the tall grass.

She carefully settles herself onto the spot she's prepared. It's a small area where she has stepped down the grass, pushing it to the ground to make a soft place.

The surrounding grass should be tall enough to hide her.

She has seen some pregnant females do this in other seasons.

She hears movement in the grass nearby. She tries to be quiet. It doesn't matter if it's a predator or one of the group. The fear is the same.

A small one from the group has found her!

More from the group arrive.

A painful muscle spasm grips her. Her baby is coming.

The baby demands all her attention now. There's nothing she can do about the others.

The pain is much worse than she expected. She fears that there is something wrong with her baby.

The group around her is agitated. It's taking a very long time.

She just wants it to be *over!*

Finally, she hears the baby cry.

She suddenly realizes that she has been screaming, from the pain—and the fear.

She glances down hesitantly.

Her heart sinks. The baby is deformed like the others. It has the big head. Its face is ugly and there's no hair anywhere on its body that she can see.

She is so deeply disappointed and confused. Her spirit is crushed. She feels like she wants to wail the howl of loss.

She tries to catch her breath. She looks down again and grimaces at this disturbing thing that has come out of her.

The First appears and approaches. The First puts a large rock in her hand, obviously so that she can kill the grotesque baby.

Instinctively, she takes the rock from the First. She rolls forward and kneels in front of the baby.

She lifts the rock over her head. The baby is wiggling around and looking back at her.

Its eyes . . . there's something about its eyes. Its eyes are looking into her eyes.

The baby is crying softly, and its little hand is reaching for her.

She lowers the rock. She doesn't want to kill it.

The others become agitated.

She wants to drop the rock. She wants to crawl away, but she's drawn to the baby's eyes and its gentle crying.

The First *roars!*

The First lunges in, grabs the baby's leg, and pulls at it.

The First tugs at the baby's leg again.

She realizes that the First is going to drag the baby away and kill it!

An impulse spurs her. A reflex. In one motion, she springs to her feet and straddles over the crying baby.

She hisses with intensity at the First. She hisses at the others.

The First charges in and knocks her away.

She hits the ground but rolls onto her feet. She looks back.

The First stands over the baby.

Some in the group are somberly circling the scene. Others are turning away.

The First raises both fists in the air, preparing to strike down on the baby. The First looks at her and smiles.

Anger and . . . something else, swell in her.

She charges and knocks the First away, before the First can hurt the baby.

Her baby!

The others are surprised and confused. A couple of the others screech and make lunging motions toward her.

She realizes that she is still holding the rock in her hand. She raises the rock over her head and hisses at the others.

She circles, keeping the baby, *her* baby, at her feet.

More of the others become agitated, whooping and screeching. A few are lunging and retreating.

She stands her ground. She feels a fierceness that she's never known before.

A male lunges at her. She aggressively hisses at him. He backs off.

The shifty First tries to charge in while her back is turned.

She sees it!

She roars and turns as the First charges. Just as the First slams into her, she swings the rock down with all her strength.

The rock strikes the First on the head.

There is a loud crack, like when the big, brown predators hit their heads against hollow, dead trees.

With the momentum from the First charging, their two bodies plummet to the ground. They roll together in the grass.

She comes up fast and quickly gets back to her baby. She circles and hisses, readying herself for another attack.

Silence falls over the group.

The First isn't getting up. The First's head is smashed and gushing blood.

The others look at the motionless First. Reactions range from shock and disbelief to relief and happiness.

They look at her. She lost the rock after she hit the First, but she is still determined!

The others slowly back away.

Keeping her eyes on the others, she picks up her crying baby. She holds the baby to her breast. The baby stops crying and begins to suckle.

She watches as the crowd fades away.

She sits on the trampled grass. Her whole body is shaking. She holds the baby's large head in her hand and allows the baby to feed.

She looks around at those of the group who are still there.

They show no aggression. They're just watching her. She realizes that they are all pregnant females.

All the babies born during the rest of the season have the same strange deformities. Some are stillborn, but nobody tries to kill any more of the babies that are born alive.

All the other females decide to care for their babies, too.

Some of the younger females even try to use a bit of mud to emulate the unique streak of lighter gray skin that she has above her right eye.

Her baby has a near-matching streak of darker gray skin above *his* right eye.

The first moment of awareness is of a light in the darkness. It isn't much, just a faint, dull glow, but the light creates a contrast.

Then the light is gone.

The darkness fades from the light, but not all the darkness. The light begins to create a sense of direction.

There is light again, and then it's gone again. It's there, then it's gone. The changing light begins to create a sense of time.

The darkness is nothing, the light is something. When the light fades to the darkness, it creates a sense of desire.

A desire for the light.

The light comes again. To go in this direction is to get closer to the light. To get closer to the light is to get more light.

With more light, there is more awareness.

Something is in the way of getting to the light.

Straining against the obstruction causes it to separate.

Moving past the barrier, seeing that the light is much brighter outside of the barrier, watching the barrier sink slowly down and into the darkness, desiring to go to the light, realizing that it's now easier to move toward the light—all of this creates a sense of self.

I am me.

There is something else. It drifts nearby. It is consumed and creates a desire to consume more, like the desire for more light.

Others drift along nearby.

The others are very large. When the others are in front of the light, they dim the light. The others are similarly shaped.

I am shaped like the others!

Now, after many passings of the light, I have learned much.

The world is divided into three parts: the water, the air, and the land.

The people live in the water between the land and where the bottom ends. Past the bottom, the water goes deeper than anybody can go.

Other things live in our water, too. There are plants, small creatures that crawl among the rocks, and many kinds of fish.

Some of the fish are very small. Some fish are about the size of one of my eyes and there are fish that are much larger.

The people eat the plants and the smaller fish.

The larger fish would not fit into our orifice.

The people have long, round bodies, tentacles, and a central orifice where the body joins the tentacles. We circulate water in and out of our orifice to breathe.

The younger people all have four tentacles and four eyes—one eye over each tentacle. Our eyes are at the middle of our bodies.

The older people have two tentacles and two eyes, also an eye over each tentacle.

There are other differences between the older and younger, too.

The older people are quiet while us younger people try to communicate with air bubbles and brief vibrations we make with our orifice.

We feel the vibrations on our skin.

The older people like to eat one type of the smaller fish. They wait for the small fish in shallower water or against the cliffs that are part of the land.

There are not very many of these fish. They can slowly change color, but they are slow swimmers and easy to catch.

Us younger people work together to catch small fish. Also, we drift into schools of the very small fish and can catch them simply by breathing in the water.

The older people have no interest in the air or the land. Us younger people are interested in the air—and *very* interested in the land.

We like to put the ends of our tentacles or even most of a tentacle into the air.

Also, we can roll our bodies upside-down and get our orifices into the air. We've learned that we only need to breathe a small amount of air, compared to a large amount of water.

The older ones never try to breathe the air.

We also like to float on the surface with an eye above the water. This is how we learned about *the land.*

The land looks very different.

Us younger people like to look at the land. When the water rises up, we can see a lot before the water drops back down.

Occasionally, one of us tries to swim closer to the land. Some have floated back dead. Some never came back at all, and we wonder about their fate.

I am very close to the land now.

I'm at the point where the water lifts me up and drops me back down. This is where we can get the best look at the land, if only for a moment.

From here, I can see the area where the water meets the land. This area looks to be without life, a blank area.

Beyond that is what looks like *land* plants. The land plants are a similar color to the water plants, only much brighter.

I am now closer to the land than I have ever been.

I see something strange that I've never noticed before. There's a weird spot between the blank area and the cliffs. Something's different.

I want to get closer.

This *is* a curious spot. The water rises and falls against the cliffs on one side. The water rises and falls against the blank area on the other side. The water seems to flow into this spot.

I must get closer.

I'm in front of the strange spot. The cliffs go up very high on one side. On the other side, the cliffs do not go very high out of the water.

The water lifts me up, and I can see into the strange spot.

There is a small blank area back in there. The rise of water is going up and down too fast. I'm unable to get a good look.

I need to get closer.

I watch for the next rise in the water with the two eyes that look away from the land. Here it comes. The water is starting to rise.

What is this?

I've never seen this before. This side of the rise of water is like a short cliff.

It's lifting me up. Up and forward. Now I'm sliding down the cliff of water.

I turn three eyes toward the land.

Searching into the strange spot, I see a small, short, blank area. Behind that, it looks like a kind of cliff, some kind of land.

I'm falling out of the water from the top of the rise. I'm completely in the air and spinning!

Then I'm back in the water and tumbling.

I'm not sure which way is to the air. I feel uneasy. I spread out my tentacles and feel air on one of them.

I turn to get an eye in the air. I see another cliff of water coming at me.

It's lifting me up. I try to swim down the cliff of water before it lifts me up and drops me through the air again.

I swim as fast as I can, but I'm stuck between the top of the rise and the water below.

The cliff of water is pushing me toward the land—very fast.

The top of the cliff of water is going over me. I'm tumbling around in the water again.

I'm scared! What have I done?

I need to get away from the land and back to the calm water.

It's another cliff of water!

I don't want to get tumbled around again. I lean my body down the cliff and swim as fast as I can.

Somehow, I'm staying in the middle of the cliff of water again.

I'm still being pushed toward the land, though. The little blank area is coming at me very fast! Is this what the others saw before they died?

The little blank area is right there! To the sides, the land cliffs are very close and getting closer. The cliff of water is pushing me faster toward the land.

Everything is happening too fast.

I'm not sure which eye to use!

The cliff of water lifts me up. I'm very high up above the—*Whaaa?*

There is no water under me. *It's the Blank!*

Uuuuhhhh, what happened?

There is an unpleasant feeling on part of my body and in one tentacle. I'm unable to move two tentacles at all. They are stuck in the Blank. I can't move.

I'm completely out of the water!

I'm stuck in the Blank! I'm going to die like the others.

Here comes another cliff of water!

Uuuhhhh, the water flows over me, and quickly drops back down again.

Now *three* of my tentacles are stuck in the Blank!

Strangely, the Blank got softer in the water. Now, the Blank is hard again.

But the water softens it. I can use my fourth tentacle to push against the Blank. I must get out of the Blank while it's softened by the water.

Here comes another cliff of water!

The water flows over me. Yes, the Blank is loosening. I swim my tentacles to get them out of the Blank.

The water drops away again, extremely fast.

I'm stuck again.

It's not as bad as it was—I think. Only one tentacle is stuck, but I'm more up the Blank and farther from the water.

I think I can get my tentacle out of the Blank. Yes! It's out. But how do I get back into the water?

Here comes another cliff of water!

This time I keep swimming as the water drops away and—I'm not stuck in the Blank. I'm just stuck *on* the Blank.

I guess I just have to wait for another cliff of water.

Something moved over there, on the Blank.

It's one of the creatures that crawls around in the rocks, only it's crawling on the Blank. It's going up the Blank. It's moving from the Blank onto the land rocks.

Here comes another cliff of water!

I'm in the water again! Oh no. The cliff of water lifts me up and over the Blank again.

I think of the land creature. It moved on the Blank. Maybe with my tentacles under me—like the rock creature does it.

Ugghhh! The cliff of water puts me on the Blank, and the water drops away.

I'm stuck in the Blank again.

This time, it's only the ends of my tentacles. Can I get them loose? There's one! There's another! Then the next. It's working.

I now have all four tentacles out of the Blank. I'm also moving across the land.

Amazing! If I move one tentacle, then another, I'm able to move across the Blank—like the rock creature!

I'm doing it. Move one tentacle, then another, then another. I'm moving on the Blank. I'm moving *on the land!*

A crashing behind me? Oh—another cliff of water. I'm so far up on the land that the water didn't even get to me.

I see the tops of land plants. The plants are just over this rise of land.

I must get closer!

Wow! This—there is land for as far as I can see!

In the far distance, the land rises very high into the air. All the land is covered with bright green plants.

I spend a long time looking at all the new sights. Then I realize that the light is passing. I should get back in the water before the darkness.

I want to tell the others about this.

Maybe I can take a piece of land plant with me, to show the others. I reach a tentacle around a small piece. It is easy to pull off a piece of the land plant.

The light has nearly passed. How do I get back into the water? The last time I tried, the cliffs of water pushed me back onto the Blank.

The big Blank area? It's way over there! Can I go that far?

If I hold the piece of land plant with one tentacle, I only have three tentacles to move across the land.

Yes, I can hold the plant with one tentacle and move with the other three.

Move one tentacle, then another, then the third, then the first again. I *can* go that far on the land. I can get to the big Blank area. I just need to keep moving.

There's very little light now. The land of the big Blank area is soft and more difficult to move across.

There are cliffs of water farther out. They fall into little rises long before they reach the Blank. The water is mostly calm along the edge with the Blank.

The outside of my body feels stiff and uncomfortable. It feels like the land plant.

I haven't been in the water for the last part of the light. I haven't had water on me! That must be why my outside feels strange.

I am dry!

Being dry is unpleasant.

The part of my tentacle that's been holding the land plant feels good.

I've crushed the part of the land plant that I have been holding. A slimy, thick water has come out of the plant. The thick water feels good on my tentacle. Smearing the thick water on my body makes that area feel better.

It's almost completely dark. The land of the Blank has become moist and firmer. I can feel the vibrations of the water moving at the edge of the Blank.

Almost there. Yes, there's the water.

Ahh, that feels very good on the ends of my tentacles. My tentacle ends sink into the soft Blank, but I can still move into the water.

I'm in deep enough water now. I can just let myself fall into it.

Aaahhh, the water feels very good on my whole body!

I'm back in the water—and I have the piece of land plant!

During the next passing of the light, I will bring some other young people back here and show them how I can go on the land—how *we can go on the land!*

R1

After a big meal, the reptiles are all lounging around in the short grass, soaking in the heat of midday. The larger reptile absentmindedly scratches at the old wound on his left arm. The wound is healed, but it still itches a lot.

Something twinkles.

There it is again—a bright shine.

The larger reptile lethargically rolls his head in the direction of the twinkling that caught his eye. He's very comfortable with a full stomach and the warmth on his skin.

He watches the twinkling of the bright shine in the distant mountains.

What *is* that bright shine?

After watching it twinkle for a good part of the day, the larger reptile decides to go and see what it is. He's in no hurry. It's just a reason to go in that direction instead of any other direction.

The larger reptile drifts toward the bright shine. The youngest hatchling follows him. With no reason to go in a different direction, the other reptiles follow in the same direction—toward the bright shine.

The larger reptile doesn't hurry toward the bright shine. He's curious about it, but he's more interested in eating. The reptiles go about their daily lives, hunting food and resting in the warmth of midday.

When the reptiles feel like moving, they simply move toward the bright shine.

Occasionally, a reptile will begin to move off in another direction. The larger reptile isn't concerned about where the other reptiles go. The reptiles go in whatever direction interests them. The larger reptile walks on, the youngest hatchling follows, and the rest follow them toward the bright shine.

It's a long journey toward the bright shine. The other reptiles notice the bright shine, too. They don't really care much, but it becomes understood that the direction they are all heading is toward the bright shine.

As the reptiles get closer, the twinkling gets brighter. The bright shine influences their movement from a general direction to a specific spot in the mountains. The curious shining is coming from an outcropping of rock on the side of the mountain.

As the mountain gets steeper, the reptiles slow their pace. Their surroundings change from dirt and trees to hard rock with an occasional tuft of grass. The terrain is rockier, and the footing becomes more unstable.

The larger reptile pauses to catch his breath. He looks for the easiest path forward.

Higher up the side of the mountain, a reptile slips in a patch of loose rocks. The reptile drops to four legs as the patch of rocks slides down the steep slope for a short distance.

Moving carefully, the reptile gets past the gravel and continues climbing.

The larger reptile finds himself on a similar patch of loose rocks. The gravel under his feet shifts slightly downhill. He puts his arms out for balance until he stops sliding.

He hears rocks falling from higher up the mountain. It's the other reptile.

The larger reptile watches as the rock crumbles under the other reptile's feet. It jumps to a ledge a little higher up. The ledge is too narrow.

The reptile jumps again, to a large foothold. Just as that large foothold starts to crumble, the reptile gets a foot onto the next foothold.

Each time the reptile moves to a newer foothold, the brittle rock crumbles underfoot.

The reptile steps to the next foothold, then the next, and the next. The scrambling reptile's pace quickens in a desperate attempt to find solid footing on the increasingly steep and crumbling mountainside.

The larger reptile sees that the other reptile is running out of places to go.

The reptile finally stops running. The reptile clings desperately to the side of the mountain. The rock crumbles under its feet. The reptile slips downward.

The reptile's claws screech against the slab of hard rock until it slides off the end of the slab.

The reptile falls through the air for a moment.

The reptile bounces off a ledge of rock and is cast into the air again.

The reptile falls a long distance through the air before merging with the steep mountainside.

The reptile tumbles and rolls down the steep slope for a long time.

The larger reptile gazes up toward the bright shine.

There's a good-sized ledge at the outcropping if he can just get to it. He would like to *see* the bright shine after all this time of moving *toward* the bright shine.

The patch of gravel, which the larger reptile is standing on, shifts downhill. He gets an uneasy feeling in his stomach.

He thinks about the other reptile who fell.

He decides that he wants to get off the side of this mountain, much more than he wants to see the bright shine.

The larger reptile high-steps it back down to firmer footing. He sees that other reptiles are already moving back down the mountain.

Now, with no reason to go in any other direction, the small band of reptiles simply drifts *away from* the bright shine.

It doesn't take long before her baby is too big to be able to return to the burrow. All the babies that season are like hers—all those who survived.

The babies are so different. They are now three times bigger than their mothers. They're purple instead of tan.

The strangest thing? They walk on only two legs.

The babies eat *a lot.* The food is getting dangerously depleted.

One of the routes she takes when looking for food is along the river. There are fruit trees here, but the remaining fruit is unreachable because it's hanging over the water.

Nobody will get near the water. Hunger is increasing, but fear of the water is far greater than the hunger.

There's a gathering of the babies around a tree that is frighteningly close to the water.

One of the babies is using a long stick to bend a fruit-laden tree branch to the side of the river. Other babies are pulling the food from the bent branch.

One baby pulls hard at a fruit. The food snaps off. In an instant, this baby slips in the mud, lands on its back, and slides down toward the edge of the water.

The baby with the long stick is pulled forward by the branch and falls *into* the water!

She's stunned! She's horrified! She's panic-stricken! She scurries back and forth. She's not sure what to do.

Then she hears the babies . . . making cheerful noises.

The baby who fell into the water is standing, on two legs of course, *in* the river. The river is nearly up to its body. Most of the baby's body is wet.

The baby at the edge of the river has its foot *in* the water. The baby splashes the water with its foot.

Disturbingly, both babies seem to be amused by the water, instead of mortally terrified.

The baby in the river grabs the end of a tree branch and bows it over to the bank. Other babies pull the fruit off.

Shockingly, more babies actually *walk* into the water to get fruit.

She watches, horrified, as the babies get all the fruit from the branches over the water.

One of the babies leaves the river, heading in her direction. She cringes and shivers at the sight of its wet legs. As it walks past, the baby stops and gives her some of the fruit.

This surprises her in one way but not in another way.

Food is to be collected and hoarded when you can find it. But the babies are different. They share food with each other and with the mothers and older ones.

The babies don't seem to learn that they should be hoarding food. They're too big to make burrows, but they could stash food in places.

As food gets more difficult to find, many of the strange young ones drift away. With their size and ability to walk on two legs, they wander to places where there's more food.

R2

The Big Blank and the land around it are increasingly part of my world.

So much is different on the land compared to life in the water. I have learned many new things during my time on the land.

There are many creatures that live on the land, and they are in strange, fun shapes. Some are very small. Others might be heavy if they were held on one tentacle.

Certain parts of many land plants are edible. Most of the land plants taste much better than the water plants.

It is very enjoyable to be on the land.

New and different sounds can be made in the air. I have started making sounds for some of the more interesting land things.

It started because I'm always happy to see my favorite plant, the one with the slimy, thick water that feels good on the skin. Putting the thick water on the body and tentacles allows people to remain on the land for much longer.

When I approach my favorite plant, I lift a tentacle and let out air in a way that sounds like "nanbay."

Now, other people make the same sound for those plants.

Someone on the Blank is repeatedly making the "Nanbay" sound.

This person sounds ill.

Three people near the Blank, among the very tall plants, are calling back, "Nanbay, Nanbay, Nanbay."

The three people appear at the edge of the Blank. They are dragging Nanbay plants. They hurry to get the Nanbay to the one calling for help.

The three people crush the soft ends of the Nanbay plant and smear the thick water on the one in trouble.

This is probably another situation of "falling asleep on the Blank."

It's easy to do. I've done it.

Being on the land is very different from being in the water.

It is such a habit to move with our tentacles behind us, instead of with our tentacles under us. People often fall over when trying to move on the land.

Even I sometimes forget where I am and fall on my side, as if I were going to swim through the air.

It has been difficult to get people to try the land.

It probably didn't help that when I first got back from the land, I was bruised, dehydrated, tired, and sore all over.

Some people have difficulty getting out of the water and standing on four tentacles.

Some people have tried being on the land and do not like it. These people usually don't come back.

I cannot understand how people do not like being on the land. There is so much to see and do.

One of my favorite things to do is squat under the tall plants at the edge of the Blank and look at the water. It is very enjoyable to see the colors of the water and watch the motion of the water's surface.

Sometimes, interesting things float into the shallow water and onto the Blank, too.

There are interesting pieces of large land plants floating in the shallow water, right now. Those pieces are from big plants, like the Nanbay. They are the big parts that rise out of the land. Most of the tentacle-like parts of the plants are gone.

The large pieces are floating together in a bunch.

I have an idea.

There is a land plant that grows long and thin. This plant is not easy to break. It grows close to the ground and often trips people as we move around on the land.

I collect some of this long, low-growing land plant.

It's a short swim to the large land-plant parts in the shallow water. I wrap the long plant around the floating parts to hold the large pieces together.

I climb onto this floating bunch. It stays together.

At first, I feel a little uneasy on the floating bunch. When I try to stand up, the floating bunch shifts around under me and I almost fall off.

The floating bunch is stable when I squat down.

It is enjoyable to be on the floating bunch. I can see far in every direction. It feels good to move up and down with the surface of the water.

Looking into the water from above is strange, yet stirring.

I see things in the water in a different way. I have seen the plants and these rocks and those fish many times from the water. But looking at them from above, out of the water, is eerily different.

I feel a strange sensation to see things this way. A sense of power.

I swim a tentacle behind me and the floating bunch moves across the water. With two tentacles in the water, I move the floating bunch down to the far end of the Blank. Then I swim it toward the Blank.

The floating bunch slides to a stop on the Blank's firm, moist edge. It's easy to move from the floating bunch to standing on four tentacles.

I think this floating bunch might be a great idea.

With a better floating thing, I'm sure more people will come to the land.

First, people can pull themselves from the water onto the floating thing. Then, they can slide off, slow and easy, to get upright on four tentacles.

Yes, this floating thing could be very helpful.

I collect more large land-plant parts and long, low-growing plants. Other people see what I'm doing. They want to help.

Some people collect plant parts. Some people provide a variety of food. A few of us do the work of wrapping the thin plants around the large parts.

Together, we are making a larger and better floating thing.

I see this one person sliding down the steep land at the end of the Blank. This one was one of the first people to try going on the land.

I haven't seen this one for many passings of the light. It is good to see this one.

This one is struggling to move and keeps falling over. This one doesn't look well.

I move to get Nanbay. Some other people are moving quickly to drag Nanbay ends toward this one.

As I approach, I let out many of the sounds that we make when we first see each other on the land. "Blurpy, Blurpy, Blurpy!"

This one looks *three eyes* at me.

Other people also make the "Blurpy" sound. I move in to help with the Nanbay.

This one lowers an eye but keeps two eyes at me.

This one tries making the "Blurpy" sound. The vibrations are a little wrong.

We keep repeating, "Blurpy, Blurpy."

This one keeps trying to make the "Blurpy" sound. This one gets much better at it.

Everybody is happy after we get this one coated with Nanbay.

Suddenly, this one wraps two tentacles firmly around one of my tentacles and pulls at me.

I look three eyes at this one.

This one makes a strange sound. This one makes the same sound again. With a struggling effort, this one points a tentacle inland.

This one repeats the strange sound over and over, while pointing toward the land.

After several days of crossing through the tall grass that grows high above his head, the larger reptile emerges into the meadow. Not long after, the youngest hatchling comes out of the grass from the same spot.

The smaller reptile must have followed in his path through the tall grass. The youngest hatchling probably ate the scraps of food he left behind instead of going into the thick grass to hunt for himself.

The larger reptile studies the new area. In the meadow, there should be some small food, but there's nothing big to eat.

Other reptiles find their way out of the grass.

There are many new reptiles in the band. Most of the newer reptiles are younger than the one he thinks of as the Youngest Hatchling, though none of them have been hatchlings for a long time.

The Larger Reptile notices a twinkling in the distance. It reminds him of the bright shine from when he was not much older than a hatchling. The original band of hatchlings were unable to reach that bright shine.

This bright shine is coming from the mountains on the other side of the valley. It's not far away, but between him and the bright shine is another large field of the tall grass.

The Larger Reptile doesn't like the tall grass.

He wants to see what makes the bright shine, but in the tall grass, it's difficult to catch even small food, and there are those little biting creatures.

The biting creatures are a concern.

They look like a small, bluish-gray fruit, on a little flat rock. Six long, stick-like legs extend from the flat part.

The biting creatures can move very fast.

Sometimes, when moving through the tall grass, you run into a few of the creatures. Sometimes, a biting creature drops onto you from the grass above your head.

It's very annoying how the little biting creatures scurry straight to the scars on his left arm and shoulder. They like to bite at his scars.

More reptiles appear in the meadow between the tall grass fields.

The Larger Reptile doesn't see many of the original hatchlings. It's difficult to know if some of them are still in the band.

Since the early days of the original hatchlings, many more reptiles like them have joined the band.

In this area of the meadow, the small food is scarce.

Some reptiles hunt along the thickening edge of the next field of tall grass. Some reptiles drift toward another area of the meadow.

The reptiles know they can't stay here. The Larger Reptile does not want to go back into the tall grass, but he does want to know about the bright shine. What is it?

That is the direction he goes, toward the bright shine.

This field of tall grass is difficult to walk through.

The grass extends to well above his head. There are patches of dense growth. In places, the grass stalks are like small trees and too overgrown to get through.

The reptiles find themselves boxed in and must backtrack out. The reptiles exit the impassible area and drift to the right side.

A few of the biting creatures appear.

The reptiles walk faster.

More creatures appear.

The reptiles quicken their pace again.

The clicking legs of the biting creatures is disturbing. The clicking sound grows louder.

The biting creatures are bad in this place.

The reptiles hear an approaching chorus of clicking legs. The frightening sound is moving toward the band from behind and the left side. The buzz of the clicking legs continues to get louder.

The creatures are coming at them fast!

The reptiles glance around at each other. Then they all bolt!

The reptiles take off running as fast as they can move through the grass.

The loud buzz of clicking legs is right behind him. The buzzing sound expands past him on both sides.

The Larger Reptile tries to run faster.

The buzzing sound is closing in.

From above, a creature lands on the Larger Reptile's shoulder. The thing immediately bites at the scar on his upper arm.

The Larger Reptile smashes the bug against a thick stalk as he hurries through a dense patch of the grass.

Ahead of him and to the left, he sees a reptile getting swarmed by the biting creatures.

At first, the running reptile thrashes around and sheds some of the creatures.

Then the reptile slows and stops running. It briefly stands on two legs before dropping forward to four legs.

The reptile disappears under a growing swarm of biting creatures as the Larger Reptile sprints past.

Several biting creatures appear in front of him. The creatures are moving in.

The Larger Reptile leaps through a gap in the grass.

The Larger Reptile feels one of the creatures crawling up his back. He lowers his head and pushes through some thicker grass.

The Larger Reptile expects the creature to go for the scar on his left shoulder. It does.

Without breaking stride, the Larger Reptile swings his right claw over. He stabs the disgusting creature through the bulbous top part of its body and into the hard, thin part where the legs are attached.

The Larger Reptile sticks the impaled creature straight out in front of him as he races through the very tall grass.

Another biting creature lands on his extended arm. He expects the creature to run straight up his arm and onto his face.

Instead, the creature skitters *down* his arm.

The second creature pounces and bites frantically into the squirming creature stuck on the Larger Reptile's claw.

As he dashes through the grass, biting creatures scurry up his body from below and land on him from above.

All the biting creatures run straight to the one on his claw.

A spastic, crawling mass of biting creatures forms at the end of his arm, voraciously consuming the shrinking lump of the impaled creature.

While still running full-on, the Larger Reptile whips his arm to the side. He flicks the remaining part of the creature off his claw.

The whole mess of swarming, feasting creatures falls into the grass.

The surrounding creatures go after the tumbling, gruesome frenzy.

The Larger Reptile doesn't see any more biting creatures in front of him.

The buzz of clicking legs fades behind him, but the Larger Reptile doesn't stop running for a long time.

The next day, the tall grass finally begins to thin out. The Larger Reptile is able to see more than the grass a few steps ahead of him.

The Larger Reptile feels a wave of relief as he steps out of the grass and into the direct sunlight.

He's tired and thirsty. He hasn't eaten in several days. He hasn't stopped to hunt or sleep since the run past the biting creatures. He hasn't even slowed down much.

Not far behind the Larger Reptile, the Youngest Hatchling emerges from the tall grass at the same spot. The smaller reptile must have followed in his path again.

The Larger Reptile scans the immediate area. He sees a river running at the bottom of the valley. It's not far away. He staggers toward the river.

The Youngest Hatchling stays behind him while taking a good look around. More reptiles exit the tall grass. They all follow the Larger Reptile toward the river.

At the river's edge, the Larger Reptile drops to four legs. He crawls forward until his upper body is in the water.

He drinks only a little water at first. Then he gulps it down.

The Larger Reptile submerges his head, arms, and torso into the water. The cool water washing over him feels very good.

The Larger Reptile opens his eyes. He's surprised to see food in the water.

The food is not much bigger than his foot. The food is long and flat on its sides. There are many of these food within his view.

One of the strange food moves through the water in front of him. The Larger Reptile brings his arms together. His arms move slowly in the water, but he's able to catch the food between his claws.

He rolls sideways out of the water.

The Larger Reptile eats half of the river food before slowing down enough to breathe.

He finishes the food and takes a moment to look around.

Many reptiles are in and around the water. There are reptiles up and down the river.

There's getting to be a lot of reptiles in the band.

Standing next to the river, the Youngest Hatchling appears stronger and healthier than the other reptiles. He has very few bite wounds compared to the others.

Many in the band have bleeding and festering sores.

Everyone is tired and hungry.

The Larger Reptile eats several more of the river food before relaxing for a moment in the midday warmth.

A twinkle.

He glances toward it. It's the bright shine! He hasn't even thought to look for it since leaving the tall grass.

The bright shine is close.

After a rejuvenating nap, the Larger Reptile eats and drinks again. He crosses the waist-deep river and heads toward the bright shine.

The Youngest Hatchling follows. Some of the other reptiles are already moving toward the bright shine.

As the daylight fades to darkness, so does the bright shine on the mountain. The reptiles find spots to sleep for the night.

The crisp morning daylight shines across the land. In the thin fog, the bright shine blazes on the mountainside.

The reptiles are slow to wake. They are irritable. There isn't any food nearby.

The band of reptiles journeys on.

The Larger Reptile heads straight toward the bright shine. It's close now, just up a short hill. He is eager to find the source of the bright shine.

Two younger reptiles run past him as he climbs the hill.

He gets to the top of the hill and stops, bewildered.

The Larger Reptile is not sure what he's seeing. It looks as if there's a puncture wound into the mountain.

It appears that the bright shine has bled out of the mountain.

Bright shiny stuff covers a small area like a frozen pond.

The Larger Reptile circles the pond of bright shine.

Along the edge, the bright shine breaks up into chunks of various sizes. In places, short streams of bright shine branch off from the pond.

The two younger reptiles step onto the bright shine pond. They wander as they inspect the strangeness. One of the two loses interest and roams off toward some nearby trees.

The Larger Reptile takes a few steps onto the pond-like surface.

He scratches a claw across the bright shine. It makes a strange, high-pitched sound. His claw leaves a thin groove on the surface.

When his claw scratches rock, the rock turns to dust.

Rock is cold. The bright shine is warm.

What is this bright shine?

The Larger Reptile walks along the edge of the pond. He finds an interesting piece of the bright shine and picks it up.

The piece is long and straight. It's nearly the length of his body.

One end looks like a thin tree branch. Near the middle is a bulge that looks like a knot in a branch. From the middle to the other end, the piece is flat—like the river food.

The piece of bright shine is much heavier than a tree branch of the same size.

The Larger Reptile decides to keep the branch of bright shine for now.

R3

The floater is almost ready. It should be done before the next light has passed.

This One has been insistent. This One keeps saying, "Blurpy" and pointing a tentacle up the hill.

Finally, This One convinces us to see what it is.

It's far down the other side of the hill.

Many people surround the large object. Some people are excitedly making "Blurpy" sounds and bobbing around.

I move in to see it.

The object is about one-quarter the size of the floater. It's thin and flat. It looks like a giant land-plant leaf only it's not green. The color is closer to that of the blank areas at the edge of the water.

This One's strange object doesn't look like a plant or a rock.

It's very bright and shiny.

I touch at it with a tentacle. The strange object is surprisingly heavy. I'm unable to lift the edge of it off the ground.

The object feels warm to the tentacle.

Someone is trying to lift it. The large object is too heavy. Others move in to help.

They manage to get the object standing upright. Two people hold it up while we look it over.

Everybody has three eyes on it.

This One's strange object is very much like a giant, shiny leaf.

A sudden wind hits the giant, shiny leaf and it falls to the ground—along with the two people who are still holding it.

This One made it seem so important. I don't see what good this thing could be.

There are a lot of new things to see on the land. The important things are those that we can eat and use to make the floater.

This One moves over to me excitedly saying, "Blurpy, Blurpy." This One points a tentacle at the giant, shiny leaf.

I look around at the others. I look up the hill that we came down. I think about the object being so heavy.

I don't see how we could use the giant, shiny leaf.

There are a few things to do before we put the floater in the water. I'm not sure what else to do here, so I start moving up the hill.

A small, furry, four-legged animal runs up the hill to my side. The playful animal goes right up a tree as if it were still running on the ground.

With tentacles, we cannot move on the land like that.

We're able to climb short distances up some trees to get the food, but it's not easy. It's also difficult to move up and down hills.

I look an eye back down the hill at the other people. Many of the people are struggling to move the giant, shiny leaf up the hill.

The people have the object with its flat side to the ground. There are people all around it. The people are using one tentacle to lift the giant, shiny leaf and three tentacles to maneuver it up the hill.

Why bother with it?

Maybe somebody has an idea about a way to use it. Maybe they just like the giant, shiny leaf because it's different.

Back at the Blank, we prepare for a big meal as we finish the work on the floater.

Later in this passing of the light, we will feast on a variety of food in anticipation of making a good floater.

We will put the floater in the water in the next passing.

The time has come to launch the floater.

We push the floater down the Blank to the edge of the water. The Blank softens and the water lifts the other end of the floater.

We give the floater a final push.

The floater moves entirely into the water.

The floater rocks gently on the surface. The floater looks big and impressive in the water. We observe the grand accomplishment with satisfaction.

We swim up and climb onto the floater. We get tentacles in the water and start swimming the floater away from the Blank.

We move the floater a short distance, but the cliffs of water keep pushing us back.

Several people jump into the water and push the floater with all their tentacles. It doesn't seem to help.

After a lot of effort, we are all too tired to try moving the floater anymore. We drift back toward the Blank.

Everybody else is standing on the Blank. They have been watching to see what happens with the floater.

We didn't get very far.

The floater drifts into the side corner of the Blank area.

We come to a stop on the Blank with a lurch. Some people climb off the floater and move away. Everybody feels exhausted and defeated.

I squat on the floater and look out at the water. I think about the difficulty we had moving the floater and being stopped by the cliffs of water.

An eye is distracted by land-plant ends blowing in the wind. I think about how we ended up at the far corner of the Blank, instead of the middle.

I have an idea.

I find This One and the Giant Shiny Leaf. I want to tell This One my thought about how the Giant Shiny Leaf could be useful.

However, given our current vocabulary, I instead say, "Blurpy, pffft, Blurpy."

After a long and strenuous effort, we get the Giant Shiny Leaf onto the floater. We lift up the Giant Shiny Leaf and position it against the side rail at the front of the floater. We secure the Giant Shiny Leaf in place with a lot of the long, low-growing plant.

The wind pushes against the Giant Shiny Leaf and the floater shifts. Because of the Giant Shiny Leaf, the wind pushes the floater back into the water.

Many people climb onto the floater.

The wind against the Giant Shiny Leaf pushes the floater away from the Blank. The Giant Shiny Leaf seems to be moving the floater very well.

The floater blasts through the cliffs of water. The floater bounces a little as it moves through cliffs of water, but it quickly settles down on the other side.

The Giant Shiny Leaf is working.

We are quickly coming up to where we want to stop. This is where we go to meet with people who still live in the water.

Sometimes people will want to go back with us to the land. Sometimes we just visit those who stay in the water.

There is a small pod waiting for us. A few tentacles wave in the air.

We arrive at the place where we want to stop. The floater zips past, going very fast.

We look back at the people in the water. It doesn't take much time before we are unable to see them anymore.

It feels like the floater just keeps moving faster.

Nobody knows what to do.

The person next to me drops a fruit stem into the water. We expect to watch the stem float away behind us. Instead, the instant the stem touches the water, it's gone!

With two eyes in the direction of the fruit stem, we look two eyes at each other. We now have a better understanding of how fast we are actually moving.

The Giant Shiny Leaf works much better at moving the floater than I would have thought. The Giant Shiny Leaf works better than I wanted.

The light passing fades to darkness.

The floater continues moving across the water, extremely fast.

As we awaken at the next light, everyone notices that the floater is not moving. The wind has stopped. The floater sits still and quiet in the water.

Then we realize that there is no land visible anywhere—in any direction. There's nothing but water all around us.

We must be over the deep water.

I stare down at the dark water with three eyes. I get a very uncomfortable feeling. Nobody knows *what* is out here.

I wonder if being afraid of the water "itches the tentacles" of anyone else.

I look at the Giant Shiny Leaf. It has shifted a little from where we tied it. It occurs to me that being able to adjust the Giant Shiny Leaf should allow better control of the floater.

I hesitate to do anything with the Giant Shiny Leaf right now, though. If it got loose and fell off the floater—what?

I'm not sure but, I think that would be very bad.

If we lost the Giant Shiny Leaf, would we be stuck out here? Maybe we could swim back, but in which direction?

As the light gets brighter, the wind increases. The floater starts moving.

It doesn't take long before the floater is moving very fast again.

The misty air begins to clear. We keep eyes looking for the land in all directions.

Several people at the front have apparently seen something interesting. They're bobbing up and down, waving tentacles, and making high-vibration "Blurpy" sounds.

Everybody turns *three eyes* to look—and that's a lot of eyes.

It's unclear in the hazy air, but it *does* look like the land.

The air gets clearer. Something is not right.

All our lives, we have seen the land—from far away while in the water to standing four tentacles on it. That is not the shape of the land.

This One moved on the land for many passings of the light before coming back to tell us about the Giant Shiny Leaf. The land might be bigger than we thought.

We can see a lot of land from standing on the hill by the Blank. Maybe there's much more land than we realized.

We must be on another side of the land. I'm very curious to see another side of the land.

Standing at the back of the floater, a person newer to the land starts bobbing up and down and making high-vibration "Blurpy" sounds.

Everybody turns to look!

It is just barely visible, but it looks like there's another land in the opposite direction. When the air clears enough, we see that the other land is *the* land, *our* land.

We can now look in opposite directions and see land both ways.

There are two lands!

The land in this direction looks like the land, our land.

The land in that direction looks like *new land!*

Another of the newer people is very agitated. The newer person bobs up and down, points a tentacle in the direction of our land, and makes "Nanbay" sounds.

I am surprised when the newer person jumps off the floater.

I move quickly to the back of the floater and search for the person who jumped in the water. All I see is water.

We are moving very fast. If the person was not injured from jumping into the water, it would still be a very long swim back.

Is there even food along the way? We are already hungry. None of us has eaten since we left the land—our land.

The new land is getting closer. It looks much wider across than our land. The tallest hill goes much higher into the air than any of ours, too.

The wind and the Giant Shiny Leaf keep us moving very fast.

The light passes to darkness and back to light again. The new land is very close.

This new land is much larger than the land that we have always seen. It is strange to see land that is shaped differently. The features and colors are different, too.

Yet, the new land seems familiar.

There are blank areas, cliffs, and hills.

The most striking thing is the rich green color of the land plants. I have become accustomed to that color, and I like it. It is a pleasant sight.

We are being pushed toward one of the blank areas.

Somebody starts bobbing up and down and making "Blurpy" sounds while pointing a tentacle at the water. Immediately, many eyes are looking in the water.

We see large schools of fish and the kinds of water plants that we usually eat. It doesn't take long to see that there is a lot of food here. A lot of it!

The floater catches in the middle of a cliff of water. The floater shakes and we are suddenly moving even faster.

Everybody wraps a tentacle around something.

The cliff of water is pushing the floater incredibly fast.

I vaguely remember the first time I left the water. That was many light passings ago. I haven't thought about it for a while.

The Blank is coming at us very fast.

Now I remember clearly. The cliffs of water hurled me onto the land, where I got stuck in the Blank. I thought I was going to die.

The Blank is very close.

Here I go again!

The cliff of water flattens down, and the floater loses speed rapidly. We skim across the shallow area to the edge of the water, still moving quite fast as we approach the Blank.

The floater slides out of the water and stops abruptly on the Blank with a lurching thud.

The sudden stop scatters people everywhere. People fall all over the floater. Some fall off the floater and onto the Blank.

We all sit where we fell and look around with all eyes.

It feels strange to be on land again.

It feels strange to look upon new land.

That plant over there. It looks like—it is! It's Nanbay!

We have a lot to do now. We need to find places where land plants block the light during its passing. We need to collect Nanbay and food.

There is much to do.

We have now been on the New Land for many passings of the light. I have just eaten another big meal. We have all been eating well.

The same long, low-growing plant grows on the New Land, too. I'm wrapping some of the long plant around loose pieces on the Floater.

The wind whips past. Water hits the ends of my tentacles.

Water! The Floater is high up on the dry Blank. There shouldn't be water up here.

I turn three eyes toward the water.

The air is dark over the water. Big cliffs of water are churning out there.

I look across the Blank and see people overwhelmed by the wind. Two people are blown over. I watch as they struggle to get back onto their tentacles.

The water rises higher on the Blank. Water gets under the Floater. The Floater shifts down the Blank.

I *do not* want to lose the Floater!

It took so much to make the Floater—a lot of plant parts and much work by many people over many passings of the light.

Also, without the Floater, we would be stuck on this New Land.

I see another person and try to get help by bobbing up and down and making "eeeep" and "ffffrrrrp" sounds.

The other person sees that I'm trying to pull the Floater up the Blank. The other person moves quickly to the back end to push.

The wind is not helping. The wind on the Giant Shiny Leaf is pushing the Floater backward, toward the water. The Floater is also turning.

The wind pushes the Floater to the edge of the water. On the firm, moist edge of the Blank, the Floater spins completely around.

I am now trying to pull the back end of the Floater up the Blank.

A large cliff of water washes onto the Blank. The water hits the Floater and knocks me down. The Floater suddenly pulls away and floats into the water.

I move as fast as I can to get to the Floater, but moving on the Blank is slow.

When I reach the water, I'm able to swim much faster.

I'm getting close to the Floater, but the wind against the Giant Shiny Leaf is making the Floater go faster.

I'm almost there, but the Floater is moving fast.

I briefly touch the Floater with the tip of a tentacle. Before I can wrap a tentacle onto it, the Floater moves away.

Four tentacles! Full swim effort! My only thought: *I must catch the Floater!*

The top of my body bumps into the Floater.

I spin and get a good wrap on the lower side rail. I get another tentacle wrapped tightly next to the first.

The water pulls at my sideways body and my other two tentacles.

I lift a tentacle out of the water. Without the water pulling on it, I get the third tentacle firmly onto the edge of the Floater.

After that, it's easy to pivot my body around. I get all four tentacles wrapped comfortably onto the back end of the Floater.

I did it. I caught the Floater!

I rest for a moment with my body hovering above the water. I am exhilarated by how fast I'm moving.

I dip an eye under the surface and watch the rocks, plants, and fish zip past. This is much faster than I could swim, even for a short distance.

This is much, much faster than I could swim.

I pull myself onto the Floater. Standing there is the person who was just helping me with the Floater on the Blank. This person is looking three big eyes back at the New Land.

I get up on four tentacles and look two eyes back at the land, then three eyes. I am shocked by how far away we are already.

The two of us stand on the Floater and watch the New Land getting smaller in the growing distance. The land fades into the misty air.

We are going into the deep, dark water again. I'm glad that we've been storing food on the Floater.

After a few light passings on the Floater, it is very good to see the land, our land, the First Land, again. The land looks like it should, like it always has.

We are coming up fast to the area where we meet with the people living in the water.

There must be many people here. The area is churning with white water from all the tentacles waving in the air.

Just like last time, the Floater zips past, going very fast.

This time though, a large pod follows us to the land.

The reptiles must find some good food soon. All the reptiles are looking sick.

The Larger Reptile notices that the grass is getting taller. The reptiles ahead of him are moving into a field of tall grass.

The Larger Reptile usually carries the branch of bright shine in his right claw because the scars on his left arm and shoulder begin to ache after a short time.

Some grass gets tangled around his branch of bright shine. He yanks on the branch and the grass falls away from it. He swings the branch out in front of him. The branch cuts or smooths away the shoulder-high grass.

As the grass gradually gets taller and thicker, the Larger Reptile increasingly swings the branch across in front of him.

The grass continues to get thicker and more difficult to walk in. He swings the branch, and the grass clears away.

He swings the branch, and the biting creatures scurry away.

The grass gets to be like thin trees and too thick to pass through. It takes a few swings, but he cuts a hole through it. He continues to chop through the dense vegetation.

The Larger Reptile pauses to rest and looks back. He's impressed by the path that he's cut through the tall grass. Not far back is the Youngest

Hatchling. Further behind, there are many reptiles following in the easy path he's made.

The branch of bright shine makes a comfortable path to walk in.

With the little field of tall grass behind them, the reptiles walk up the slope between two mountain peaks. They get to the top of the slope and look out across a huge expanse.

The land gradually slopes down to a large lake at the left edge of his vision. To the right, a twinkle of bright shine catches his attention.

The twinkle is coming from a nearby mountain.

The Larger Reptile thinks about the bright shine. Now that he has been to a bright shine place and seen it, he's not very interested in going toward the bright shine.

Good food is the concern now.

The reptiles search across the hills and valleys for any sign of food. Somewhere out there must be some good, big food.

However, with no good reason to go in any other direction, the band of reptiles drifts toward the bright shine.

As the reptiles are nearing the bright shine, they notice that it's twinkling more. Then the shining stops. The bright shine should still be shining.

The Larger Reptile thinks he sees some movement near the area where they were seeing the bright shine. The other reptiles see it, too. It must be big food.

Late in the day, the reptiles approach the area where they saw the bright shine. They see some good, big food in a small valley, just down the hill. The food is sizeable, but not big enough to share.

The Larger Reptile drops his branch of bright shine on the ground. The reptiles move down the hill and spread out. He's only seen four of the food. There are many more reptiles than food.

The Larger Reptile begins to select his next meal. He focuses on one of the food. He charges into the little valley.

He's going to get this one!

He really needs a good meal. The others can share the rest.

She rubs the patch of lighter skin above her right eye. She pulls another fruit from the tree and takes a bite. She gazes around the gulley as she chews.

Several others are also gathering fruits and nuts. There's a creek with good water running through here. There's good shade. This is a good spot.

Two of the others are staring toward the mountain. One of them suddenly wails the howl of warning.

Looking up, she sees a scattering of strange, green creatures. Predators! The large predators are charging down the hill. The unfamiliar predators are moving fast.

She and the others scatter for cover.

One of the predators is after her. She's older now and slower. With a feeling of dread, she realizes that she will not be able to reach safety in time.

She's trying to run, but she can't move fast. The predator's shadow darkens the ground around her. Her leg muscles spasm in fear!

The food sees him and starts running. The Larger Reptile chases. The food is slow. He closes in. As the food is running, he kicks one of the food's two legs. The food trips.

The food goes down and tumbles. The Larger Reptile can take his time now. His food has a severely injured leg.

The Larger Reptile sees another reptile catching food.

New food appears at the top of the little valley. Maybe there is enough food for everybody.

The new food is a little bigger than the one he caught. The new food doesn't have hair. Otherwise, the new food looks about the same.

Strangely, instead of running away, the new food stays at the top of the little valley. Now the new food is making a weird noise.

This new food is somehow emitting rocks and sticks.

Some of the rocks and sticks are hitting a reptile while it's eating, but the reptile only flinches at the annoyance.

The reptile is focused on its meal.

She tries to get up, but her leg is injured. When she tries to stand, a sharp pain stabs down her leg. With a short wail, she falls back to the ground.

Her leg is broken. She can't run.

As she rolls onto her back, she sees that one of the others is caught by a predator.

She looks up at the predator moving slowly toward her. Her body tenses in panic and shakes with fear.

The predator is going to kill her and eat her!

Something else draws the predator's attention. It's a sound.

The predator stares up the hill.

She glances to where the predator is looking.

Some of the young are standing on the hill and making noises. Strangely, the young are *not* running away from the predators!

Even though the predator is standing right in front of her, one of the young is running toward her.

It's her son!

By reflex, she looks at the patch of darker skin above his right eye.

He and the others should be running away or hiding. She is *stunned* to see him getting so close to the predator.

Inconceivably, her son runs right up to the predator and stabs it with a stick!

It poked him with a stick!

He's bleeding!

With an angry roar, the Larger Reptile swipes angrily at the offending food. He connects with a backhand and smacks it away.

The new food looks injured, but it gets back up and circles.

The first food he caught is still there. His original food makes a feeble attempt to get away, but it can't move much.

Some of the new food are still emitting rocks and sticks from the top of the little shallow valley.

Strangely, a few more of the new food are now running down into the valley.

He's distracted by the unusual behavior of this new food.

While the predator is distracted, she attempts to crawl away.

She doesn't understand why her son is not running away from the predators.

The young on the hill are throwing rocks and sticks at the predators. A few more of the young run down the hill *toward* the predators.

She is baffled by the actions of the strange young people, yet again.

The malformed younger people are often bewildering, but not running from a predator is the most bizarre behavior she's ever seen.

Her child moves away from her, but not away from the predator.

The predator turns away from him and back to her.

Then, her son runs up to the predator and stabs it with the stick again!

The Larger Reptile flinches from another sharp stab. The new food hits him with the stick across the scar on his left arm, then again.

This new food is becoming a nuisance. The Larger Reptile lunges at the new food, but it quickly sidesteps and moves away.

The Larger Reptile tracks the new food as it circles.

Behind the new food, he notices that a bunch of the food have surrounded a reptile. The food are hitting the other reptile with rocks and sticks.

The other reptile seems unable to catch any of the food that are hitting him with sticks. The other reptile stops chasing the food and slumps to the ground.

The Larger Reptile glances in the other direction. A reptile is running up the hill and out of the little valley, carrying away its food.

This reminds him of his hunger. He turns back to his original food and moves toward it.

It's time to eat.

The predator moves toward her again.

She realizes that she has not been trying to get away. She's in a lot of pain, but more than that, she is shocked and confused.

She has never seen anything like this.

Her son runs in and hits the predator with his stick again. Her son lunges back as the predator swings at him.

The predator is bleeding profusely now, and it staggers.

Her son runs up to her.

She sees blood on his chest. He's injured!

Her son kneels beside her. He sweeps his gaze over her. He takes a long look at her broken leg.

She can't help but look at his patch of darker skin above his right eye, like the patch of lighter skin above her right eye.

As her son looks at her injuries, his face turns red, angry, and mean.

The annoying new food is between him and his meal. The new food has its attention on the original food with the injured leg.

The Larger Reptile is getting angry! He's hungry.

The Larger Reptile is eager to give the chase, end the hunt, and eat. If this new food wants to be his meal, then he will kill *it*, too.

He growls and charges!

The predator roars. The predator charges toward them.

Her son needs to get away! She looks at him, hoping he will run away.

Her child is angry in a way that she has never seen before.

His head snaps around—toward the predator.

Then, she watches the most *unimaginable* thing happen.

Her son roars!

He jumps to his feet. He continues to roar as he charges at the much larger predator, who is roaring and charging at them.

Disturbingly, the new food doesn't begin the chase. The Larger Reptile would rather avoid a long chase right now, but what is this?

The new food is growling and charging *straight at him*.

Just before her son and the predator slam into each other, her son leaps in the air, swings his stick, and hits the predator on the side of its head, very hard.

The stick hitting the predator's head makes a sound like when she hit the First on the head with a rock.

Her son and the predator collide.

They both fall to the ground.

Her son is faster to get up and he jumps on the predator's back. The predator stands and tries to shake him off, but her son has an arm around its neck.

The predator coughs and moves slower. As the predator falls forward onto four legs, her son is thrown over its head.

Her son lands on his back, in front of the predator.

It looks as though the predator is going to pin her son to the ground and bring its big, teeth-filled mouth down for the kill.

The predator sluggishly lunges its arms forward and begins to drop.

Her son pivots and yells, "DAAAHHHNNN!"

He thrusts the point of his stick up into the predator's throat.

With the predator's downward motion, the bottom end of the stick sinks into the ground and the other end stabs into the predator's throat, all the way to the top of the inside of its skull.

The stick breaks, and the predator drops while her son is still under it.

Her son rolls to the side, but he doesn't make it all the way. He disappears under the larger reptile.

Everything seems to stop.

An ominous hush descends over the gulley.

The other predators run away.

The young gather into groups on the hill and in the gulley.

Bodies of both kinds lay on the ground. Silence frames stunned expressions on the faces of the primates.

A voice rises as if from under the ground.

"mmmMMMAAAHHH!"

Her son roars as he lifts the big, heavy predator enough to get out from under it. He pulls himself up and gets on his feet.

He stands, hands on knees, leaning over the dead body of the reptile.

He gasps for breath, and he's drenched in blood.

The others stare at her son and the dead predator in front of him.

One of the young utters in a rough, raspy voice, "Daaahhhnnn . . . Mm . . . Mmaaahhh."

He looks around. "Daahhnnn . . . Maahhh?"

Another raises his fist in the air and repeats, "Daahhnn Maahhh."

All around, others start murmuring, "Daahhnn Maahhh."

Her son stands fully upright and looks at her. He looks up and down the gulley.

The predator's blood is running off him like water after a swim.

The young begin raising their arms until most of them have an arm in the air. More of them begin muttering, "Daahhnn Maahhh."

Her son raises both of his fists straight up into the air. He roars out loud and long. "AAAAHHHHRRRRGGG!"

Whooping and hollering voices join the increasingly louder chants.

"Daahhnn Mah, Daahhnn Mah!"

She lays on the ground in the gulley, propped on one elbow, a hand on her broken leg, in great pain, confusion, disbelief, and awe.

Her head slightly shaking, her face subtly twitching, she marvels at the scene.

"Daahhnn Mah, Daahhnn Mah!"

The air is *loud* with the victory chant.

"Dahn Mah, Dahn Mah, Dahn Mah!"

R4

The retreating reptiles hear the voices rising behind them.

"Dahn Mah, Dahn Mah."

The Youngest Hatchling and the other reptiles slink back in the direction from which they had come. They are not thinking about which way to go. It's simply a reflex.

The reptiles are shocked about what just happened.

The Youngest Hatchling, now the oldest in the band of reptiles, watched with the others as the Larger Reptile was killed by food!

Nothing like this has ever happened.

Sometimes the reptiles would fall or kill each other in a fight or get bitten by a bug, but food never *killed* his kind. Food was simply there for the taking.

They kill the food.

The food doesn't kill *them*.

The reptiles walk in silence. Their heads swivel around, looking for unknown dangers. They're unsure of themselves, and they're afraid.

Their world is suddenly a very different place.

The Youngest Hatchling finds the strange shiny branch where the Larger Reptile dropped it. He picks it up. He's surprised by the weight of it. It's very heavy.

The Youngest Hatchling swings it a few times. Holding the shiny branch, he feels a sense of power.

The reptiles continue to move back. Without the Larger Reptile leading the way, the reptiles drift off in various directions.

The Youngest Hatchling wanders into a field of grass. The grass gets taller and thicker. He tries using the shiny branch to clear a path, like the Larger Reptile did.

Swinging the branch feels awkward. Chopping through the grass is tiring. It's still better than not clearing a path, though.

Before long, the Youngest Hatchling notices that some of the other reptiles are following him on the path he's making.

As the daylight fades, exhaustion catches up with him. With the last of his energy, the Youngest Hatchling chops a clear area and is soon asleep.

The next morning, the Youngest Hatchling wakes in his small clearing. The shiny branch is gone!

A path has been cut leading away.

The Youngest Hatchling hurries down the path cut in the tall grass. He passes the other reptiles. As he comes up to the front of the path, he sees a reptile swinging the shiny branch clumsily at the tall grass.

This reptile looks tired and drops the branch. Another reptile moves up to the front, picks up the branch, and begins clearing more path.

The Youngest Hatchling rubs his sore muscles as he watches the other reptile struggle to clear a path.

He decides to let the others clear the path.

The reptiles in the north have had trouble with a type of large creature. When the reptiles began moving into this area, many reptiles were killed by the creatures.

Even now, a reptile is occasionally injured while hunting one of the creatures or killed by a group of them.

These creatures are about the same size as the reptiles. The furry creatures have claws like the reptiles. They also have big, sharp teeth, but their mouths are smaller.

The large creatures are good, big food, if you can kill them without getting injured or killed yourself.

When he was a hatchling, he found the bright, shiny stick. The piece is long, thin, straight, and round. It comes to a sharp point at one end.

At the time, the bright, shiny stick was nearly three times longer than his little body. Now, the piece is about twice the length of his arm.

He feels that there is something special about the bright, shiny thing. The furry creatures avoid him when he carries the bright, shiny stick into the mountains.

It seems like the bright, shiny stick could be useful for something, but all he does is carry it around. He never uses it for any purpose. There just hasn't been any reason to use the thing for anything in particular.

In his lifetime, he never did.

At first, she doesn't think much about the newest reptiles coming up from the south. Then she sees that they have a large piece of the bright and shiny.

Their piece looks like a tall, thin scrub bush, only made of twig-sized, overlapping strands of the bright and shiny material. Small chunks of rock are stuck to it in places.

When she was a hatchling, an old reptile had a long piece of the bright and shiny.

She thinks about looking for the piece that the old reptile carried around. That was a long time ago. She doesn't know where to look.

As she goes through her daily life, she occasionally thinks about the old bright and shiny piece and sometimes looks for it.

The more she thinks about it, the more she remembers. She remembers some places where she saw the old reptile with the piece.

She recalls that most of the time, the old reptile seemed to be in an area of the forest near the river. She begins hunting in that area. She finds herself spending more time in the area and looking closer for the old reptile's bright and shiny piece.

When the reptiles from the south first arrived, their new piece of the bright and shiny seemed special. One of the new reptiles was always around the bush-like piece.

There were a few short fights near the rocks where the piece was placed.

Now, the bright and shiny piece just sits there. Nobody even thinks about it anymore.

The piece is not very bright or shiny, either. Dirt covers the entire piece. The bottom and most of one side are completely buried. Grass and bushes have grown around it.

Unless you knew where to look, you would never know that the piece is there.

Now, in her waning years, she spends most of her time in this area near the river. The tree cover is good. There's good food here, including the small food she finds in the river water.

She sees a cave opening that she's never noticed before. The grass there is very tall, taller than her. Large rocks are piled in front of the cave.

She gets closer and sees that the cave goes back farther than the usual reptile's dugout in the side of a hill.

Wanting to avoid the tall grass, she circles to the side of the hill. As she gets closer to the cave, she realizes that she's on an old path.

She approaches the stack of rocks in front of the cave. The ground hasn't been disturbed for a long time.

She decides to go in. She has to lower her head to enter the cave. A short distance inside, she can stand up again.

Inside the cave, there's an old pile of grass bedding—mostly turned to dust now. There's a large pile of bones—small creatures and river food. In the corner, under a pile of dried tree branches, she finds the long piece of the bright and shiny.

Now that she's found it, she doesn't know what to do with this piece of the bright and shiny. It's heavier than she expected.

She doesn't know why the old reptile would carry the thing around. She places it back in the corner. She's not sure why, but she carefully piles the tree branches back over the bright and shiny piece before she leaves the cave.

She walks over to the other piece of the bright and shiny. It's mostly buried and still ignored.

The thought strikes her to put this round piece in the cave with the long piece. She digs out the round piece.

There seems to be something special about the bright and shiny, so she puts the two pieces together in the cave.

When he was a young reptile, he went to the strange cave many times. That's where he found the two pieces of bright-shiny, in the corner of the cave.

The pieces were buried under a layer of dirt and the powdery remnants of tree branches. Apparently, the pieces had been hidden there for a very long time.

During most of his life, he's tinkered with the bright-shiny pieces. He's found some occasional uses for them.

The smaller, bush-like piece he uses to catch the small food in the river. He puts the piece in the water and river food gets caught in it.

The long piece he uses mostly for knocking small food out of the trees. Once in a while, he's able to stab small food right out of a tree or from under a bush.

New reptiles arrive in the area. It's a sizeable band, and they're not much older than hatchlings.

They have an interesting piece of bright-shiny. It looks like a tree branch at one end, and the other end is flat, like the river food. The new reptiles are showing some of the other reptiles how they swing the branch-like piece to clear grass and scrub bushes.

Why would anybody want to do that? There's some tall grass and scrub bush around, but not so much that there would be a reason to cut it down.

He gets closer to look at their piece of bright-shiny. It's interesting how the flat end is sharp along its edges. It reminds him of the reptile's third, pincer claw that they use to cut food or hold things.

Back at the cave, he considers his two pieces of bright-shiny and thinks about the other piece. He clacks his two front and third pincer claws together. He tries to think of ways to combine the three pieces to make something helpful.

He stands the short, bush-like piece up and puts the long piece on top of it. He circles around, looking at them.

Over the years, he has tried many different ways to combine his two pieces of bright-shiny. Now, he tries to think of a way that the third piece could be combined with his pieces.

He sits in the cave, considering possibilities. He clacks his two front and third pincer claws together while looking at the two pieces of bright-shiny.

He looks down at his claws. He looks back at the two pieces. He thinks about the third piece. An idea seems to be forming, but he's not sure exactly what it is.

He wants to see all three pieces together.

He searches for the band of new reptiles and discovers that they're gone. They left!

He sees their trail going over the hill. It looks like someone is dragging the piece of bright-shiny with the flat side to the ground.

He needs to see all three pieces together. How long ago did they leave?

He decides that he needs to catch up with the new reptiles. As he runs back to the cave, he formulates a basic plan.

He quickly puts together a small bag of personal items. He slings the bag over his head and one shoulder. He picks up his two pieces of bright-shiny with one in each hand. He hurries out of the cave and gets on their trail.

Several days later, he reaches the top of a long uphill walk. On the other side of the pass is a large valley.

He stops to look it over. The mountains on the other side of the valley are very far away.

He sees the trail left by the new reptiles. Their trail goes down into the flatland, but he doesn't see the reptiles. How far ahead can they be?

As he gets closer to the bottom of the slope, he's surprised by the large amount of vegetation. It's not like this where he lives. In this place, there are trees everywhere, and the grass and scrub bush are thick.

Following the trail leads him into increasingly taller grass. He sees where the reptiles have cleared a path in the grass with their branch of bright-shiny. The grass is getting so tall that the path becomes a tunnel.

Now he understands why the new reptiles thought it was so important to be able to clear away the grass.

He's been in the tunnel for most of the day. The daylight is fading.

He hears the reptiles ahead. They're very close.

The tunnel suddenly opens into a small, cleared area. Around the corner, it's the new reptiles!

They see him. A few of the new reptiles lift their heads and let out a short, soft growl, more of a trill. A couple of the other reptiles look over and do the same.

They are not aggressive or passive. It is just an acknowledgment. Then they look away and return to what they were doing.

As he moves from the tunnel opening into the cleared area, he tries to mimic the sound they made.

He finds a small open spot at the edge of the clearing. He sets down his two pieces of bright-shiny. He settles into a comfortable position.

It's good to be off the feet.

He's relieved to be able to rest. He closes his eyes. His arms are sore from carrying the bright-shiny. His legs are throbbing from the fast walking. He hasn't slowed down to get much food, either.

In the fading daylight, he notices a faint shadow over him. He opens his eyes to see one of the new reptiles standing over him, holding their branch of bright-shiny.

The reptile is looking at his two pieces of bright-shiny. He looks at their shiny branch piece. It's interesting how the piece is flat on one half.

He looks up to see that the new reptile is looking at him, looking at their shiny branch. The new reptile lets out that short, soft trill, walks away, and sits down at the other end of the cleared area inside the tall grass.

The next day starts with the sound of a reptile swinging the branch of bright-shiny, cutting a path through the tall grass. One reptile swings for a while before dropping back to the end of the line. Then the next reptile in line swings for a while.

Suddenly, all the reptiles stop and get quiet. Some of them slip quietly into the tall grass. There's a lot of rustling in the grass to the side. Then there's a wail and growling. It sounds like they just got food!

The reptiles return to the tunnel, dragging a sizable food. The food is about half his size. It's covered with fur, and it has a small mouth with some sharp teeth in it.

A reptile uses the flat end of the branch to cut off pieces of food. Now *that* is a good use of the bright-shiny.

The reptile cuts off two pieces and walks over to other reptiles. The cutter gives them the two pieces of food.

He's never seen a reptile give food to another—leave extra food for others, yes, but not so organized as this.

The cutter walks over to him, hands him a small piece of food, and walks back to cut some more pieces.

The food tastes very good. It isn't much, but he's glad to eat.

When the food is gone, the reptiles line up in the tunnel and continue swinging the branch to clear a path. He's getting close to the front when the line stops.

There's a small area of less vegetation, then there's very thick vegetation. It looks like many small trees growing very close together with grass growing throughout it.

At the front of the line is the new reptile who was looking at his two pieces of bright-shiny. The reptile swings the branch of bright-shiny repeatedly at the thick line of vegetation. The reptile pauses for a moment.

The new reptile aggressively swings the branch a few more times and inspects the meager progress. The frustrated reptile glances around at the vegetation and at the other reptiles. Then the reptile focuses on his two pieces of bright-shiny.

The new reptile walks over to him and extends the branch. He already has a piece of bright-shiny in each hand, plus the shoulder bag containing his personal stuff. The new reptile steps closer and extends the branch again.

He walks over to the line of thick vegetation and sets down the smaller, bush-like piece of bright-shiny. He sets down the long piece next to the first piece. He sets down his shoulder bag. He steps back and takes the third piece.

This is the first time that he's held the third piece. It's heavier than he would have thought. The edges of the flat part are sharp, and the end of the piece is very sharp.

Near the middle, where the flat part changes to the round part, there's an interesting bulge with a hole going all the way through it. He sticks the tip of a claw in the hole.

He looks down at the piece of bright-shiny that looks like a tall, thin bush. There's a short peg of bright-shiny on the top that points upward. The short peg is a little smaller than the size of the hole in the branch piece.

He positions the hole through the bulge on the branch piece over the peg of the bush-like piece. With a little twisting, the branch piece fits onto the upward-sticking peg.

The branch piece swivels.

He takes the two attached pieces up to the thick line of vegetation and sets them down. He swivels the branch piece on the bush-like piece. It chops into the vegetation.

The sharp end of the branch cuts into the thick plants. It doesn't take much effort to swivel the branch piece when it's fitted onto the bush-like piece. He easily chops away.

A hole begins to form in the thick vegetation. The thin trees and bushes are cut through, but some of the grass remains.

He stops chopping and takes a look.

He pulls back the two pieces of bright-shiny. He looks at the opening in the thicker vegetation. He peers through the grass to the other side. There's an area of less vegetation on the other side, like it is on this side.

Other reptiles come up to look through the hole.

As he's walking back toward the two attached pieces of bright-shiny, his attention is drawn to the long piece on the ground. The long, straight piece resembles the thin trees that he just cut down.

He picks up the long piece and searches for a way to attach it to the other two pieces. He's thinking that he might be able to cut the grass against it with the branch.

He's standing behind the branch and bush-like pieces, holding the long piece pointed toward the opening.

Some reptiles in front of him are looking through the opening in the thicker vegetation. The reptiles suddenly dart away from the opening.

He glances up and sees something large squeezing through the hole. The creature looks like the food they just ate, only much larger. It's as large as a reptile.

By reflex, he quickly considers the situation. This could be good food, or it could be dangerous, or it could be both. As he's considering this, the furry creature bursts through the opening and lunges straight at him.

He's standing there, holding the long, thin, straight piece of bright-shiny that comes to a sharp point at the other end. It's pointed toward the hole.

The creature runs right into the end of the long piece. The creature's mid-body goes onto the point, and it runs a couple of steps up the piece before it stops.

He's surprised and not sure what to do. He looks at the creature. The creature looks down at the thing stuck through its body.

A second creature bursts through the opening. The creature looks at him. The creature charges toward him.

The branch is right there on top of the bush-like piece. With his other claw, he swivels it, pointing the sharp end of the branch at the second creature. Just like the first creature on the long piece, the charging second creature stabs itself into the sharp end of the branch and continues forward a step.

A third creature comes through and turns to the side to run around the other creatures.

He clamps the branch piece and the long piece together. The branch cuts through both creatures until it hits the long piece. The sliced-through bodies of the first two creatures fall away to each side.

As the third creature runs past him, he swings the long piece around. The bright-shiny catches the creature in the back of the head and the creature tumbles forward to a stop.

The other reptiles are astounded. They look at all the food. They look at him.

The branch. He has the branch! They need the branch to cut the food into pieces.

He turns and sets the long piece on top of the bush-like piece.

He's about to remove the branch piece from the bush-like piece when a fourth creature emerges from the opening. The creature steps forward, stops, and looks around.

The long piece is pointing past the creature's left side. On the creature's right side is the branch piece with the sharp edge.

Realizing the situation, he *snaps* together his two ends of the X made by the branch and the long piece.

Thus was created the first Special Weapon on the planet—giant scissors.

Gishey Donmaru travels on both sides of the mountain. Her family travels from the lake to the desert. They trade things from one end for things from the other end. They trade everything and everywhere between the two ends.

Gishey's family has homes in all three Regions, not counting the new Region people are talking about. Gishey has never been there, and she doesn't care to go.

The line of carts stops along the road for a midday food break. After eating, Gishey goes looking around in the trees along the road. Her father lets her run around whenever they stop. Gishey knows not to go very far.

Her mother acts like she doesn't like it, but Gishey thinks that her mother secretly does like when Gishey goes out exploring.

Sometimes Gishey finds things to bring back and talk about.

Gishey hears a whimpering sound further into the trees. She quietly sneaks up to see what it is.

It's a tiny baby icenna. Icennas are hairy, four-legged predators.

The fuzzy little baby is trying to nurse from its dead mother. The mother icenna had been injured, probably while hunting.

Gishey knows that the baby will not survive for long without its mother.

They're calling her. The food stop is over. They're ready to go.

Gishey's heart breaks for the little icenna. She slides over, scoops up the crying baby and cradles it in the pocket along the bottom of her shirt.

The tiny, fuzzy animal blinks its squinty eyes at her. It gets quiet and looks like it's going to go to sleep.

Her father calls her name again.

Gishey swiftly and carefully hurries back to the carts. She waves to several people, including her father and the assistant who pushes the cart she rides in. Her father watches as she climbs inside and closes the door.

Gishey settles into her spot, with the sleeping baby icenna hidden in her shirt.

Gishey is weary of all the traveling that they do. She thinks her family visits too many places. She wishes that they could just live in one place.

Sometimes traveling is fun, though. The people are generally nice everywhere they go. Her family is respected. Most of her group has the family "patch." It's a birthmark of slightly darker skin above the right eye.

When people see their Donma patch, they usually become even friendlier.

When Gishey tries to talk with her father about cutting down on traveling so much, he always says something like, "If we didn't travel, we wouldn't be eating as good as we do," or "If we didn't travel, you wouldn't have those nice clothes," or "If we didn't travel, we wouldn't have so many good friends," or "If we didn't travel, we wouldn't see so many wonderful places."

There's one of her father's sayings that Gishey can't argue with.

"If we didn't travel, you would not have found Nicena."

Nicena is her faithful and best friend, her pet icenna. Icennas are a little over knee-high to an adult. The animals walk on four legs and are covered with hair.

Icennas are predators in the wild. Nicena is not like that, though. Gishey has cared for and raised her ever since she rescued Nicena as a baby.

At first, many people did not like that Gishey was keeping an icenna as a pet. It's well known that icennas can be dangerous. However, the baby Nicena was accepted by most and generally considered to be something unique.

Also, Nicena is so friendly and nice that nobody should *not* like her, really. That's how Gishey thought of Nicena's name. She's a *nice* icenna. She's "Nice—eena!"

Lately, the talk has been about a large piece of dolg that was found in the new Region. It has a lot of people excited, specially in Gishey's family. Two other large pieces of dolg are kept in the family storage building, right next to the house.

As soon as they got to this town, her father rushed over to check on the dolg.

Her father has been working with their two pieces of dolg ever since. He's almost always at the storage building.

On most days, Gishey makes lunches to share with her father. Gishey is bringing lunch today. As always, Nicena is happily trotting along at Gishey's side.

As they like to do, Gishey sits at one end of the pile of dolg, and her father sits at the other. They look across the pile of weird shapes as they eat and talk.

Today is what Gishey calls a "start over" day. The pile of dolg has been taken apart and the pieces are re-arranged, again.

Her father's mood changes. Gishey recognizes the look of concern on his face. He looks her in the eye.

He speaks with a serious and worried voice. "Gishey, have you heard about all the terropad attacks, recently?"

Gishey squirms in her chair, uncomfortable with the thought of people getting hurt by those wild animals.

Her father is always concerned about Gishey getting hurt, but with Nicena always nearby, Gishey doesn't think that *she* would be attacked.

He continues in the same tone. "It's been happening more frequently. You have to be careful, Gishey!"

Gishey answers in her most serious tone. "We *are* careful, Nicena and me."

Her father looks over at Nicena and smiles. Nicena smiles back and wags her tail.

Terropads are just a little smaller than icennas.

The terropads come in from the unclaimed Region to the west. The wild predators lived in this area before people started the town.

The first settlers got the terropads under control as they Claimed the Region. Now, it seems the terropads are coming back.

Her father keeps staring at the dolg. He gets that "faraway" look on his face. He subconsciously reaches for something until he glances at Gishey.

She is giving him the "not during lunch" look.

He puts his hand down, looking guilty.

Gishey giggles.

Gishey teases him. "Are you *sure* about what you're trying to do?"

Her father chuckles. "Like I said many times, Gishey, I am *not* sure about what I'm trying to do. It just seems like there's something special, something important about this *dolg*. It's fascinating."

Gishey doesn't see what's so fascinating about the dolg. It's just a bunch of weird stuff—and it's heavy. Although, if you look at it for long enough, it sort-of . . . draws you in.

Her father whispers, "What are you thinking, Gishey?"

Gishey feels disturbed somehow. "I don't know. I was just looking at the strange way it's shaped, the little curves and twists and . . ."

Her father sits back slowly, studying what Gishey says.

Gishey continues, unsure of herself. "Have you ever seen it, sort-of . . . glow?"

The longer they're here, the more Gishey likes this house. They've stayed in this town for much longer than they usually stay anywhere. There isn't even talk about traveling again. Gishey thinks it's because of the dolg.

Her father still spends most of his time trying to do something with the two large pieces of dolg. That's fine with her. Gishey likes how so many things have settled into routines. This house and this town are starting to feel like a home.

The people of the town are mostly nice and friendly. Gishey is well known around town because of Nicena. Many people are curious about the icenna. They want to see the icenna. When they are comfortable enough, they want to touch the icenna.

Nicena happily lets anyone touch her. If someone is unsure, she will sidestep over to them or lean her head forward, making it easier for people to touch her long fur.

For a Species with no hair (except for the rare occasion), Nicena is something of a novelty. People are amused by such a friendly animal, covered in soft hair, and walking on four legs.

When they first meet Nicena, the people of the town are usually surprised and thrilled that she is so friendly. Then it's like they are all part of a club, "Friends of Nicena."

Most people find her large mouth with dangerous teeth to be an irony.

Nicena thrives on the attention, and she genuinely wants to make people happy. Nicena greets everybody as if she's saying, "Hi, I know you. You're a member of the club."

Not everybody likes Nicena, though. Some people are afraid of her. They don't give her a chance. They just hate that she's an icenna.

Some people even act like they're deathly afraid of her or something, getting all excited and waving their arms in the air. On rare occasions, somebody will get angry and call Nicena "that dangerous, wild animal in our town."

Nicena mostly ignores anybody who doesn't appear to be interested in liking her. Nicena doesn't act aggressive or snobbish. It's more like, "Oh, I'm just looking for another member of the club."

Gishey is happy to know that there are many members of the club, and not many of those panicky, angry people.

Gishey has made regular friends for the first time, too. She spends a lot of time with her neighbor down the hill, his girlfriend, and Yergis. Yergis was one of her first friends here.

Of course, they are all members of the club.

There's been a lot of excitement lately. They're bringing in that third large piece of dolg from the fourth Region. Her father gets a little crazy every time he talks about it.

Gishey Donmaru doesn't care about dolg. She's more interested in Yergis.

Yergis is a Donmahu. The Donmahu family patch, above the right eye, is the darkest of all the "Donmas."

There are other "Donma-somethings" and variations of "Donma-somethings." The various families of "Donmas" branched off from each other long ago.

It is interesting what they say, that if you go back far enough, all the different "Donmas" came from a common ancestor.

Whoever that was.

Something's happened!

There's a lot of shouting and wailing coming from down the mountain. It's not good. You can feel the pain in their voices.

Yergis goes to see what's happened. He's gone a long time before he finally gets back. He runs up to Gishey and the small group of friends.

Yergis is almost out of breath. "A baby's been taken. There's some blood and muddy animal tracks. Some people are going after the baby. That's all I was able to find out."

At the mention of animal tracks, Gishey wonders about Nicena. When Gishey is with Yergis, Nicena roams farther away.

Nicena usually isn't very far away, though. She's been absent long enough that Gishey thinks Nicena is probably taking a nap in Gishey's room.

There's a scream from down the mountain, then many loud voices. Everyone looks around at each other.

Gishey's neighbor begins to drift down the mountain. His girlfriend takes a few steps down the mountain. Gishey leans in that direction while she and Yergis look at each other. Then they all break into a trot to go and see what's happening.

Gishey glances back at the home to see if Nicena is following, but she's not there. Gishey is concerned about Nicena's absence. She considers going back home to look for Nicena. Instead, Gishey follows her friends toward the commotion.

Gishey keeps looking back, hoping to see Nicena running to catch up with them.

As the group clears the trees at the bottom of the mountain, they see a crowd gathered around something. People are talking loudly and waving their arms in the air.

Yergis runs ahead and disappears into the crowd.

Gishey and her friends hear voices from the crowd. "What did it do to the baby?" "Somebody stop it." "I knew something like this was going to happen. I *knew* it!"

Suddenly, most of the crowd cheers and runs off as a group.

Yergis runs in the other direction, toward something in the grass by the road.

It's Nicena!

Gishey gasps and takes off running. She doesn't notice the mean stares coming from a few people who are still there.

Yergis scoops Nicena out of the grass. Yergis is struggling to carry the heavy Nicena, but he looks determined. He hurries past Gishey toward her home.

As Yergis goes past, Gishey sees that Nicena is hurt. There is blood all over her. Nicena is hanging loosely in Yergis's arms.

Gishey pivots and quickly catches up with them.

Yergis tries to speak while running. "People were standing there, when Nicena went limping past, heading toward your house."

Yergis slows down a little to catch his breath. He tries to talk while keeping up a hurried pace. "Then, they saw that Nicena . . . had the boy, in her mouth."

Gishey is shocked and confused. She mumbles while she's running, "Whaaat?"

As they approach the house, Yergis slows down to a lumbering walk. He's struggling with the weight of Nicena.

Gishey runs ahead of him. She sprints to the front door and throws it open.

Yergis enters the house.

He looks around for a place to put Nicena. "When they ran over to her, Nicena set down the kid at the feet of a member of the club."

Gishey tries to absorb it all. She recoils from the sight of the blood all over Nicena. "Who did this to her?!"

Yergis goes into the washroom.

Gishey follows.

Yergis carefully places Nicena in the washing area. "Nobody got near her. She was already like this. By the time I realized what was going on, Nicena was limping away. When she saw me, she just collapsed in the grass."

Yergis backs away as Gishey approaches the washing area. Nicena is bleeding *a lot!*

Gishey shouts with anger and fear. "Get some wet towels!"

Yergis leaves to get the towels.

He continues from the kitchen. "Someone said Nicena's tracks were at the boy's house, in the dirt, going away from the house. They said Nicena's tracks were on top of a trail of blood, like the kid was bleeding, then Nicena was stepping in it."

Gishey's anger rises. "Then how did she get like this?! You know like I do that Nicena would *not* hurt anybody, particularly a small child!"

Yergis takes an armful of towels over to the kitchen window and dunks them halfway into the pot of warm water. After each towel is mostly wet, he sets them next to Gishey.

Yergis tugs at his blood-soaked green shirt. "It doesn't make sense . . . unless a terropad took the kid. I don't think Nicena hurt the boy. She acted like she was caring for him."

Gishey starts gently wiping the blood out of Nicena's fur. Nicena stirs, then begins breathing heavily.

Nicena looks up at Gishey. When their eyes meet, the pain on Nicena's face fades for a moment.

Nicena gives Gishey that *look*, as if she's saying, "Hi, I know you. You're a member of the club."

Then the moment is past. Nicena slumps her head back down.

Yergis brings Gishey a cup of drinking water. He sets the cup on a table near the washing area.

Yergis glances at Nicena. "Nicena needs help. I think I know who to ask. I'll be back as fast as I can."

Yergis is gone before Gishey can think of anything to say.

Gishey gets most of the old blood wiped off. Now she can see the wounds better with just the fresh blood. They look like terropad wounds.

With a determined effort, Gishey picks up Nicena in a bundle of towels. She struggles to carry Nicena into her room and over to Gishey's bed. Nicena offers no resistance.

Gishey walks across the room to get the bag of bandages and medicines. When she tries to pick up the bag, Gishey realizes that her hands are shaking.

Gishey hurries back over to Nicena and kneels next to the bed. Nicena's eyes are half open, and her tongue is hanging partway out of her mouth. Nicena is still breathing heavily, but not as bad.

Gishey is heartbroken. "Now Nicena, I'm going to bandage you up, so let me take care of you."

Nicena lifts her head. Like they have so many times before, Gishey and Nicena look into each other's eyes. There is understanding, a connection.

Nicena licks her upper lip in the way that seems to say, "I love you." Then Nicena drops her head back down to the bed.

Gishey loosely places a temporary bandage over all the wounds that are bleeding. With a closer look at the wounds, she knows better where to start and what to do. The family teaches these kinds of things so that everybody knows when they need to.

Even at a glance, Gishey can tell that the wounds are bites and claw cuts. As she cleans and re-bandages the injuries, Gishey is certain that the wounds came from a terropad. Gishey has seen these kinds of wounds on the people of the town, many times.

Nicena is being great about letting Gishey help. Nicena winces and flinches a few times but allows Gishey to treat the wounds.

When Gishey is done bandaging, Nicena closes her eyes and continues to breathe heavily.

Gishey sits on the floor next to the bed.

She knows that Nicena is hurting and scared. Gishey is exhausted, physically and emotionally. She starts crying.

Gishey's relieved that Nicena is alive but frightened by the thought that Nicena might not survive.

Gishey hears the approach of loud voices. One of the voices is her mother!

Suddenly, the door to Gishey's room bursts open. A man stands in the doorway. He looks mean-angry!

Behind him, Gishey sees her mother struggling with someone else.

Gishey springs to her feet. The man leaps over and pushes her away so hard that her head and arms snap forward.

Gishey is flung backward.

She glances off the bedside table before slamming hard against the wall. As she hits the table, she hears a bone crack in her lower arm. Then her head slams against the wall.

Pain shoots through her. Everything is blurry. Her thoughts are fuzzy.

She vaguely observes two people move from the doorway to the bed. The man is standing beside the bed. The two people are carrying sticks. The man has a stick.

The man is beating the stick down on the bed. The other two begin beating on the bed . . . *where Nicena is!*

All around hear Gishey, "*SSSHHHRRRIIIIEEEEEEKKK!*"

The nurse examines Gishey, who is still sleeping. The nurse checks the bandages. She reports back to the doctor.

The nurse is indignant. "I can understand why they did that to the icenna. But they should not have hurt that young woman!"

The doctor replies with compassion. "What they did to her pet will probably hurt her more than the broken arm and bruised head."

The nurse continues, "Well, if it attacked the boy . . . How is the child?"

The doctor sighs in relief. "He's good. He will have some scars from the cuts, but I think most of the bite marks will be unremarkable."

The doctor shakes his head. "We stitched that kid back together. I have seen those kinds of wounds far too often. Those wounds were caused by a terropad. The teeth and claw marks were all made by a terropad! I have no doubt."

The nurse begins to understand. "Then, that would mean . . . Oh, no."

When Gishey wakes, she's not sure where she is.

She hears Yergis talking in the other room. She hopes that her father is in the other room. She wishes her father were here.

Gishey slowly gets up and staggers toward the door. She feels so dizzy. She scans the doctor's lobby. Her father is not here.

Yergis is talking quietly with the doctor and nurse. Gishey drifts up behind Yergis. Just as she reaches over to him, Yergis stands up and hurries out the door.

Yergis leans his head back into the open doorway and starts to say something. When he sees Gishey standing in the room, Yergis turns to her and shows his hand. "A crowd is gathering around the circle in the road. I'm going to see what's happening."

Then he's gone.

The nurse walks over to the window and peers outside.

Gishey numbly follows Yergis.

Her broken arm bumps the door jamb. She knows that pain just shot up her arm, but that pain barely registers through all of the other pain.

Gishey shuffles toward the circle in the road. There are a lot of people gathering. Half of the town must be here.

An older man offers Gishey his seat on a bench. He allows Gishey to brace herself on his forearm as she gets seated.

Gishey is close enough to the group of town leaders to hear what they're saying. She's also high enough on the hill so she can see that her father is with a group of people coming back into town. Her father runs up to the town leaders.

Her father looks determined as he speaks to the leaders. "Nicena didn't do it!"

A large man pushes his way to the front. Gishey doesn't recognize him. She doesn't think she's seen him before.

The man approaches the town leaders but speaks loud enough for everybody to hear. "We followed that icenna's tracks from the boy's house, all the way and back. It is clear that a *terropad* took the boy, and the icenna chased after. The icenna caught up to the terropad before it got very far, just into the trees."

Another man blurts out excitedly, "They got in a fight, too!"

The large man glares at him, obviously annoyed. "I was just about to say that part!"

The large man turns back to the town leaders. "We found a place where the ground was all stirred up. Blood trails going in circles, bits of terropad hide. We saw the trails of both animals leading away in opposite directions."

The large man swivels as he addresses the gathered crowd. "The icenna fought the terropad to get the boy back!"

Her father sums it up. "And what did Nicena do then? She was bringing the child straight to Gishey for help! Nicena didn't take the boy, she *rescued* the boy!"

Her father smiles at Gishey and nods his head as if to say, "It's going to be good."

Gishey can't help it. She bursts into tears. She doubles over as if unable to sit upright. She mumbles with heavy sobs. "Ni-ce-na . . . uuhh!"

She gasps for breath.

Stunned, her father notices the bandages on Gishey's arm. He sees the blood on her shirt. He anguishes at the sight of his daughter.

She is in great pain.

With veins throbbing under his Donma patch, Gishey's father growls, slow and loud through clenched teeth. "What . . . *WHAT HAS HAPPENED?!*"

Silence sweeps through the group. Heads turn downward.

Yergis angrily tugs at his clean blue shirt, two sizes too big for him. There's a sadness in his voice. "They thought Nicena killed the little boy."

Yergis turns away from Gishey's father and speaks louder to the group. "The boy isn't dead, and he isn't going to die! I just came from there. The doctor bandaged him up!"

Yergis scowls at the group. He looks into the eyes of friends and strangers.

Yergis announces, "The boy is going to be good!"

Yergis accuses in righteous indignation, "What about *Gishey*?"

Yergis turns sympathetically to Gishey's father. "They killed Nicena."

What follows is a blur.

Gishey is lost without Nicena. The absence is a hole in her world. Nicena was such an important part of her life for so long.

Her father takes time to hear the whole story. He questions a lot of people about what they know and what they think. He spends several days alone, locked in the storage building, not wanting to see anybody.

Then her father goes looking for the one who broke her arm and killed Nicena.

Gishey's father is killed.

Nobody knows what her father was going to say or do. They didn't give him a chance to say or do anything. That group just attacked him before he even got to the house.

Even with so many against him, her father killed three of them before the rest killed him.

Gishey is unable to comprehend a world without her father. He isn't gone forever. He just isn't here at the moment.

Sometimes she gets upset with him when she wants to talk with her father or needs his help and he's not there.

Her mother is devastated. Gishey wishes she could go to her mother, but it's too much pain in the same place. Instead of supporting each other, they drift apart.

Her mother doesn't blame Gishey or Nicena for anything that's happened. Her mother assigns all the blame where it properly belongs—the Gemishay. It's their fault that her father and Nicena aren't here.

Her mother calls them "those vile idiots."

Some extended family arrives in town in a Traveling Group. Gishey avoids them.

Her mother decides to join their Group when they leave. Gishey isn't sure if her mother is going to another town or back to traveling.

Her mother asks Gishey to go with her. Gishey is old enough now to decide for herself.

To Gishey, leaving isn't even a possibility. She can't imagine leaving without her father and Nicena. She would feel like she's leaving them behind.

Also, Yergis is here.

Yergis tries to be helpful and understanding. He cares for her and does a lot to help. For a while, Gishey relies on him heavily.

Gishey is grateful to Yergis, but she doesn't show it. She isn't sure how to. She isn't sure about anything.

Occasionally, Gishey overhears his friends murmuring things like, "We know you care about her, but you're doing too much. Look at yourself, Yergis."

One day, Yergis touches her arm and Gishey flinches away from him. Her reaction startles both of them.

Yergis sounds frustrated and frightened. "I want *my* Gishey back."

Gishey realizes that they haven't touched each other in a long time.

She hears Yergis's friends openly say things like, "Well, she doesn't seem to care about you, Yergis. Look at the way she treats you."

Gishey knows she should be acting differently. But she feels numb, about everything.

Since her mother left, Gishey has supported herself by selling the inventory in the storage building.

It's always awkward dealing with the people of the town, whether she's selling or buying. She hates going into town.

Most people try to be nice, but they usually say something that reminds Gishey of the loss of her family. Sometimes it's about Nicena. Usually it's about her father or mother.

Gishey feels uncomfortable when they sometimes give her a little extra in a deal. When she realizes that they're doing it, she doesn't know how to refuse their kindness and generosity. She doesn't know how to thank them, either.

One day, having just completed a sale, Gishey is in the lower end of town. Gishey stops at a restaurant for lunch before going home.

As Gishey walks in, she is startled to see Yergis at the far end of the eating area. He's with three other people. Two of them seem to be a couple, and the third is a young woman Gishey has never seen before.

Someone is talking nearby. The restaurant greeter is talking to her.

The greeter seems concerned. "Are you good?"

Gishey steps away so that Yergis and his group can't see her. She's uncomfortable and unsure of herself. "Yes, I'm sorry. I, uh, I was looking for someone."

The greeter is glad to be talking business. "Ah, how many are going to be in your group?"

Gishey scrambles to think of something to say. She strongly does not want to be here. She wants to leave, *now!*

Gishey rushes toward the door. "This isn't the right place. I'm sorry."

Gishey dashes quickly up the road a short distance. She wonders about Yergis.

Surprising herself, Gishey stops at the corner of a building. She hides around the corner and watches the entrance of the restaurant.

She feels foolish, but she waits and watches anyway. A few other groups of people leave the restaurant. Then she sees Yergis's friends.

The couple walks out first. They link arms—the sign of being a couple.

Then she sees Yergis and the fourth one. They turn and walk in the other direction.

Gishey sees Yergis and the woman link arms.

Gishey isn't sure what to think. She realizes that she hasn't seen him in a long time. She hasn't even thought about him. Yet, she is still surprised.

Gishey is gripped by a sense of loss.

She basically knew deep down, but she never acknowledged it. It wasn't officially over.

What hurts the most is the finality of it.

She has now lost Yergis, too.

Gishey thinks back to that time, so long ago.

Sometimes it is still mind-numbing to think about how much and how fast life can change—for the worse. In such a short time, she lost her best friend and longtime companion, and then her father, and her mother, and then Yergis.

Gishey has been alone since then.

It took a long time before Gishey stopped expecting to see Nicena. So many times, Gishey wished that she could just sit with Nicena and talk with her again. Even after all this time, it still hurts *so much.*

Also, the senselessness and the injustice of what happened still stings deep.

Sometimes, completely unexpected, it hits her as if it has just happened—or is happening. Gishey still has nightmares about "that day" and the events that unfolded immediately after.

Gishey remembers hearing people say that her father got killed over the icenna, but she knows it wasn't that. He was going there because someone hurt his daughter.

Gishey only vaguely remembers the last time she saw her mother. Thinking back, Gishey envisions two strangers, both numb with deep, wrenching pain. They stand in front of each other, not knowing what to say and looking curiously at each other.

Gishey does not remember a lot of things from that time. She doesn't remember when they removed the bandages from her broken arm. She doesn't remember what her father's or mother's faces looked like.

Gishey doesn't remember exactly when Yergis stopped staying at her house. She doesn't remember the last time she and Yergis were together.

She can't even remember what it was like.

Gishey sits, slumped down in her chair, in the shop at the back of the storage building. She stares unfocused at the pile of three large pieces of dolg.

Gishey walks into the food store. She glances at the line in front of the raised pay table to her right. She notices a boy in the middle of the line. People are usually in groups of two or three and usually her age or older.

The boy is clearly by himself. Nobody is even near him. The boy is just standing in line, by himself, with his head down. Gishey senses a sadness about him.

As usual, people are talking about various divisions and conflicts among the people of the three Regions. One group wants this, others do not. One group likes that, others do not. One group wants to Claim the fourth Region, and others do not.

Gishey doesn't care either way about the fourth Region.

By habit, Gishey starts at the back of the store. She collects her items and works her way toward the door.

One group does want to Claim the fifth Region and another group does not. Of course, the "Claim the fifth" group includes many from the "Claim the fourth" group, but not all of them. Typical.

Any news about the fifth Region is always big around here. The town is in the northwest corner of the third Region, at the border with the fifth Region's southeast corner.

Gishey tells herself that she doesn't care about the fifth Region either, but she does care in a way. Nobody knows what's out there. That makes it interesting.

What could they be living next to?

It's really that she doesn't want to care what anybody else thinks—about anything.

After "that day," some people supported the boy's father.

In town, where everybody knew Nicena and the boy's family—the Gemishay and that group—most people supported the Donmarus. But not everybody.

Across the rest of the three Regions, where people didn't know Nicena or the others, most people supported the Gemishay.

Gishey approaches the front of the store. The sad boy is now standing to the side of the pay table. The last of the people who were behind him are paying now. The boy is alone, with his head down, being ignored.

Gishey waits until the last people finish paying and go out the door. Then Gishey moves toward the pay table.

The clerk sitting at the pay table impatiently waves her forward.

Gishey points to the boy. "He was here before me."

Irritated, the clerk looks at the boy for a moment. The clerk's expression changes to an ugly, satisfied-looking smile—like he's made a point. He waves the boy forward.

The boy glances at her as he steps forward. He places money and something she can't see on the table. The clerk nods, the boy picks up the item and sprints out the door.

Gishey wonders what all that was about.

While Gishey is paying, the clerk keeps giving her strange looks. At first, Gishey ignores it. She's been treated like this ever since "that day." However, this seems different.

They nod to each other in completion of the transaction. The clerk has a strange expression on his face, like he wants to ask a question.

It occurs to her that she could probably learn what the strange looks are about with a simple, "What?" Instead, Gishey leaves the store and heads toward home. She stopped caring, a long time ago, about all the looks she gets from everybody.

But the clerk was different.

The clerk wasn't being unfriendly or overly sympathetic.

Briefly, she wonders what was going on with the clerk. Then she dismisses the thought. She doesn't care what anybody else thinks, about anything.

Gishey turns the first corner on her long walk home. The boy from the store is standing on the other side of the road. He's eating something.

This is the third time their paths have crossed today.

Her curiosity returns. She decides to ask the boy about what just happened in the store.

As Gishey approaches, the boy glances sideways at her.

The boy speaks first and sounds friendly. "Thanks for what you did in the store, letting me pay before you."

As he's speaking, the boy turns his face toward her. He's smiling—AAHH! Gishey involuntarily flinches at the sight of the other side of his face.

It's disfigured. There are deep scars, and his right eye is lower than the left. He's not a Donma. There's no patch above his right eye.

The boy drops his head again and shuffles away. Gishey realizes that she was staring at the malformed side of his face. She didn't even say anything in response to his "thank you."

She just stood there gawking at him.

Gishey regrets it for two reasons: his disfigurement is probably why he gets treated unfairly, and because she made the boy feel bad, too.

Well, it surprised her.

A few years later, Gishey is in town on errands. Near her first stop, she sees a group of older kids gathered in a circle. They're talking loudly and cheering about something. She ignores them.

Yet, they seem to be having fun. She's mildly curious. She drifts toward them. Some of them appear to be young adults.

Gishey moves closer and sees that two boys are kicking another boy, who is curled up on the ground.

Gishey is wondering if she should break it up. Then she recognizes the boy on the ground. He's the disfigured boy from the store a while back.

By a reflex, Gishey yells at the group. "Hey, what are you doing? Stop it!"

The kids scatter and run away.

The boy on the ground looks up. When he understands that the attack is over, he drops his arms from his head. He casually gets up, dusting off his clothes.

When the disfigured boy sees Gishey, he jerks the bad side of his face away from her, but he doesn't run off.

They both stand there for a moment in an awkward silence.

Gishey still regrets her response to his face when she saw his scars for the first time.

Gishey breaks the silence. "I'm sorry about my reaction to your scars that time at the food store. You probably don't even remember. But it just surprised me."

The boy glances at her several times. He's not sure what to say. He keeps the left side of his face toward her.

The boy tries to be gracious. "At least you don't want to hurt me because of it."

Gishey is puzzled. "Is that why those kids were hitting you just now—and why the clerk acted like he did? Or did you do something?"

The boy replies sadly. "I never do anything bad to anybody. I don't even try to fight back anymore. Other than trying to block the really bad stuff."

Gishey is familiar with terropad scars. Terropad attacks are a part of life here. For most of her life, she's overheard people talking about how they got their scars.

Even though a terropad attack is a traumatizing experience, some people of the town talk openly and casually about it. Others *do not* like to talk about it.

Gishey raises the subject. "How did you get your scars?"

The boy hesitates and seems confused. "Accident when I was little."

Gishey assumes he's uncomfortable talking about it. "That doesn't seem like a good reason to be mean to somebody."

The boy partially smiles. "Yeah. It doesn't seem like a good reason to me, either."

Gishey can't think of anything else to say, so she decides to get back to her errands.

She starts to walk away. "Well, stay out of trouble."

The boy, now a young adult, tilts his head to the side and raises his eyebrows in the "Are you joking?" gesture.

A few days later, Gishey quietly sits in the shop, as usual. She spends much of her time in the shop, ignoring her father's dolg, not really doing anything.

She's startled by a knock at the storage building's front door.

She isn't expecting anybody. Nobody ever comes here unless it's by appointment.

She peeks out. It's the disfigured boy.

She doesn't really care to see him here. She considers ignoring him and going back to what she was doing. Well, she wasn't really doing anything.

Maybe it's something important.

Gishey opens the door.

The boy stammers a bit. "Hi. I thought I should visit and thank you for stopping those kids the other day."

He steps closer and peers past Gishey into the storage building. "*What's in there?*"

Gishey's reflex action is to pull the door to her side. "Some stuff my family left."

The boy deadpans at her.

She comments further. "Selling it is how I live."

He seems to understand.

They are both surprised when Gishey turns and walks inside, leaving the door open.

The boy follows her inside the large building. He takes a sweeping look around the whole room. The space is mostly empty.

There are some building materials and supplies, some large rolls of stymeyfruzzy leaf for making clothes, various sizes of boxes and crates, and a few other things.

It isn't much. Gishey is running out of inventory to sell.

The boy shares. "I scavenge and trade. There are a few people who will buy stuff from me—as long as nobody else knows about it."

He drifts toward a corner with a cluster of boxes and crates, casually looking around as he slowly walks. Now, Gishey is following him.

He stops at a wood pile. "Have you been down to the river lately?"

Gishey hasn't even thought about it for years. "No, not in a long time."

He chats. "Somebody just started offering raft rentals."

He says in a mocking voice, "You can rent a raft for half the day, a full day, or longer—with oars, a pole, or both."

Gishey smiles. "I heard somebody say that when I was in town. I didn't know what they were talking about."

The boy returns her smile and walks while he talks. "The rafts look like fun. I have a rope tied to a tree branch that's over the river. It's fun to swing out of the tree and into the water."

Gishey vaguely recalls some distant memories of having fun at the river with Yergis and their friends. "We used to jump from the cliffs and sled down the mud hills into the river."

The memories become a little clearer. Of course, Nicena was always there. She seemed to patrol the area while Gishey played in the water.

Nicena would play in the water at times, too.

Gishey smiles at the thought of Nicena with wet hair. Nicena looked too skinny compared to when her hair was dry and puffed out.

The boy's voice snaps Gishey back to the present. "I've jumped from the cliffs—haven't tried the mud hills yet."

It's nice to talk with somebody about something other than a business transaction. Gishey starts to feel comfortable with the boy. He has a friendly honesty about him.

He stops walking and stares to his left. Gishey walks up behind him.

She sees that she left the door open to the shop at the back. They're both staring at the pile of dolg.

The boy asks excitedly. "What's *that*?"

Nobody except her has seen the dolg in many years. Gishey feels more than a little uncomfortable about the boy seeing it now.

When people come here to haul off something or to drop off something, Gishey always makes sure that the pile of dolg is covered, the window shutters are closed, and the shop door is shut and locked.

She wasn't expecting anybody today.

It isn't really a secret, though. The whole town knew about the dolg when they brought the third piece here.

Gishey recalls more memories. "My father thought he could make something with it. He tried making something to scoop water from the river, some kind of vegetable picker, a few other things."

Gishey switches from concerned that the boy had seen the dolg to blabbering about it. "The last thing he talked about was using it to kill terropads"—the boy stiffens at the word—"though I don't see how."

Gishey remembers now. "He said he thought it could be used to throw rocks."

Gishey is melancholy. "I've been looking at it for years. I don't see how this stuff could be used for any of the things my father tried doing with it."

Gishey said a lot before she realized it. Then she feels a sense of relief from having shared her thoughts with somebody.

The boy speaks with a tone of experience. "Throwing rocks only discourages the terropads, slightly."

Gishey is glad for the company and conversation. The boy is easy to be with.

She keeps thinking of him as the boy from the store. Now, he's a young adult.

She doesn't know his name. She never asks anybody their name. She usually doesn't care about anyone's name.

He continues, anxiously trying to be casual. "May I look at it? I might have an idea that you haven't thought of yet."

Gishey is actually considering it. She must know his name first. "My name is Gishey."

He dodges her prompt. "I know. Everybody knows you."

Gishey waits. He looks at her from his left side. She gives him the "I'm waiting" look.

He hesitates. "My name is Druno. Most people know my name. I thought you did, too."

Gishey shrugs one shoulder and shakes her head.

Druno moves toward the dolg. "You would need a lot of people, each throwing as many rocks as they're able, just to get the terropads to leave."

Druno looks over the pieces. "After they stand there for a while, looking at you, and thinking about it."

He continues, somewhat distracted. "The terropads, I mean."

One piece of the dolg is roughly A-shaped. One piece looks like a giant spoon, and the third piece is, well, strange. It's a weird shape. He is intrigued.

Druno circles the dolg. "I think what might work on the terropads is something like—setting many large rocks on top of a hill, catching the terropads halfway up the hill, and rolling the large rocks down the hill at them."

Druno half turns to Gishey, always his left side to her. "The problem with that idea is, you would also need a lot of people."

Over the next several tenths of a year, Druno and Gishey work together with the dolg.

Actually, Gishey doesn't do much. Druno studies the dolg, fiddles with her father's tools, and explores the shop.

Mostly, Gishey and Druno talk about many different things. Neither of them has had anybody to talk with for a long time. However, they are both careful not to talk about or ask about their personal histories. It's as though they have an unspoken agreement.

Sometimes, they don't talk for long periods of time. They both seem comfortable with the long silences, too.

Druno finds her father's dolg notebooks in an old desk. Druno excitedly shows Gishey an entry in one of the notebooks.

When she sees her father's handwriting, Gishey feels sick to her stomach.

Druno is talking enthusiastically about something.

Gishey isn't paying attention. His voice sounds like a fading echo.

Gishey has to leave.

She makes her way home.

Gishey doesn't go back to the shop for several days. After that, Druno will only look at the notebooks when she's not there. He's still friendly, but cautious.

Druno has an idea. "If we move the pieces out of the shop and into the storage building, between the shop and the stacks of crates, it would be easier to work with them."

Gishey is staggered by the thought. "Move the pieces?"

This is the last arrangement made by her father. None of the dolg has moved since he touched it last.

Druno is focused on the dolg. "It's a larger area and we can spread it out more, try different things."

Druno continues talking, but Gishey isn't listening. She's contemplating the concept of moving the pieces. She has been looking at this shape for so long.

Gishey glances at Druno. He stopped talking. He's smiling at her.

Gishey feels numb and detached from the moment.

Gishey is surprised when she hears the word "yes." She's further surprised when she realizes that *she* said it.

Gishey finds herself *helping* Druno move the pieces.

Her motions are sluggish, like she's underwater.

It doesn't seem like she's actually doing these things. It feels more like she's watching herself do them.

Druno keeps trying to arrange the pieces in a U shape somehow. Gishey thinks it's because of something he read in her father's notes.

After being so alone for so long, it was good to have some company, at first. But now, it's starting to feel oppressive. Druno is here all the time working with the dolg pieces.

Sometimes he seems too friendly. Sometimes he acts as though she's not even there. Sometimes it's just—awkward.

Gishey brings lunch into the dolg area. She stands next to the dolg holding the food. Druno doesn't even seem to notice her. He keeps examining the pile of dolg pieces from different angles.

Druno mumbles, "I can see how something like this could work. Your father was trying to build a kind of rock-throwing machine. It looks promising."

At the mention of her father, Gishey stiffens. Druno cringes, instantly regretting that he mentioned her father.

With a little more force than she intended, Gishey slams down the lunch without caring where she's putting the plate—which happens to be on the end of the dolg piece that looks like a giant spoon.

The pile of dolg shifts. The other end of the spoon piece flips up, then down.

Suddenly, the spoon end, with the lunch on it, flings up fast and stops with a *thud* against the top of the A piece.

There's a faint flash of light as the food launches across the room, passing very close to Druno's head. The lunch splatters across the wall.

Gishey is surprised, frustrated, and embarrassed.

Druno stands stiff with his mouth hanging open and stares at the food on the wall. He laughs. He thinks it's funny!

What if he got hit by the food? He could've been hurt. What if the swinging dolg piece had hit *her*, broken her arm again or something?

Druno beams with excitement. "Wow! Ha ha ha."

Druno looks at the pile of dolg pieces again. He touches it, affectionately. "I thought I saw a flash of light when the food went zinging past my head!"

Fuming, but without saying a word, Gishey stomps away. She marches straight out of the storage building and back to the house.

Gishey fidgets around in the house for the rest of the day—cleaning, organizing, and reorganizing miscellaneous items. She makes herself dinner and eats half of it.

Gishey goes to bed early. She sleeps restlessly. She has very bad nightmares the whole long night.

Something wakes her up—banging noises. Gishey is irritated. Druno is already making noise in the shop.

Gishey gets up, very annoyed. She is going to tell Druno to leave!

Gishey yanks on her robe and kicks on her slippers. She stomps toward the storage building, tired and grumpy.

Suddenly there's a loud *BOOM!*

Gishey jumps, kicking a slipper off her foot. The fluffy slipper flings up into the air and rolls to a stop about halfway to the storage building.

Add frightened and angry to tired and grumpy.

Gishey storms into the building in a fury. With the one slipper in her hand, she stomps up to Druno—who's fawning over the pile of dolg.

Gishey grumbles. "What are you doing here so early? Why are you in here without me?"

Druno turns toward her, startled. His demeanor shifts from elated to sad and defensive. "I . . . I thought it was good that I could be here."

Gishey points her slipper at him. "Well, it's not good that you're here so much!"

Gishey vents, not really expecting an answer. "Why are you here all the time?"

Druno pauses, then he stands tall and firm.

He looks straight into Gishey's eyes. "I want to kill the terropads, every one of them! They are dangerous pests that have been terrorizing us and killing us for generations."

Druno is resolute. "They need to be eliminated!"

Druno turns his head a little, trying to hide the right side of his face. Gishey doesn't care about his face. She's familiar with it, and his scars don't bother her.

Gishey is not sure what to do. She feels like she can't think . . . with him looking at her.

Gishey doesn't want to deal with this right now. "Would you just leave? Please."

Gishey can tell that Druno is looking at her, but she's not looking at him. Gishey is looking away, avoiding eye contact.

Druno seems to deflate. He walks away sullenly.

Gishey hobbles on one slipper as she wanders in no particular direction.

Gishey glances at the pile of dolg. Then she does a double-take. The pieces are in a slightly different shape.

She notices a pile of rocks. There's a scoopful missing.

Gishey gasps when she sees a hole through the wall—a hole the size of a window!

Gishey hobbles over and peers through the hole in the wall. She considers the many rocks stuck in the trees on the other side of the wall.

Huh! He did it. He figured it out.

Druno somehow got the machine to work!

Then, in his moment of triumph, she stomps in, all whiny, and sends him away.

A few days later, Gishey is in a gloomy mood as she strolls along her garden path. The path circles around the house and storage building.

She's been avoiding the storage building.

Gishey walks slowly while rubbing at the occasional mild soreness in her previously broken arm. She is staring ahead at nothing in particular when she hears distant warning shouts of "*Terropads!*" come from down the mountain.

Over the years, Gishey has noticed signs that terropads have passed through her area of the mountain, but the terropads are usually seen in the lower parts of the town.

She hears a warning shout again. The voice is louder. The terropads must be getting closer.

Something is coming up the road! Thinking about running for safety, Gishey begins to move toward the storage building.

Then she sees that it's Druno.

Druno stumbles up the road, breathing heavily. "They're coming this way!" He gasps for air several times, then finally spits out, "The machine . . ."

Gishey instantly understands. She turns and runs for the big door on the side of the storage building. Gishey has the door open enough for Druno to fit through by the time he gets there. She swings the big door the rest of the way open and secures it.

Druno struggles to push the machine toward the door.

Gishey sprints over to help him.

The combined pieces of dolg are heavy and awkward. Working together, they finally manage to slide the machine out the door and into the open.

Druno makes several adjustments to the machine. He runs back inside. He returns with a scoopful of rocks, which he carefully places on the wide part of the spoon piece.

Druno is focused on what he's doing.

Gishey backs away.

Druno's voice is intense. "Keep watch for the terropads!"

Druno pivots the machine in different directions, testing it. He meticulously examines the machine.

Gishey turns to the sound of movement in the bushes behind them. The sound of rustling bushes stops. She hears two terropads snarling with each other. They're in the storage yard.

The predators are just around the corner!

Gishey is petrified. She holds her breath, not wanting to attract their attention.

Druno does the exact opposite.

He yells and jumps around. Druno turns the machine while he shouts. "Over here! Over here!"

Three terropads peek around the corner. The animals move cautiously forward, sniffing the air. The terropads focus straight at Gishey and Druno.

The terropads begin to approach. The predators assume a hunting posture.

Gishey is frozen in place.

Druno is struggling with the machine. He doesn't have it pointing in the right direction yet, and the terropads are getting closer.

One terropad breaks into a run, straight toward Druno. The other two terropads quickly jump in behind the first.

Gishey can see that Druno is *not* going to get the machine turned around in time.

Gishey lunges against the machine. Her pushing is helping.

She glances over at Druno. His face is pale, and he looks like he's near panic.

Gishey leans into the machine with her shoulder. She grunts and pushes with all her strength.

The machine turns abruptly. Gishey slides off the machine and falls to the ground.

She hits the ground hard, landing on top of her previously broken arm.

Gishey feels a sharp stab of pain shoot up her arm. It stuns her. She rolls away from the machine and props herself up on her other elbow.

The momentary concern for her arm evaporates.

Looking up from the ground, Gishey makes eye contact with the fast-approaching second terropad.

The leading terropad prepares to leap over the machine and onto Druno.

FLASH/BOOM! Riiinnnngggg.

Gishey is jolted backward.

She blinks her eyes, trying to clear her vision. She sits up and swivels her head to clear her hearing.

Her attention is drawn to the cloud of dust in front of the machine. Dust, where the terropads were.

Druno runs around to the front of the machine and into the swirling cloud of dust.

Gishey smiles when she hears Druno's whooping and cheering. He saunters back through the thinning dust, arms raised in the air in the sign of victory!

The sight at the machine is really amazing. There are two shredded terropad bodies and what is left of a third body—just its back end.

A clear path is swept from the front of the machine, straight to the trees. There is even some damage to the trees and the ground vegetation.

It isn't long before the people of the town show up, wanting to find out what happened. At first, it's a few kids, then a bunch of people, then too many people.

People are crawling all over her home. Some seem to only want to snoop around.

Gishey begins to feel like she went from being attacked by terropads to being attacked by the people of the town.

They keep asking her the same questions, over and over.

Gishey's temper is getting short. "I don't know how it works. You'll have to ask Druno."

Gishey tries to move away from a pushy business owner.

The builder's shop owner presses. "Well, will you need parts for it?"

She ignores the shop owner's question. Gishey has been watching four young adults hovering near the front door to the storage building.

She anchors her hands on her hips and stares at them. It doesn't work. The door is opening.

Gishey shouts at the group. "You! Stay out of there!"

The group shuffles away.

Gishey yells at the retreating group. "You could've shut the door!"

The builder's shop owner pesters. "We have some interesting new fasteners coming in."

Gishey goes into a speed-walk to close the storage building's front door. She responds sarcastically to the shop owner. "Good to know. I love fasteners."

Before she can get to the open door, a boy drifts closer and gazes into the storage building. Gishey is about to bark at him when she sees two others peeking through a window into her house.

Gishey turns and stomps toward the two at the window. "You! Get away from there! What're you doing? That's my home."

The two scurry off. Gishey turns back to the storage building. Several more people have managed to get in front of the open door.

Gishey points a stiff arm. "The machine is over there!"

The people in front of the open door try to act innocent as they slowly drift away. A couple of them peek back, to get one last look.

Gishey stands in front of the open door with her hands anchored on her hips. She gives a long, mean stare to the departing intruders.

Then, two kids bump past her on their way *out* of the storage building.

Gishey is even more infuriated because the two kids ran off before she had a chance to yell at them.

While Gishey has been trying, with mixed results, to keep people out of where they shouldn't be, Druno has been standing guard over the machine.

Well, not exactly standing guard. Druno is talking excitedly to everybody and waving his arms in what looks like an attempted explanation of how the machine works.

He seems to be more than willing to tell the story to anyone who walks up.

Gishey notices that Druno stays within touching distance of the machine.

Gishey slams shut the front door to the storage building.

Three startled-looking people appear from around the corner of the building. They were probably trying to peek through the shop windows.

A commotion stirs at the machine. Gishey is relieved when everybody moves that way to see what's happening.

She barks at a few stragglers and checks the house before moving closer to the machine herself.

Druno and four other people are pushing the machine over to the trees in front of the hill. They line up the machine to point at the hill.

For a better view, Gishey steps up to the top of a mound of dirt near the storage building.

Most of the town leaders are standing next to the machine. They're talking excitedly with Druno. Druno gestures repeatedly and one of the town leaders stutter-steps closer to the back of the machine.

Gishey thinks, *Nobody seems to care about his scars now.* It's good to see.

It looks like they're going to set it off again.

Gishey is very curious to see the machine work from standing a short distance away, rather than from the ground next to it, while staring into the eyes of an attacking terropad.

There's the *FLASH!* and *BOOM!* The flash looks different from farther away. It's more of a *beam* of light that goes from the machine to the hill. The rocks are launched along the path of the beam.

The trees in front of the machine poof off clouds of dust.

One tree is cut clear through at about knee high. The tree bounces backward and its bottom end sticks into the ground behind its stump.

The tree stands there, like it's going to stay that way. Then it starts to tip in the direction of a group of people standing off to the side.

The people scream and scatter. The tree falls. The top of the tree slaps to the ground, right where they were just standing.

Several other trees are badly damaged. One tree is cut through most of its trunk. The trunk is split the rest of the way to the ground and the tree is only upright because it's leaning against another tree.

Over the next several days, many people of the town come to talk with Gishey. Most are overly friendly. They thank her for killing the terropads and compliment her for inventing the machine.

In town, everyone is talking about "The Machine and Gishey Donmaru."

She tries to explain that Druno actually built the machine. The people of the town brush off her explanations and continue to credit Gishey. Some act like she's just being modest about her achievement.

Gishey grows disgusted, quickly.

Over the next tenth of a year, the town settles back into the usual. As Gishey is walking up to a restaurant for lunch, she finds Druno standing outside, eating.

Gishey smiles as she approaches. "Why are you standing out here?"

Druno finishes chewing a bite before answering. "They don't let me eat inside."

Gishey's smile disappears. "Why don't you eat someplace else?"

Druno shakes his head. "No place lets me eat inside."

Gishey goes into the restaurant, gets a plate of food, and pays for it. Instead of going to sit at a table, she walks outside and joins Druno.

They chat as Druno finishes his meal. Then he does most of the talking while Gishey eats.

Druno tries to sound convincing. "The machine can be mounted on a cart. That way, it could be turned faster and easier. You could put the rocks on the cart. One person could push it easily on a road."

Gishey nods, swallows a bite. "I think that's a good idea."

Druno turns serious. "Gishey, I want to take the machine out to the fifth Region, to kill terropads."

Gishey is stunned by the thought. Take her father's dolg? Druno out there alone? "Well, I don't know about that."

Druno leans forward intently. "They're a danger. If we don't stop the terropads, they will continue killing people—and ruining our lives."

Gishey nods in understanding. "I agree but, we could use it whenever a terropad tries coming into town."

Druno shakes his head. "That won't be very effective. The terropads could kill a lot of people before we even get it out of the storage building. Then we have to move it to wherever the terropads are. Or were. If we have to chase them around the town . . ."

Gishey can see his point. No, she still doesn't like the idea. It would be too dangerous, anyway.

She shakes her head while she chews.

Druno smiles. "I know what you're thinking. It's too much for me to do by myself."

Gishey is intrigued. *Wow, does he really know me that well?*

Druno smiles big and shows his upturned hands. "That's why I want you to go with me."

Gishey coughs. If she hadn't just swallowed her mouthful of food, she would've spit it out. Gishey shakes her head vigorously. What a ridiculous idea.

Gishey thinks about it. They could roll the machine out a short distance, to see if the cart works. Maybe set it off a few times.

Druno leans back against the building. He's being very quiet. He's just watching her think—and he's smiling.

Gishey shakes her head, 'No'. "We could take it on a short trip. To test the cart and the machine. But that's it."

Druno doesn't respond. Still casually leaning against the building, he just smiles his friendly smile at her.

It takes several tenths to build the cart and mount the machine the way Druno wants it.

It takes more time to load a light cart with food and other supplies. They plan to be back in four days, so they supply for eight days—something the family taught Gishey.

They start with a small amount of rocks on the cart. Rocks can be collected from the river when they get there.

Finally, they're off. Druno pushes the machine and Gishey pushes the supplies. Occasionally, they need to team up on the carts to get them past a difficult spot.

A few times before, Druno has scouted this border area of the fifth Region. He knows where some of the easiest traveling will be, and several areas to avoid.

Traveling with the carts is much slower than walking. Without the supplies, they wouldn't get very far before they would need to head back.

Without the machine, they wouldn't be doing this at all.

Gishey is enjoying the short travel. It's nice out here. It's fascinating to see the new terrain. It brings back some good memories of traveling when she was a little girl.

On the third morning, Druno packs up the camp to continue traveling. Gishey was expecting that this would be their campsite until they returned to town.

Well, a little farther does sound interesting.

Halfway through the fifth day, Druno spots fresh terropad tracks. They decide to set up camp and check the area from here.

The daylight fades. After taking time to rest, Gishey becomes increasingly nervous about the whole idea. They are among terropads!

They each find a good stick for protection through the night. They agree to take turns on watch. Gishey volunteers to be first watch.

There is no way she can sleep right now, anyway.

Gishey curls up in her bedding on one side of the machine cart. Druno is sleeping on the other side of the cart—and she's ready to wake him by poking him with her stick if she sees or hears anything that might be a terropad. Or anything else.

The next day, as Gishey and Druno are finishing their morning meal, they hear what might be terropads heading in their direction. They both jump to their feet. They quietly get the machine ready and pointed at the approaching sound.

With a big, confident smile for Gishey, Druno shouts and makes loud sounds to attract attention—a laugh, some one- and two-word shouts.

It works. Two terropads stroll into the camp area. They look around, unafraid.

Behind the machine, Druno taunts the predators. "Over here, you repulsive bugs."

The terropads see him. They assume a hunting posture.

Before the terropads can take three steps, Druno blasts them back into the underbrush, leaving a tunnel into the bushes. Druno only needs a moment to check the results.

The machine on a cart works, and it was easy.

They both feel that it was a lot of work, anticipation, and suspense for something that was over so fast.

Gishey and Druno decide to leave their supplies at the campsite and go out with just the machine. Early in the day, they come across a large pack of terropads.

Druno points the machine in the direction of the terropads and sets it off. He is able to quickly reload the machine and pull the lever, repeatedly.

Druno eliminates a lot of terropads in the area and tracks down several more as the day passes. They stay out too long and get back to the campsite just after sunset.

Pushing the machine cart over rough terrain and collecting rocks is hard work. They're exhausted.

Neither of them is thinking about standing a watch. They roll the machine cart to its spot, collect their bedding, and both are soon asleep.

Days pass. Without coming to a conscious decision, Gishey and Druno continue to travel. Druno eliminates terropads occasionally along the way.

It's obvious that the testing of the machine was over a long time ago.

Gishey realizes a decision should be made about going back to town. Gishey isn't completely comfortable washing in the river. She misses her washing area at home.

They were only supposed to be out for a few days, and it is now closer to a tenth of a year. The time traveling out is how long it will take to get back.

She hints at it, but Druno avoids the topic and involves himself with the machine.

The evening meal is quiet. They are tired and muscle-sore from all the traveling. Mostly though, Gishey and Druno are avoiding the pending conversation about going back to town.

Gishey does enjoy being out here. It's so beautiful and peaceful—well, except for the occasional flash/boom.

Food is abundant and easy to collect in the fifth Region. Gishey hasn't gone a day without her favorite fruit, the one with purple juice.

They still have much of their original eight days of supplies on the light cart.

Druno suggests going to look in another area.

Gishey quickly agrees.

Gishey realizes that it must be getting close to three tenths of a year since they began this travel. This is their eighth or ninth night now, at this latest campsite.

It's been fun, but Gishey is ready to go home and relax for a while—get clean and relax.

Gishey peels her bedding back and tries to get comfortable on her side of the machine cart. In the faint starlight, she watches Druno settle into his bedding on the other side.

Gishey brings it up. "I would really enjoy a long wash, and my own bed, right now."

Druno starts talking about rechecking areas they have previously cleared. Gishey realizes that he's trying to avoid the subject of going home, again.

She doesn't fault him for not wanting to go back. The people of the town have never treated him well.

Gishey isn't bothered by Druno's scars. They look like scars from a terropad attack. A lot of people have them—though not nearly as bad as Druno.

She knows how the people of the town can be, but Gishey has always wondered if there's more to the situation than just the scars.

Now she's curious.

Gishey asks with a soft voice, "Druno, you never really told me about . . . how you got your scars."

Gishey realizes that Druno was talking, and she just interrupted him. She doesn't even know what he was talking about. It's awkward.

She lets her comment-that's-really-a-question stand.

Druno is quiet. He looks off to the trees at the edge of the darkness. He looks back at Gishey. He half-shrugs his shoulders.

Druno is wary. "You really don't know, do you?"

Now Gishey is suspicious. "Know what?"

Druno hesitates. He starts speaking, but in the direction of the trees. "I got attacked by a terropad when I was a little boy. It chewed me up and hauled me off to the trees."

Gishey stiffens. She sits up straight, a flood of memories pouring over her.

Druno shifts onto an elbow and looks directly at Gishey. "I'm Druno . . . Gemishay. You know the story. Your pet icenna saved my life."

Gishey is *spun!*

It feels like her world is imploding—like it did "that day." She flinches at the grip tightening around her.

Druno's voice pierces the moment. "I thought that you probly knew. I wanted to talk about it, and I tried to a few times, but I wasn't sure if I should bring it up."

Gishey feels like she, that he . . . something—she's not sure what.

Anger becomes the dominant emotion.

Gishey tries to pull herself together. She searches for something to say. "Why didn't you think you could talk about it?"

Druno replies with concern, "I was afraid this would happen—that you would be angry."

Druno shifts onto his back, sounding sad. "I was afraid that you might . . . hate me—like everyone else does."

Druno turns his head slightly, as if to hide his scars.

Gishey hasn't really noticed the scars on his face in a long time. Without even realizing it, she has been seeing—or picturing in her mind—his right side looking like the left side.

The undamaged side of his face is pleasant, friendly, understandable . . . attractive.

Druno is a little older than Yergis was when Yergis and Gishey—started being a couple.

Gishey still feels angry about being lied to! Well, he didn't actually lie, and she understands why he hesitated to bring it up.

Gishey looks over at Druno. He's quietly waiting to find out what's going to happen. He doesn't look optimistic.

Gishey sympathizes with him. "Druno, I don't hate you."

Gishey retreats inward. "I'm angry about everything that's happened. All of it!"

Gishey thinks back. “I'm angry about what happened to me, to you . . . to Nicena.”

Tears swell in Gishey's eyes. “More than anything, I'm angry about what happened to my father.”

Gishey has never talked about this with anyone. Gishey's voice quivers as it slips out. “Did I get him killed?”

Druno starts to speak but pauses for a moment.

Druno states comfortingly, but firmly, “Gishey, you didn't kill him. Some friends of my father did.”

Druno explains, “Those idiots thought they would impress my father and the group they were in. My father had nothing to do with it. He was trying to find a way to apologize to your family.”

Druno trails off a bit. “They said they did it for him. That they only went there to stop your father, and the situation got out of control. My father still felt guilty about it, though. He disassociated with the people who attacked your father, and it caused a split in their group.”

Druno slumps apologetically. “More than anything, my father regretted what he did to you and Nicena, after he found out the whole truth.”

Druno recalls the memories. “Many times, I saw the regret and anguish in his face when he talked about it. Sometimes I saw that look when he *wasn't* talking, and I knew he was thinking about it.”

Gishey wipes tears from her eyes. “If I hadn't taken Nicena from where I found her, none of this would have happened.”

Druno sighs. “I have thought a lot about ‘if things didn't happen the way they did.’ It doesn't help.”

Druno's tone is philosophical yet comforting. “You can't fault yourself, Gishey. You rescued Nicena from a very near death, after a very short life.”

Friendliness returns to Druno's voice. “From what I heard—and I hear a lot because people ignore me, and I listen instead of talk. What I heard is that most people liked Nicena, and still do.”

Druno glances back to the trees. “Nicena saved my life—something I'm hoping to be grateful for some day.”

Tears stream down Gishey's face. "I still miss her so much. She was so good—to just be around."

Druno agrees. "A lot of people felt that way. Nicena brought a lot of happiness to people. I saw it in their faces when they talked about her."

Neither speaks for a long moment, lost in their own thoughts.

Druno finally shares what he was thinking. "My father was never the same after 'what happened with the Donmarus.' As it was called."

Tears well in his eyes. "He started hating both sides of the group, then he started hating himself."

Druno pulls a rock from under his bedding and tosses it into the darkness. "Then he started hating me. Then, everybody started hating me."

Neither of them feels like talking anymore. They quietly settle into their bedding and eventually fall asleep.

The next morning, Gishey mentions going back to town. She knows that Druno doesn't want to go back yet.

Druno rambles about wanting to look for terropads in the next valley.

Gishey agrees to take a quick look in the next valley. But that's it. After that, it's time to go home—to her washing area.

They have been traveling for another tenth of a year.

Neither of them knew how far it was to the "next valley", but Gishey had no idea that it was going to be this far.

Gishey knows that they are going deep into the fifth Region.

Gishey feels the town pulling at her to go back, yet she really does love it out here.

The last fifteen days have not been as much fun, though. They have been pushing the carts up this same hill for that long. Gishey started counting on the third uphill day.

Druno chatters as they push on. His favorite topics are ideas he has for changes to the machine cart and his thoughts about terropads.

When they pause to rest, Gishey often gazes back down the hill. The view is stunning. The vast grassland extends to the far-distant horizon.

So much land. It's amazing to see it all at once.

Gishey ponders the land behind them. If she can see this much land from her spot on the hill, how much land is there . . . on the whole world?

Lately, Druno has been talking about how the grassland is turning. They're seeing more scrub bush, and the waist-high grass is thinning.

A short distance ahead of Gishey, Druno stops suddenly. He's intently looking ahead at something. It must be important.

Gishey leans into pushing her cart. She covers most of the distance, then walks up to stand beside Druno.

The sight she beholds causes her to stutter-step and gasp a short breath.

They stand on the rim of an immense valley. The amount of land Gishey can see is many times larger than the views of the grassland.

A large river runs through the bottom of the valley. For as far as she can see, streams feed into the river from both sides.

Next Valley is beautiful!

Gishey can make out huge fields of familiar nut trees, vegetables, roots, and fruits. Almost certainly, they will find other food.

Gishey gazes across Next Valley. The distant mountains on the other side are merely vague shadows.

They are both lost in the moment. To look upon this amount of land . . . is stirring. To see this much green, mixed with so many other colors . . . is awe-inspiring.

To her right, Gishey is drawn to a large flat area. The flat is a good distance down from the rim. On the other side of the flat, a stream runs past.

Gishey notices that Druno is eyeing the same spot. At the same time, they both say, "There's our campsite."

They reach the flat late in the day and hurry to set up camp before it gets dark.

Well, Gishey is trying to hurry.

Druno drifts over to the edge of the flat to take in the view. He gazes to his left. He scans across to his right. His head turns forward and he stares into the valley.

Gishey clears the rocks from her side of the machine cart and rolls out her bedding. She tries to prompt Druno into getting set up by anchoring her hands on her hips and giving him the "Are you going to help?" look.

Druno turns back to her. He appears more serious than she has ever seen him. "I'm not going back, Gishey. There's nothing for me in that town."

Druno sweeps his hand across the horizon. "Here, I have all this."

Druno is gracious. "If you want to go back, I'll help you with the machine. Then I'm coming straight back here. I'll find another way to eliminate the terropads."

Gishey walks over and stands next to Druno. She doesn't know what to say.

Druno breathes a heartfelt whisper. "I hope you don't go back, Gishey."

In the fading light, they witness the sunset across Next Valley, together.

Thus was created the second Special Weapon on the planet—a catapult.

Tubells have expanded from First Land, the island of our origin, westward to the Big Island, and now, north to this new Big Land. There is much land to see and explore.

Transportation is a problem. Traveling by tentacle is very slow.

Supplies need to be transported until we find the things we need in the new places.

Also, people are acquiring more and more things as we travel. People have collected all kinds of tree trunks and branches, a variety of large leaves, strange rocks, and other things that people have found on the new land.

Bestal Tenluce thinks that there is too much stuff to carry and a lot of it is unnecessary. They don't need to collect seashells or tree branches.

Even the large, flat piece of Giant Shiny, which was used on the first Boat, is being dragged along.

Bestal believes the Giant Shiny is an unnecessary burden. That thing is very heavy, and it's not useful.

The Giant Shiny piece was replaced when it was discovered that many large leaves could be sewn together and used as a sail. Leaf sails are lighter, easier to control, more effective, and replaceable.

The Giant Shiny hasn't been used for anything in a very long time. Yet people refuse to leave the Giant Shiny Leaf behind. When we move into new lands, many people will struggle to push and pull the large sled with the Giant Shiny on it.

People can move stuff with sleds, but it is difficult and requires a lot of tentacle strength.

Transportation is a problem. We must find ways to travel faster and easier.

Bestal wobbles over to the large Blank, near the cliffs, where people have been accumulating materials and testing new ideas.

Bestal spools down to rest the tentacles and scans the area with three eyes.

Nothing Bestal sees will work. Everybody keeps trying variations on sleds. No matter what they try, sleds are still heavy and slow.

There have been attempts to make a kind of "land boat." These were sleds with sails attached. The air would not push them.

Bestal notices the Second Shiny piece. It was found here on the Big Land, not long ago. This piece looks like a long, thin tree trunk.

People have placed the Second Shiny piece on the sled with the Giant Shiny Leaf. The sled sits on top of a bunch of tree trunks. Actually, the sled is at one end of a long row of tree trunks.

The Giant Shiny Leaf is standing upright at the front of the sled. To Bestal, it looks like they are trying to use the Giant Shiny Leaf as a sail again.

It won't work. That sled is too heavy. The air will not push it.

Bestal rolls the eye that is looking at the sled.

Bestal moves to the cliff edge and spools down in the shade of a tree. Bestal likes to look out at the water. Bestal spends a lot of time just watching the water move.

Bestal is intrigued by how the water pushes things. Is there a way that water could push a land boat?

Several times, Bestal has tried to use the water that falls from the air. Bestal tried pushing a sled while the water was on the land. The sled was easier to push at first, but the land got gooey, and the sled got stuck.

One time, when water was falling from the air, Bestal tried using a sail on a sled. The sled barely moved before it got stuck in the gooey land again.

Also, the water that falls from the air is unreliable.

Usually, it isn't much water. Sometimes it's too much. The water either doesn't fall often enough or it falls too often.

Nobody likes to travel when water falls from the air, anyway.

Bestal continues to watch the movement of the amazing cliffs of water. The water gets a little higher or lower on the Blank, but there are always many cliffs of water moving toward the land.

Bestal watches a cliff of water rise higher as it gets closer to the Blank. The top of the cliff falls forward and drops to the bottom.

It looks like the water that falls to the bottom goes right back up to the top of the cliff and falls to the bottom again, in a revolving circle.

Bestal considers that this revolving is how the cliffs of water might push things. There must be a way to do something like that on the land.

Bestal detects sounds of activity coming from the Blank, where people are working on the better transportation ideas. Many of the people down there are making loud squealing and "Blurpy" sounds.

Bestal moves toward the Blank to see what's happening.

From the path on the cliff, Bestal sees a large pod of people trying to carry something. It must be a tree trunk.

They move the object a short distance. Then the people lose their tentacle holds and it drops to the land. They lift it up again, move the thing forward a little, and drop it again.

Then Bestal sees the light reflect off the object. They found a third piece of Giant Shiny.

Bestal loses interest. That stuff is just too heavy to be useful for transportation.

Still though, it's fun to watch the people work together for a common purpose. Bestal keeps one eye on them as they maneuver the Third Giant Shiny piece toward the sled with the other two pieces.

Many people repeatedly lift the Third Giant Shiny, heave the thing forward, lose control, and drop it. Bestal mutters a few "Blurpys" in amusement. Those people are exerting a lot of effort for something that is of no use.

Strangely, the more Bestal watches the procession, the more interesting it becomes. Bestal turns two eyes toward the spectacle.

Bestal moves down the path to get a closer look.

Then Bestal detects the thumping sound of the Third Giant Shiny being dropped to the ground. Not only is the sound in the air, but the sound can also be felt on the bottom of Bestal's tentacles. The sound is coming from the land, too. The Third Giant Shiny must be very heavy to cause sound from the land.

Bestal continues to observe the people carrying the Third Giant Shiny. They are trying to put it on the sled with the other two pieces of Shiny.

Bestal has seen enough. Watching the cliffs of water is much more interesting. Bestal begins to move back up the path. Still slightly amused, Bestal keeps one eye looking in their direction.

FLASH/BOOM! Riiinnnnggggg.

What was THAT?!

Whatever those people are doing, they have Bestal's attention *now.*

The people at the sled with the Giant Shiny are very excited. The sled appears to have moved forward.

Bestal approaches the scene. Some people reposition the direction of the sled, as it sits on the tree trunks. Other people are lining up more tree trunks in front of the sled.

People gather around the Third Giant Shiny piece. With a lot of commotion, "Blurpys" and a few words Bestal hasn't heard before, the people lift the new Shiny and line it up behind the sled.

The people move the Third Shiny piece quickly toward the sled.

FLASH/BOOM! Riiinnnnggggg.

Bestal's vision is blurred in the two eyes that were watching. Bestal spins around to look with the other two eyes.

The Third Giant Shiny has dropped to the land. People are spilled on the land along both sides of the Third Shiny.

The sled. The sled is *moving!* The sled moves to the end of the assembled row of tree trunks, the front tips down onto the land, and the sled stops.

Whoa! Bestal mentally replays the movement of the sled.

The Third Shiny hits one end of the Second Shiny on the sled—the other end of the Second Shiny is against the Giant Shiny Leaf.

The tree trunks under the sled roll like the cliffs of water. The sled moves across the tree trunks until it falls off the last trunk.

The tree trunks roll.

You can't keep moving tree trunks to the front of the sled. That would be too slow and too much work.

But what if you have rolling tree trunks that stay under the sled?

There are some pieces of tree trunks in the piles of collected junk. Bestal has the beginning of an idea.

Bestal moves as fast as possible on four tentacles. Bestal hurries over a hill, stumbles in the soft Blank, falls over, and rolls down the hill . . . like a tree trunk rolls.

Bestal works on his idea for many passings of the light.

After many attempts and variations, Bestal has a working wheel-and-axle combination. It consists of a long, thin tree trunk with two short, thick pieces of trunks on each end. It took a lot of effort to hollow out the centers of the short pieces and position them onto the ends of the long trunk.

Bestal can push against the middle of the long trunk with a tentacle and the two short pieces at each end roll across the land. It rolls like the cliffs of water.

Satisfied that the wheels and axle will work, Bestal rolls the assembly toward the sled with the Shiny pieces.

It takes a lot of effort for Bestal to push the axle up a short hill of Blank.

At the top of the hill, Bestal pauses to rest and looks three eyes toward the sled.

The sled is sitting on one end of a long assembly of tree trunks.

The Third Shiny is mounted at the back end, sticking up like a short tree.

The Giant Shiny Leaf is still at the front of the sled.

Bestal looks again at the tree trunks lined up in front of the sled. The series of tree trunks are spaced evenly apart for about four or five sled-lengths.

Bestal pushes the axle off the top of the hill. The axle rolls to the bottom of the hill and keeps rolling for a good distance.

When Bestal gets to the bottom of the hill, the Second Shiny piece becomes visible. The Second Shiny is still where it was on the sled, but the Shiny has been boxed over with tree branches.

Something's happening. People are talking excitedly and bobbing up and down.

Two people climb onto the sled. They both wrap a tentacle tightly around a side rail.

The Third Shiny at the back end begins to move. It's pivoting, swinging back and forth. When the Third Shiny hits the Second Shiny, there's a flash of light that grows brighter with each strike.

Bestal is intrigued as the Third Shiny bounces repeatedly against the Second Shiny and a glow of light flashes across the Giant Shiny Leaf.

The sled begins to move across the assembly of tree trunks. The light continues to flash across the Giant Shiny Leaf.

With the Third Shiny at the back thumping against the Second Shiny and the light flashing on the Giant Shiny Leaf at the front, the sled moves all the way across the rolling trunks until it gets to the last one.

The front end of the sled tips down onto the land. The Third Shiny stops moving. The flashing light vanishes from the Giant Shiny Leaf.

It worked!

The sled traveled on the land.

Across the Blank, people cheer excitedly. The two people on the sled enthusiastically wave happy tentacles.

Bestal rolls the axle to the front of the sled. Several people turn three eyes to Bestal. Bestal attempts to position the axle under the front of the sled.

Other people understand what Bestal is trying to do and move in to help. More people move in to lift the front of the sled.

They manage to maneuver the axle under the front of the sled. Bestal and a few others push the sled backward.

The axle wheels roll, the last trunk rolls, and the sled travels backward until the axle bumps into the last trunk.

The sled rests level on three of the tree trunks and the axle.

The axle works!

After many more light passings, the sled with the Shiny sits on two axles. Four people stand in the sled, each with a tentacle wrapped tightly around a side rail.

Two people get the Third Shiny piece rocking and thumping. Bright light flashes across the Giant Shiny Leaf. The sled begins moving.

The sled rolls slowly at first, then faster and faster. The sled travels about fifty sled lengths across the Blank.

The people on the sled wave happy tentacles.

The sled begins going up the gradual hill away from the Blank. It travels a good distance before veering off to the side.

The land levels off and the sled bounces across a rough area with tufts of grass. One of the people falls off the sled and into the grass.

A wheel wobbles off the back axle. The sled grinds to a sudden, swerving stop, and flings off two more people.

The fourth and only person still on the sled excitedly waves a happy tentacle while bobbing up and down and blabbering cheers of "Blurpy!"

Thus was created the third Special Weapon on the planet—a car.

A gathering of young Drels is collecting the low-hanging fruit from the trees along the river when they notice all the shiny yellow rocks at the bottom of the knee-deep water.

These rocks are very different from the rocks they've seen before. They seem to glow underwater. When pulled out of the water, these rocks still seem to glow. They don't look like or feel like other rocks.

The young ones collect the glowing rocks and put them in a pile on the bank.

Instead of carrying a larger glowing rock out of the water, someone throws it onto the bank. When the large rock lands on the pile of other glowing rocks, it makes a sharp, crackling sound, and sparks of light shoot out of the pile.

The kids are throwing glow rocks.

When he was young, he threw glow rocks to make them spark, too. It seems to fascinate everyone at that age. It's still interesting in a way and fun to do once in a while.

He watches his kids playing with their friends through the side window of his upramps office—upramps being ground level. Aside from knowing that they're safe, he enjoys watching their carefree activities.

The kids will occasionally pick fruit and sit around eating it. They explore their world of the neighborhood and surrounding hills. Of course, one of their favorite things to do is "throw glow rocks" in the ditch at the bottom of the mountain.

He's impressed to see that the kids have found a large piece of glow rock. A bunch of the kids are dragging the piece down the side of the mountain. It takes a while, but they get the piece down the hill, through the nut trees and into the "glow rock throwing ditch."

Good for them.

Days later, he sees the kids dragging a second large piece of glow rock down the mountain. They manage to maneuver this large piece into the ditch.

The kids seem quite happy with their accomplishment.

He chuckles to himself. He imagines the fun the kids are having throwing glow rocks at the large pieces.

He thinks about going out there and throwing some glow rocks with the kids. It's been a while since he's done that.

A few tenths of a year later, he notices that the kids are dragging a third large piece of glow rock down the mountain. The kids are still quite a distance up the mountain when they lose control of the large chunk of glow rock.

The very large piece rolls slowly a few times, then it picks up speed fast.

It could be dangerous.

He hurries from the room, waddling as fast as he can. He's moving quickly, for a Drel, as he exits the home and turns toward the ditch.

He glances up at the large piece of glow rock. It's careening down the steep mountainside extremely fast. It's heading straight for the ditch.

A bunch of kids are standing well back, but watching to see what happens. The large piece goes hurtling into the ditch.

FLASH/BOOM! Riiinnnngggg.

He's stunned, but he saw it. A beam of light shot out of the ditch and into the trees.

What . . . is *that?* There's something wrong with the trees. Something peculiar is on them. The bizarre something is growing bigger.

They all stand and watch the strange phenomenon in the trees. It continues to move up the hill and onto other trees.

Sometimes the phenomenon moves slowly up the hill and sometimes it goes up the hill very quickly.

The strange, flickering yellow-orange glow leaves blackened and barren trees in its path.

More people show up. Some are fascinated. Some are frightened. Everyone is in awe of what they are witnessing.

A few people walk into the blackened area to investigate. They come back reeking of a strange odor, and with black dust all over them.

One of them has some nuts from the blackened area and is showing the food to others. People are intrigued by how the nuts have changed. The nut shells are easier to open. He watches as people eat the food and smile.

Curious, he tries one, too. The food is softer and tastes better.

Thus was created the fourth Special Weapon on the planet—fire.

Word of the amazing new machine that kills terropads spreads across the four Regions. People are excited about it, for a while.

But when the story becomes "the Machine and its inventor have mysteriously vanished," people are skeptical.

After many years, "the Machine and Gishey Donmaru" becomes a myth.

One man knows it isn't a myth. He was in that town on that day when he was a young boy. His Traveling Group was there at the time.

He had touched the Machine and watched it take down two tall trees.

He even saw Gishey Donmaru.

She was standing to the side, near a storage building. Gishey Donmaru was overseeing everything from there.

A weird assistant was doing a bad job of explaining the Machine to the town leaders, before Gishey Donmaru had the assistant conduct the demonstration.

After the demonstration, he and a bunch of other kids pried rocks from the Machine out of the trees to keep as souvenirs. After all these years, he still carries his Machine-rock in his pocket.

One day, he crosses paths with a traveler who was also there that day. They talk about what happened and he shows the other man his Machine-rock.

The other man slips a concealed neck chain out of his shirt. His Machine-rock is mounted in a pendant. The two discuss where exactly it was in the trees that they each pulled their Machine-rocks.

Nearly a year later, the two Machine-rock friends organize a Traveling Group to search for "The Machine and Gishey Donmaru."

Many in the group have "rocks from the Machine."

For years, the Traveling Group searches probable locations across the five Regions.

One bright morning, the Traveling Group reaches the top of a days-long slope. The travelers pause to behold a startlingly immense and beautifully green valley. A large river runs through the bottom of the valley.

To the right and a good distance down from the rim, there's a large flat area. On the flat are a large home, a storage building, and some small structures. A tributary river runs by on the other side of the flat.

As the travelers descend into the valley, they notice a strange column of whitish-gray dust rising continuously from the home. They can't imagine what this dust is, what could be causing it, or why it's coming out of a spot on the top of the home.

The travelers find a trail that might lead to the home on the flat. They follow the trail toward the home.

As the travelers are going over a hill, they see two Geminy figures emerge from the home and begin walking toward them. The travelers stop in a clearing near the home and wait for the two people to arrive.

A boy and a girl approach, calling to their camp. By appearances, the boy will likely be a young adult soon. The girl is maybe a year or two younger.

They both have a light Donma patch.

The kids are very curious about everything. They ask the travelers about things in the camp and about the travelers themselves. In particular, the two young ones want to know about the rest of the known world.

The two, mostly the girl, ask a lot of questions and listen attentively.

The travelers are happy to answer their questions. The travelers, by long-standing tradition, talk freely, openly, and in detail about the world that they are traveling in.

The kids seem to like one traveler in particular—a kind, older woman with a Donma patch. The woman talks easily with the kids from the home on the flat.

A nervous murmur rises from the back of the group. An icenna stands on top of the hill behind them. It's looking down at the camp.

The travelers are naturally afraid of the animal. They scan the hills with concern. Where there's one icenna, the rest of the pack is always nearby.

The boy makes a whistling sound. The icenna begins to casually descend the hill.

Startled, the older woman turns to the girl and asks, "Do you know the icenna?"

The girl giggles. "Ya, that's Cienna."

The travelers quietly stare at the icenna as the animal walks calmly through the camp. The travelers move back and allow the predator plenty of space.

When the icenna gets close to the kids, it trots up to the girl.

She kneels down and embraces the creature. She circles her arms around its hairy neck and leans her head against the animal.

The icenna wags its tail while it looks around at the crowd.

The girl is happy to talk about the icenna. "She's part of our family. She's usually around my mother, but we all love her. Cienna watches over us, too."

The woman is surprised, and curious. "How . . . how is it that you . . . have an icenna?"

The icenna sits its back end down. The predator seems happy and friendly.

As she prepares to talk, the girl anchors a hand on her hip and tilts her head to the side.

The girl recalls the story. "My father says she just followed him home one day, but my mother says Cienna was already familiar with taking food from him. She says he must have been trying to get her to follow him for a while before she finally did."

The travelers are still uncomfortable in the presence of the potentially dangerous animal. The icenna stays close to the girl and watches all the travelers, but it does not appear aggressive or threatening. Most of the travelers slowly become more at ease with the hairy, four-legged visitor—a *little* more at ease.

Then the girl asks the question that the travelers have been waiting for.

"Why are you here?"

The woman smiles and opens her hands upward. "We're looking for a friend. Her name is Gishey Donmaru."

The girl gasps with a big smile. "Our *mother's* name is Gishey!"

The woman's face brightens. "Oh, we will be so glad to see her."

Smiles break out among the travelers. They are hopeful that Gishey Donmaru is still alive and that they have found her. Their quest may be at an end!

The boy sees everybody smiling. He smiles too, even though he's not sure why.

The older woman speaks fondly. "I wonder what ever happened to that machine she built out of dolg pieces?"

The boy jumps into the conversation. "We have one in storage."

The girl glances at the boy. "Father hasn't used it much since *we* came along." She giggles and looks back at the older woman.

The boy responds proudly. "Father took me out with him three times."

His posture changes to a somewhat disappointed demeanor. "But we never saw a terropad."

That confirms it. Gishey, the Machine, and terropads. The travelers touch their Machine-rocks and nod to each other.

The travelers feel a kinship. They have a unique bond involving a myth.

The travelers feel that Gishey Donmaru is part of this special bond. However, they're not sure how she will feel about them.

Yet, the travelers still anticipate meeting Gishey Donmaru. Maybe she will let them see the Machine, too.

One of the travelers has another goal in mind. He wants to bring the Machine back to civilization.

Whatever happens next, the travelers are pleased and profoundly moved to learn the fate of "The Machine and Gishey Donmaru."

R5

Young Beel Tectalnus likes to make new things.

Beel made wooden paddles that can be held in the tentacles while swimming. The "Beel Paddles" can be used to swim faster, stop faster, and turn sharper in the water.

Beel Paddles are a lot of fun.

In the past, Tubells applied Nanbay oil directly to the skin from husk containers. With industrial advances, the ointment and containers changed, but getting it onto the skin was still messy. Beel had the great idea to apply Nanbay oil using a small piece of the material made for carry-bags and boat sails.

Now, everybody seems to be using the "Beel Wipe."

Beel had a similar idea for a small piece of the netting used to collect tiny food from the water. Beel bent the end of a stick into a four-sided loop and attached a small net bag to the loop.

The "Beel Net" can be used for many helpful purposes, from catching a snack in the water and plucking fruit, to relocating little creatures away from the shelter and generally cleaning up.

Beel and others keep finding more and more uses for it.

The Beel Net is a great idea.

Old Beel Tectalnus has believed for many light passings that there must be a better way to cross the channel between the Big Island and the Big Land. Beel has been working on a new kind of boat to do just that.

The new "Beel Boat" uses specially made materials that are stronger and lighter. In addition to the sail, Beel has made a large balloon that's positioned above the craft. This way, they can travel above the water and through the air.

Beel is certain that the Beel Boat will be a better way to cross the channel. In the water, Boats are subject to the cliffs of water and the shifting water currents.

The Beel Boat should be much easier and a lot faster in the air.

Beel has tested the new Beel Boat by taking the invention a short distance into the air several times. It's amazing how much can be seen up there, with three eyes looking out of the boat.

From high above the island, Beel has studied the channel and the features of the Big Land's coastline.

The last test included having a heavy car on board. The Beel Boat was a little slower, but it handled the additional weight effectively.

The Beel Boat works!

Beel has put a lot of time and effort into this project. Beel cannot think of anything else that could be done before traveling the Beel Boat across the channel.

This is going to be *great!*

Two younger people have been helping Beel with the project. Beel has been trying to convince them to go along on this first crossing.

Beel tries to be reassuring. "It's going to be safer, easier, and faster than crossing in the water. We have enough supplies to get there, stay for a long time, and get back. There is plenty of food over there. Our supplies are just to get started and have as a backup."

The two young ones are not quite convinced.

Beel tries to be compelling. "We have been working on this for many light passings. You both have the opportunity to be a part of this historic trip. Do you think I would be going if I didn't know that this is a great idea?"

The two young ones are still reluctant. They look an eye at each other. They look an eye at Beel. They look two eyes at the Beel Boat. One of them drifts an eye from the Beel Boat to look two eyes at Beel.

Beel tries to be encouraging. "This is a great idea, you'll see."

The young ones look two eyes at each other. One of them lifts a tentacle in a shrug-like gesture. They both move slowly toward the Beel Boat.

Beel goes to the tie-down anchor point and unties the line holding the Beel Boat.

The two young ones move onto the Beel Boat and take positions near the control panel.

The space is a bit crowded. Eyes shift between the control panel, the instruments, out the windows, at the pile of supplies, at the car, at each other.

One of the young ones bumps *into* the control panel. The harmonic resonance initiates. The Beel Boat begins to rise.

Beel is coiling the tie-down line loosely around a tentacle. Beel is startled when the coil is suddenly yanked away.

Beel follows the tie-down line with three eyes and is shocked to see that the Beel Boat is already in the air.

Beel panics! "No! NOOO! Wait! Wait for me!"

The two young ones peek out windows and down at Beel. As they watch, Beel becomes a shrinking dot on the land.

Beel realizes that the Beel Boat is not going to come back. Accepting it, Beel hopes for the next best thing—their success.

Beel lifts a tentacle and shouts, "It's good! It's just a short trip over the channel! I'll take a water Boat and meet you on the Big Land!"

The Beel Boat rises higher. It slowly drifts out, over the water. Beel stands on the Blank, watching it go.

Beel thinks, *It's working, this is a great idea.*

A short distance out, the Beel Boat begins to rise sharply higher. The Beel Boat appears to stop in place. Beel isn't sure but, it looks like it's coming back.

Yes. The Beel Boat is definitely heading back. It's very high in the air, though. Beel watches as it continues to rise.

The Beel Boat drifts out over the big water. The Beel Boat becomes a shrinking dot in the air and disappears from sight, going the wrong way.

Beel spools down to rest the tentacles. Beel stares two eyes toward the Big Land and two eyes in the opposite direction, along the path of the Beel Boat.

"Um, maybe this wasn't such a great idea."

The two in the Beel Boat look back and forth between each other and the huge expanse of water in every direction. There is no land in sight.

What would the water be like if the Beel Boat went down? What might be living in that water?

After numerous light passings, the two in the Beel Boat see land on the horizon. The Beel Boat is drifting in a direction that will put them over that land.

The two watch as they slowly approach the land. It feels like a long time before they reach the land.

This land looks very different from any land they've seen before. It is green in places, but it's also covered by a strange whiteness in other areas.

The large white areas remind them of the tan Blanks at the land's edges with the water. This Blank is white, and it's on the tops of the mountains.

The wind shifts direction and pushes the Beel Boat sideways and downward. The two look down and see a lot of trees. They also see what can only be an area of Shiny.

Now it seems like the Beel Boat is falling too fast. The two look at each other with concern.

The balloon billows and wavers. The Beel Boat plunges toward the land.

To slow their descent, the two desperately attempt to get the Shiny to push the balloon more. They disregard the frequent warnings from Beel about the delicate balance of the assemblage of Shiny pieces.

One of the two looks three eyes out the fore window.

The land is coming at them very fast.

A strong wind hits the Beel Boat. The Boat swings and sways. The balloon swells full. Their rate of descent slows quickly.

The Beel Boat skims the ground and lurches to a stop in a field of grass.

They are safely down!

The two are curious about this land. They investigate the surrounding area. They gather some local plants they've never seen before.

The two collect a piece of Shiny and carry the piece onto the Beel Boat. They replace a weak Shiny in the car.

One of the two goes to get more plants. The other one is still on board when the wind gusts and lifts the Beel Boat off the ground.

The Beel Boat floats along the ground for a short distance before gaining altitude. The one in the Beel Boat rushes to the controls in an attempt to stop.

It's not working.

The one in the Beel Boat looks three eyes down at the one on the ground. The one on the ground looks three eyes up at the one in the Beel Boat. Neither is sure if they would want to trade places with the other.

The Beel Boat, with the one Tubell, drifts over the big water. The Beel Boat resumes traveling in its previous direction.

After more light passings than it took to reach the last land, the one in the Beel Boat sees land again.

The Beel Boat floats up and over a white Blank on top of a mountain, down the other side, past an area of tan Blank, and back up into the air again.

The Beel Boat finally drifts downward and stops on the ground. The lone passenger gets out and secures the tie-down line to nearby trees.

There's nothing else to do but explore the surrounding area.

During the next light passing, the one sees other Tubells moving over a nearby hill.

The one shouts "Blurpys" and waves desperate tentacles.

The other Tubells see the one near the Beel Boat. They "Blurpy" back and wave happy tentacles.

The one from the Beel Boat is happy and relieved to learn that this *is* the Big Land, across the channel from the Big Island!

R6

It is a very sad time for the Tubellstacene.

A massive catastrophe has occurred on the island of our origin. All life on the island and in the shallow waters to the west has perished.

Extensive investigations, using the latest technology, have revealed startling information.

The place where Tubells originated was a volcanic vent. The island that Tubells have always called "First Land" was part of a volcanic shelf.

Another island to the east is also part of the same volcanic vent. However, First Land and the shallow waters to the west were a thin shelf of volcanic material that extended outward into the water.

A recent seismic event has caused the shelf to break off and sink.

We mourn the loss of the Tubells on the island and the Tubells who chose to stay in those waters, instead of moving onto the new lands.

The people reflect on the actions and contributions of our ancestors.

There would be no Tubells alive anywhere if the first Tubells had not ventured from the water, adapted to life on land, and bravely expanded to other lands.

We can only imagine the courage it took for the first Tubell to leave the presumed safety of the water and set tentacles on land.

In this solemn time of great loss, we recognize that we are able to live the wondrous lives that we do because of the efforts of those who came before us. We are grateful for the multitude of inventions and contributions to the advancement of life on our world.

In honor of our predecessors and the lives lost in this map-altering Catastrophic Event, we vow to continue advancing Tubell civilization.

As the achievements of our predecessors provided a better world for us, we will endeavor to achieve for our descendants.

The Geminy have disagreements over just about everything. People are not always consistent with their opinions, either. It isn't like "these people" all believe this and "those people" all believe that.

Opinions on a variety of topics typically put people with differing opinions on any given topic in the same groups on other topics.

One of the most prevalent divisions among the people has resulted in the formation of the demographic known as the "Roshuda."

The Roshuda are people who prefer to live near and play in bodies of water. The Roshuda gravitate to islands or areas near rivers, lakes, and beaches.

It's estimated that the Roshuda are less than half of the total population, but with varying degrees of "Roshuda tendencies," it's not an exact number.

The Geminy, which means "the people," includes the Roshuda, unless the term is used in contrast with the Roshuda.

There are many Geminy who live near water but have little or no interest in it.

There are Roshuda who live far from any body of water. But they will visit the water often or find a way to move to where there's water.

There are no specific arguments, debates, or conflicts between the Roshuda and Geminy. It's simply a matter of tendencies toward being drawn to and enjoying the water.

Formally, the people are referred to as the Roshuda Geminy. This is supposed to recognize all the people as one species.

One group of Roshuda lives to the north, near the southern end of the Great Lake. Staying near the shore, they begin to expand farther northward, along the eastern side of the lake.

This northern migration will put them in contact with the powerful reptilian Species called the Serpilgeneret. The Serpils occupy much of the northern lands and are migrating southward.

The bright, shiny, and powerful material is becoming commonly known as "NRG." All four civilizations were built with this resource. NRG is increasingly important.

At about the same time, the Roshuda and the Serpils both discover that there is NRG in an unclaimed Region on the eastern side of the Great Lake.

The NRG discovery puts the Serpils and the Roshuda on a collision course.

Conflict is inevitable.

The northernmost limit of Roshuda Geminy habitation is at the southeastern corner of the Great Lake. A small, remote community of Roshuda lives a simple existence. They enjoy the peace and tranquility of living in relative harmony with the land and water.

However, not everybody is content.

Many of the young adults are restless. They hear of the greater Geminy civilization and the technological advancements that offer a better way of life. Many of the young are frustrated with their circumstances.

They yearn for more opportunities and excitement.

Mingo Rashudey is unhappy with what he feels is "living in the past." His angst is compounded by the older people who are always telling his generation what to do.

Mingo has been very interested in recent talk about some NRG being discovered nearby. NRG is what the Geminy use to enjoy better lives. Mingo and a few of his friends have been talking about trying to find the NRG.

Mingo and several of his friends are sitting at a table in the restaurant, discussing how they could get the NRG. As usual, some old people are eavesdropping and butting in on their conversation.

The old people are always dismissive of their ideas. Also, most of the older people are skeptical about the NRG discovery, too. An elder at the next table keeps scoffing as Mingo and his friends talk about the NRG.

The elder turns and speaks directly to Mingo's table. "There's none of that NRG around here."

Mingo corrects him. "It's confirmed! There's a large deposit of NRG in the Region just north of us."

The uneasy elder adds, "I still don't like it. I think the risk of running into the Serpils is too high."

Mingo replies disdainfully, "I'm not worried about the Serpils. They're just a bunch of stupid reptiles. Sure, they're big . . . and ugly"—his friends laugh—"but they're much farther to the north. We're just going to take a small group, slip into the Region, load up the NRG, and truck it back here."

The elder is unconvinced. "You say that, Mingo, but I've heard some of the others talking about wanting to Claim the Region."

The elder is angrily authoritative. "We've lived here peacefully for many generations. We've enjoyed the benefits of the land and the Great Lake for a long time. Life is good. We don't need the NRG."

Mingo snorts in disagreement. "Yeah, I've heard that so many times from people of your generation. Well, many of my generation believe there should be more to life than eating until we're fat, floating around on the lake, and doing nothing."

The irritated elder nearly shouts. "Doing nothing? You don't know what you're talking about, Mingo! We've grown the village, built homes and roads, improved food supplies, and much, much more. We've made life better for everyone, including the ungrateful younger generations. You live in a much easier world than I did at your age."

Mingo is tired of hearing it. "So, we're supposed to just sit here and thank the elders, whenever one walks past?"

Mingo's friends laugh and slap hands.

Mingo vents his frustration. "The Geminy to the south are living a lot better than we are up here. They heat their homes with NRG! They travel in luxurious vehicles. The Geminy built craft that travel through the air. The Geminy are advancing civilization."

Mingo sneers in the direction of the elder's table. "We still chop wood for fires."

Mingo's friends murmur their agreement. They all look to Mingo.

Mingo feels emboldened by the support of his friends. Mingo speaks to both his friends and the elders at the next table. "Have you noticed that there's getting to be more people and less trees around here?"

As usual, the elder is dismissive. "There's no shortage of trees. You just have to go a little farther for them. Besides, as the trees thin, there's more places to build on."

The elder mocks Mingo's praise of the Geminy. "And grow!"

Mingo mirrors the elder's dismissive tone. "Grow into what?"

Mingo doesn't care what the timid people think. There are a lot of people who feel like he does. He and his friends could do it themselves. They could go get the NRG and prove to the others that their way is better.

Throughout known history, the Serpils have advanced their civilization across the large continent.

The Serpils have harnessed the power of NRG—a term for the bright-shiny that was introduced by the Drels, though nobody likes to admit it. The reptiles have built industry, large cities, impressive NRG weapons, and a grand culture known as the Serpilgeneret.

Sreep Reetgiln knows it's inevitable that the Serpilgeneret will eventually Claim the entire continent. Then, they will simply continue expanding into other areas.

The Serpilgeneret does know about the increasing population of primates to the south. The primates are generally regarded as a growing food supply for future Serpils, not really something to think much about.

The Serpils continue to move into the Regions of the north, the east, and the south. It doesn't really matter which way they move. The Serpilgeneret *will* Claim it all.

Sreep is part of a band moving southward. They're going to where NRG was recently discovered. After that, they'll Claim the surrounding Regions.

Mingo is encouraged that the small group he leads has made so much progress. He laughs about how his friends snuck away with the vehicles and supplies.

Mingo is proud of his mate, Rodu Gemnayshi. She helped Mingo get the Special Weapon from the storage building and out of the village without anyone catching them.

The elders are going to be unhappy about Mingo's group taking the Special Weapon and the vehicles. Mingo enjoys a spiteful laugh.

People will be happy when he returns with the NRG. They will forget about any punishment for "borrowing" the vehicles.

Now that they are into the border area and far enough away, the group stops to take a break. They set up a good camp.

Some of the others found an area with good fruits and vegetables. Rodu has gone to collect some of the food.

This is the first time that any of them have been in a Traveling Group. Mingo and the others want to enjoy the trip.

Mingo sits back and relaxes. He's enjoying the view of the new Region and the glow of the cooking fire.

Mingo watches the smoke rising into the air.

It reminds him of the smoke they made to enter a ravine at the base of the first mountain. They used the Special Weapon to blast a path through a pile of boulders.

Even more impressive was the huge plume of smoke from blasting a path through the thick trees and bushes on their way over the first mountain.

Mingo laughs to himself at the thought that the elders could probably see that smoke and know it was from Mingo's Traveling Group.

Sreep is enjoying a meal of the local foods—several different kinds of small animals. He watches without expression as the messenger approaches.

"Sreep, the Forward Effort has completed the initial movement over the mountain range. They report smoke rising from the far end of the Region."

Sreep is curious, but unconcerned. "Smoke? It's probably nothing."

Sreep considers the smoke. The primates make smoke. The smoke could have something to do with the recent ground shakes.

The young Roshuda are thrilled with their new independence.

They're beginning to realize the beauty of this new, untouched Region. The Great Lake is to their left.

Some people in the group talk of not going back.

Rodu turns to Mingo with a loving and suggestive smile. "Some of my friends are thinking about staying here, in this Region. They're talking about building homes and starting families."

Mingo smiles back. "I like that idea."

Rodu considers the prospect dreamily. "We could start our own village."

Mingo nods. "We could do what we want, without interference from the elders."

Rodu is feeling optimistic. "Life could be much better here."

Mingo is feeling seriously optimistic. "First, we need to get the NRG. We can keep track of good places as we travel and take a long look around the area of the NRG. We can decide what to do then."

Rodu glows with contentment. "That sounds like a good idea. I'm so happy to be out here with you, Mingo."

Standing on the summit of a mountain range, Sreep studies the vast Region ahead. They've been making steady progress, though they still have a long way to go to get to where the NRG is reported to be.

The time and distance are not a concern. They will follow the historical precedent. They will expand into the new lands.

All the Serpils feel the same way.

A messenger is circulating among the Serpils, passing along the latest news to everybody. The messenger approaches. "Sreep, the Forward Effort in the next sector suspects the presence of primates in the Region."

Sreep pauses and considers this curious development. "How far . . .?"

The messenger is concerned. "My understanding is they would be about as far from the NRG as the Forward Effort."

Sreep is intrigued. "I think I would like to close on the next sector."

The messenger agrees. "I hear others saying the same. Some have already begun moving toward the Forward Effort."

Mingo is thrilled to be on this Traveling Group adventure with his mate and friends. They revel in each other's company and the camaraderie of their combined efforts.

The group pauses together to stand on the summit of a mountain pass. They gaze across the vast and beautiful landscape.

Mingo takes in the majestic view.

Some of the others are animated about something. They talk louder and point to something in the distance.

Mingo and Rodu drift over to them, curious, but not concerned.

There is a strange movement on the distant mountains to their right. It's like the vegetation is shaking across a large area. It's difficult to tell what could be causing it. It doesn't appear to be a landslide.

It's probably just the wind.

The Forward Effort is camped on the summit leading into the valley where the NRG is located. They wait for the others to join them.

Sreep and the rest are approaching the summit when the messenger reports again.

"The smoke was coming from near the bottom of the mountain across the valley from the NRG. It's in one spot, then it goes away, then it reappears in another spot. Each time the smoke reappears, it's closer to the NRG."

Sreep is struck by the realization. "It seems likely that it's a group of the primates moving toward the NRG."

The messenger agrees. "That's the only explanation anyone can think of."

Now that they're down in the valley, the Roshuda can tell that the movement in the mountains to their right is not just the wind. It's animals—a lot of them.

But why are so many animals hurrying down the mountain and skirting the valley floor?

There's something else. The Roshuda didn't see it when they were up on the summit, but from the valley floor, they can see something on that distant mountain top. It's like a vague reflection off something.

It doesn't look like a reflection of NRG, which has a yellowish glow.

The Roshuda keep watching that distant mountain top. They also decide to pick up the pace toward the NRG.

As they travel, the young Roshuda occasionally catch a glimpse of the NRG (and their hopes and dreams) waiting for them on the other side of the valley.

The valley is beautiful and filled with available foods, but the Roshuda don't take time to ponder or collect the food. The group relies on their supplies and travels quickly in a straight line toward the NRG.

The strange reflections from the top of the mountain at the end of the valley have moved down the mountain. The Roshuda grow concerned. Someone raises the possibility that it could be Serpils.

The mood of the travelers changes drastically. For the first time since they set out, there's division among them. Some suggest that they forget about the NRG and turn back.

Most feel that, even if it is the Serpils, they are still very far away.

They have been watching the bright, shiny area of the NRG getting closer for many days. The NRG is much closer than the strange reflections moving down the mountain to their right.

The Traveling Group of Roshuda continues moving toward the NRG.

Sreep stands on a hill near the valley floor and doesn't like what he sees. A dust trail indicates that something is moving across the other end of the valley, and it's moving quickly.

If the Forward Effort had not stopped to wait for the rest of the band, the reptiles would be ahead of the dust trail.

Sreep doesn't consider that there's any fault with the Forward Effort. They were proceeding as usual, slow and steady progress.

Serpils are not accustomed to being in a hurry. The Serpils are in a hurry now, though.

They want that NRG.

The nagging thought of food taking the NRG from them is . . . unpleasant.

As the Serpils descend the mountain, they track the fast-moving dust trail in the valley. When the Serpils reach the valley floor, they lose their sight advantage, and the dust cloud disappears.

It's unnerving, not knowing where the primates are. If it *is* primates.

Sreep watches the normally casual demeanor of the Serpils be replaced by uncertainty and worry. It is rare for Serpils to experience these emotions, which makes it even more disturbing.

Mingo stands on the ledge with his back to the NRG. There is a good amount of NRG here. It's a good find, but not a large deposit. They load the last of the big stuff and prepare to leave.

Mingo looks down to the valley floor in the direction of the approaching dust trail. Everyone in the Traveling Group is convinced that it's the Serpilgeneret.

Mingo worries about the possibility of an encounter with the Serpils.

Nobody in the Traveling Group has ever seen a Serpil. Based on what he's heard, the reptiles will think nothing of killing and eating everybody in the Group.

Mingo looks at the Special Weapon. They have used it five times to clear dense vegetation or piles of rock in their path. But it would be very different trying to use it against attacking Serpils.

A sense of dread fills Mingo. Outwardly, Mingo tries not to show how uneasy he feels.

Mingo laughs. "When the Serpils get here, our Group will be gone. We will be traveling back to the other side of the mountains—with the NRG!"

Some of the others in the group laugh at this. Mingo wonders if *his* laugh sounds as nervous and hollow as theirs.

Some of the Roshuda are *not* laughing.

Sreep inspects the site. The best of the NRG has been removed. There are remnants, of course, but the expected large pieces are gone.

Tracks and scat left by those who took the NRG leave no doubt. The Serpils have been robbed by the pathetic food from the south.

Some of the Serpils return to the northern Regions with the Special Weaponry. Sreep and some others go east.

The band heading east is more than unhappy. Their anger grows as they travel.

There is no more talk of staying in the Region or starting a new town.

All the Roshuda are in agreement. The unanimous opinion—get out of there as fast as possible.

They have the NRG. They can return home victorious.

The young Roshuda's Traveling Group remains focused on running. Even transporting the heavy load, they make the return journey in half the time.

Avoiding contact with Serpils is very motivating.

As they approach their village, everyone in the NRG Traveling Group feels a great relief, even Mingo. They made it!

It's good to be back home, again.

Primates from the south snuck off with the NRG.

News of the atrocity spreads throughout the Serpilgeneret. Being robbed of the NRG is viewed by all Serpils as an outrage and not to be tolerated.

For a long time, Serpils who live on the western side of the lake have been considering hunting some of the primates. After hearing the appalling news, some of the western Serpils decide to attack.

The western Serpils commence a raid to their east into the Roshuda Geminy Region. Serpils kill and eat many of the primates before returning home.

Then messages arrive in the west of an effort to coordinate an attack on the primates to the south.

The proposal sounds delicious.

The plan of the eastern Serpil, Sreep Reetgiln, is to converge on the offending primates using a "Scissor Tactical" from the west and the east.

The western Serpils are asked to wait until the eastern Serpils are in position. The western Serpils are content to wait and would enjoy being part of such an operation.

Scissors are a traditional weapon going back into history farther than anyone knows. Scissors have always been used as a personal weapon. Most Serpils still have scissors that can be used as a weapon.

Scissors are effective for hunting and cleaning prey. Serpils have scissors that are routinely used for preparing food. Scissors are also used as eating utensils.

Some scissors are simply decorations.

Whether functional or symbolic, scissors are prevalent in Serpilgeneret culture.

Yes, it will be a great pleasure for the western Serpils to be involved in a Serpilgeneret Scissor Tactical.

It's time for a harvest.

The returning group of young Roshuda expected to be honored for getting the NRG. They are greatly disappointed.

The villagers are furious that the Special Weapon was taken without their agreement. The Special Weapon is a communal item for their common defense.

The villagers also feel disrespected.

Additionally, the villagers consider the small amount of NRG brought back to be unimportant.

When news comes to the village of the Serpil raid on their ancestral Region to the west, the adventurous Roshuda lose some friends and make some enemies. They are seen as the ones who brought this raid down upon the Roshuda.

When news comes of the approach of a large number of Serpils from the east, all the Roshuda who had participated in the NRG Traveling Group are treated with disdain.

The villagers decide to seek safety from the approaching Serpils in their ancestral homeland to the west, at the southern end of the Great Lake.

Everything that these Roshuda have worked for and built, over so many generations, will have to be abandoned.

Mingo and Rodu are no longer mates. In fact, none of those from the NRG Traveling Group want to associate with any of the others from the Group.

When the fleeing Roshuda reach the ancestral homeland, Mingo finds no place to go, and the NRG is confiscated.

Mingo doesn't know what to do. He's unable to get housing, food, or services anywhere. Everyone from his former Traveling Group is being ostracized.

Mingo tries to get the Traveling Group back together. Of the few he's able to find, nobody will even talk with him.

One night, angry and desperate, Mingo breaks into the storage building and takes back what he considers *his* NRG.

Mingo flees to the south with the NRG and a stolen truck.

The people in the Region to the south learn what has happened, of course. When he shows up with a relatively large amount of NRG, the Geminy take the NRG and send Mingo into exile.

Then, news comes that the Serpilgeneret have taken the former village and are continuing to move toward their ancestral homeland at the south end of the Great Lake. The Roshuda also become aware of the western Serpils moving toward them again.

The Roshuda are willing to stay and fight, rather than give up their homes and the land that the Geminy have lived on for all of known history.

The Drelstenprupo culture has been transformed by the utilization of NRG—the new name for glow rocks.

One of the most impactful applications was the fire machine.

Before fire machines, it took a lot of effort to cross the mountains, if you even wanted to bother. The fire opened many new areas of land, particularly in the rugged mountains and dense vegetation along the eastern coast of their continent.

Fire machines enabled the Drels to inhabit new lands. Drels now live throughout their continent, on two islands, and on the edge of another continent.

From the time of the discovery of fire, the Drelstenprupo have flourished. Invention and technology boomed.

The Drels have created a sophisticated and stable civilization.

A meteor suddenly appears.

The object streaks through the sky in a straight line toward the Drel home continent. The meteor is very low in the sky as it passes overhead. It is stunning how extremely fast the meteor is moving.

The large object disappears into its smoke trail. The Drels across the middle of the continent can feel the sudden and dramatic increase in the air temperature.

The meteor goes down behind the mountains to the east.

A blinding flash. A deafening roar. The ground shakes violently.

In the Regions near where the meteor landed, there is a lot of damage and destruction. Burrows are devastated. Forests of trees are flattened.

The air is filled with smoke and the skies are darkened for many days.

Drels investigate what has happened to the eastern lands, where the meteor struck. It is discovered that the Region is simply no longer there. What was once a large Region of land is now part of the ocean.

There was some loss of life, though the remote land was sparsely populated. If the meteor had hit near one of the heavily populated valleys, the loss would have been severe.

R7

The tiny reptile emerges from her shell into the bright light. There are many strange sounds surrounding her.

She smells food.

Her vision is blurry, but she can tell which direction to go by the smell of the food.

She nibbles at the food. She eats several large bites before another hatchling bites her front leg and pushes her away from the food.

While her wound is healing, she learns her surroundings. There are many like her—hatchlings about her size, and a few who are very large.

The very large ones dump food in certain places. The hatchlings compete for the food. Some hatchlings do not get enough food.

She learns to fight for food.

She grows and discovers that she can leave the large room. There are passageways that lead to many other rooms.

Over time, she learns to speak by listening to the bigger hatchlings and the Full Grown. By listening and talking, she's able to get more and better food without having to fight as much.

Writing has an advantage. It leads to more and better food. She learns to understand the writings. At first, the important writings are the ones that describe where food can be found. Later, she discovers much more about her world from the writings.

Some of the larger, stronger, and smarter hatchlings are given names. The hatchlings with names are treated better and given more and better food. She asks some of the Full Grown if she can have a name.

The Full Grown begin to call her "Linrep Sreeget."

Linrep's whole existence is the Hatching Facility. However, she knows that there is a much larger world out there. Other Full Growns bring food and things to the Facility in large vehicles. Writings teach of an enormous society of the Serpilgeneret.

All the hatchlings who are bigger than her gradually disappear from the Facility. Then Linrep becomes one of the bigger hatchlings.

Linrep begins to wonder what happens to the bigger hatchlings. She asks one of the Full Grown about this.

The Full Grown distractedly says, "Hatchlings leave the Facility when the time is appropriate."

Linrep is confused. "Where do we go when we leave here?"

The Full Grown recites by rote, "You go to where you can be useful. You are provided with food and shelter by those you help."

Linrep is curious. "Where will *I* go?"

The Full Grown appraises her for a moment. "I don't know where you will go. It seems that your time will be soon. Do you want to leave here?"

Linrep thinks about this. Yes. She would like to see the larger world out there. She looks back at the Full Grown, but she's not sure what to say.

The Full Grown knows with a casual glance. She has seen this hundreds of times. "You will be leaving here soon, Linrep Sreeget."

Linrep spends much of her time outside the Facility now. She usually sees a few of the other bigger hatchlings outside, too.

It feels good to be outside. They explore the surrounding hills and swim in the rivers. One of the males likes to catch small furry animals for food.

Linrep prefers to eat the prepared food inside the Facility. She's walking back inside to find something to eat when a Full Grown approaches her.

The Full Grown speaks authoritatively. “Linrep Sreeget. You are leaving the Facility. Follow me.”

Linrep is surprised and concerned. She was not prepared for this to happen today. “Where am I going?”

The Full Grown is bored with the question. The hatchlings always ask that, and she never knows. “You will learn about it when you get there.”

Linrep is led to the area of the Facility where supplies are brought in, and waste is taken away. She’s directed into one of the large vehicles.

Five larger hatchlings are already sitting in the box of the vehicle. Linrep gets in and finds a place to sit.

Two more big hatchlings are escorted into the back of the vehicle. She recognizes one of them. Linrep has seen her outside.

Before the last two have time to sit down, the door is shut, and the hatchlings are plunged into total darkness. At nearly the same instant, the vehicle begins to move.

The vehicle travels for a long time. A very long time. Then the vehicle finally stops. The back door opens. They’re inside a building.

The hatchlings are led to a narrow passageway. As they walk down the passageway, they’re sprayed with water coming from all directions. The water smells pungent.

Past the water, the narrow passageway is very warm. By the time Linrep gets to the end, she’s mostly dry.

At the end of the passageway, a Full Grown gives each hatchling a body-covering garment.

The hatchlings exit the passageway into a large room. There they are instructed to put on their robes.

The clothing feels strange and confining. The hatchlings look at themselves and at each other. They now look like smaller versions of the Full Grown.

The hatchlings begin to feel less like hatchlings and more like young Serpils.

The former hatchlings are shown other rooms where they can eat, sleep, and relieve themselves. Then, the Full Growns leave.

The young Serpils begin to settle into their new surroundings.

Someone opens a door that leads outside. They all shuffle outside, but it's very dark. They're unable to see anything past the light coming from the doorway.

The next day, the young Serpils are sent through a series of rooms where they are informed of their fates.

The place is a food farm. It covers a very large and vaguely defined area. The farm encompasses the surrounding valley and mountains.

The food consists of a variety of small, medium, and large animals.

The farm periodically sweeps areas for breeding and harvesting purposes. After breeding, the animals are released into designated areas. After harvesting, the carcasses are trucked out and contribute to the Serpilgeneret food supply.

This is to be Linrep's new life.

Linrep and the other workers help with whatever needs to be done.

Every so often, more workers arrive. Some workers leave the farm. Some workers are killed by the animals or the machinery. More workers are always needed.

Over the many years, Linrep has performed nearly all the tasks involved. Lately, she has been put on the more responsible tasks.

New workers with fewer skills can do the mundane, strenuous, and repetitive tasks.

Today, Linrep is riding in a delivery truck. The destination is three days away from the farm. This will be the first time that she has ever seen a city of her people.

Linrep is able to see a brief glimpse of the city as the truck goes over a hill.

From what she saw, there were many buildings and roads. An amazing amount. She knows there are a large number of Serpils living here. She is left with the impression that there is much more city beyond what she saw.

It's interesting to consider that this is just one of many Serpil cities across a very large continent.

Their delivery stop is at the outer edge of the city. They park the full delivery truck and acquire an empty truck for the return to the farm. The driver goes into the city a short distance so they can eat at a food dispensary.

She is in the city!

There is so much more of everything—more buildings, more roads, more noise. Vehicles of various sizes are everywhere. In any direction, there is a buzz of activity.

The number of people is shocking! There are reptiles, a lot of them, everywhere you look.

After they eat, Linrep and the driver walk back toward the door. In the opposite corner from where they ate is a sizable band of people.

Among them is a Drel.

It's the first time she's ever seen a Drel. Linrep and the driver stop and observe the Drel.

The Drel doesn't seem very impressive. Linrep ponders the Drel as she would the food animals that she has been around for most of her life.

Linrep notices that the other Serpils, including her driver, seem uncomfortable with the Drel. Everybody gets even more unnerved when it speaks in the Serpil language.

The Drel is difficult to understand at times, but it knows how to *talk!*

The other Serpils seem to be uncomfortable with it even when it isn't speaking.

An older Serpil casually approaches her. He says in a friendly manner, "You don't seem bothered by the presence of the Drel?"

Linrep shrugs. "I have been around many kinds of Species as part of my work on the farm."

The older Serpil studies her for a moment. He decides to take a chance. "The Drels have been trying to organize meetings with us, the Geminy, and the Tubells. Some don't like the idea. Most don't care either way."

Linrep is curious. "Meetings about what?"

The older Serpil shares. "The Drels say they have some ideas about the planet. They say the conferences will be about common concerns."

Linrep is dubious. Common concerns? The prevalent attitude among Serpils is that all other Species are food. She has never considered the idea that the Serpils would have "common concerns" with any other Species.

What a bizarre concept.

Linrep has to ask. "What do you think about it?"

The older Serpil answers in a conspiratorial tone. "The Drels can be useful. They have provided us with some valuable information. I believe attending their conferences would be beneficial. It's a simple thing we could do to continue getting help and information from the Drels."

The older Serpil continues: "It's good to allow the Drels to have a little of what they want sometimes. This makes it easier for the Serpilgeneret to get what we want from them."

Linrep is losing interest in the conversation. "I think I don't care either way."

The older Serpil appears uncomfortable. "I deal with certain Drel individuals occasionally. I don't like it. I do not want to attend the meetings with the Drels and the other Species. So far, no Serpil is willing to go to their conferences."

The older Serpil looks at Linrep with a mix of interest and hope. "How do you feel about it? Would you be willing to attend the meetings? Would you be able to sit in a room with the other Species while they talk with each other?"

Linrep is surprised by most of what he just said. She's trying to process the revelations about the Serpilgeneret working with the Drels. Did he ask her to go to those meetings with the Drels, and the others?

Linrep asks about the thing that struck her most. "They can talk with each other?"

The older Serpil rolls his shoulders. "The Drels have learned how to speak in our language and the languages of the other two. As far as I know, the Drels are the only ones who can speak the language of another Species."

The older Serpil tries to encourage Linrep. "The conferences will be in a neutral location. All you need to do is listen to what's being talked about and report back to me."

Linrep considers the possibility. She's not completely opposed to the idea.

The older Serpil assumes a more friendly manner. "When the conferences are over, you can go back to what you were doing if you want. Or we can find something else that you might prefer to do. If you do this, you will have your choice of accommodations."

Linrep likes the sound of that. She hasn't been offered many choices in life.

Linrep knows a little about the Geminy. People occasionally talk about the pathetic primates.

She's aware of the current conflict with the Geminy at the south end of the Great Lake. It doesn't even occur to her to be concerned about her personal safety regarding reprisals from the Geminy.

Serpils fear no Species.

Linrep wonders about the Tubellstacene. She knows very little about the Drels and almost nothing about the Tubells. Her knowledge of lower Species pertains mostly to those that she's been farming.

Linrep looks at her truck driver. She thinks about returning to life at the farm compared to what the cities might be like. She doesn't know what "her choice of accommodations" could be, but she thinks that she would like to learn.

Linrep is interested. She says casually, "I'm willing to go to the conferences."

In that instant, Linrep Sreeget's life changes forever.

Soon, existence on the planet will change forever.

As usual, the Geminy are divided as to what to do.

The Geminy are holding a meeting in the Region that has been designated as Region 3 of Continent 6. This Region is south of their ancestral homelands, which are now designated as Continent 4.

Some people want to go west into the mountains, and some want to go east to the plains. The "easterners" say the plains offer better land and the west is too dangerous. The "westerners" say that the mountains offer better potential, and that the danger is minimal.

The eastern proponent argues, "Early explorers brought back stories of large predators in the mountains. These new predators may end up being more dangerous than the Serpils."

The Westerner counters this concern. "The use of Special Weapons mitigates any threats that may await us in the mountains."

The Westerner continues, "Special Weapons have advanced a lot since Gishey Donmaru invented the first one. We understand NRG better. We're able to control it more. We now have handheld units that rival her huge machine on a cart."

A second Westerner elaborates, "It took Gishey a generation to eradicate the terropads from Region 1 of 4. With today's technology, we could do it in less than a year."

The Westerner qualifies, "Of course, we wouldn't want to. It's a shame about the extinction of the terropads."

Someone from the back of the room speaks out off-topic. "What about helping the Roshuda in the north?"

The Easterner dismisses the interruption. "We have been sending them food and supplies for a long time. They have Special Weaponry. What else should we really do to help?"

In agreement with the Easterner, the Westerner adds, "The Roshuda should not have walked out of the Conferences."

Another attendee joins in. "They said that the Conferences were not helping—that nothing was being considered except ideas that only made their situation worse."

The Westerner opines defensively. "The Conferences were helpful in a lot of ways. For the first time, the Geminy, Tubells, Drels, and Serpils all met in a peaceful setting to discuss global issues."

The Easterner supports the Westerner's comment. "Everyone else agrees that the establishment of the Global Region and Island Designations system, based on geography for land and expanded to include the water, is a good thing."

The second Westerner also supports the Agreements made at the Conferences. "And other benefits like the use of a common calendar and standardizing bookkeeping."

The attendee responds, "Yes, but the G.R.I.D. System Agreements also denied the Roshuda's request for Region 12 of 13."

The Westerner grows irritated. "The G.R.I.D. Agreements are for identification purposes only. They are not for things like claims of ownership or settling disputes."

The Easterner speaks to the reality of the situation. "The Roshuda in 12 of 13 should recognize that the Region is in Serpilgeneret territory and that the Serpils will not stop until they have it."

The Westerner concludes discussion on the topic. "Many of us have been appealing to the Roshuda to withdraw from that Region for a long time."

The battle still rages for parts of the ancestral Roshuda Geminy Region at the southern end of the Great Lake. The Serpilgeneret have conducted a synchronized attack from both sides, to a devastating effect.

The Roshuda have put up a valiant fight. However, after years of fighting, victory seems very unlikely. The Roshuda Claim on Region 12 of 13 is doomed.

Most of the Roshuda towns have been demolished. Many lives have been lost. The Serpils seem more interested in killing the Roshuda than simply taking the land.

Roshuda survivors are increasingly fleeing southward.

Someone made an effort to convert the cellar into a hidden shelter. The Roshuda doesn't know who they were or what happened to them. Maybe they perished in the house when it burned down. Maybe they already fled south.

His heart breaks at the sight of the small group of Roshuda huddling in the cellar.

He doesn't know any of these people personally, but they are his people. He doesn't know where any of them are from, but he knows how they all got here.

Like him, they have suffered great loss. He can see it in their faces.

Now, this random group of strangers takes temporary refuge in a dark, dank cellar. They are grateful to be here.

He found this place when he was in the forest, looking for food. As he gathered edible roots under some bushes, he stumbled across the hidden passage leading to the shelter.

In the eight days since then, he has kept a watch through cracks in the overhead door.

Occasionally, Geminy, in small groups or alone, will sneak through the yard. If he thinks it safe, he invites them down here.

It's a good place to hide, and there's a small cache of food.

He is always careful to brush away any tracks leading to the small shed over the door to the underground shelter. When he lowers the door, he makes sure that the broken chair is placed so that the door appears to be nothing more than part of the wooden floor.

He hasn't talked much with any of the people here. Nothing really needs to be said, and it's better to be quiet.

They all have the same goal. Bide their time. Stay quiet. Wait them out.

Right now, Serpils are everywhere.

The Roshuda in the shelter are united in their hope for escape. So far, they have eluded the Serpil patrols.

They pass the time in silence and move as little as possible. Even the small child knows not to make any unnecessary sound.

A Serpil patrol walks past the underground cellar behind the burned-out house. Every Roshuda becomes as still as stone.

In this moment, their greatest fear is to be discovered.

At this time, their greatest fear is realized.

The overhead door bursts inward. Daylight floods into the cellar. Serpils descend into the shelter two stairsteps at a time.

The group scrambles to the back of the shelter. Escape through the underground tunnel is the only option.

The Roshuda stands in front of the Serpils, blocking them, to give the people more time to get into the tunnel. He locks eyes with the leading Serpil.

With one arm, the reptile flings him aside. He slams into the wall headfirst and crumbles to the floor in a broken, bleeding heap.

The Serpils follow the Roshuda down the narrow tunnel. The much larger Serpil have difficulty in the tight space and the Roshuda are able to lengthen their lead.

The Roshuda begin to emerge from the tunnel on the other side of the nearby hill. The first ones out help the others get out.

A mother, father, and their child, about five years old, exit the tunnel in the middle of the line.

The father carries the child, and the mother helps clear the path in front of them.

They hear the trilling sounds of Serpil voices nearby. The Roshuda stop and drop to the ground.

Judging by the sounds of rustling leaves and bushes, the Serpil are getting close.

A Serpil spots the small group and lets out a loud trill. The Roshuda jump to their feet and take off running in several directions.

As he's running, the father hears the crashing of bushes right behind him. He glances back. The person behind him is taken down by a Serpil.

The father shifts the child from his right arm to his front, using both arms to hold the boy. The father focuses on his singular goal—follow wherever the mother leads.

Suddenly, a Serpil bursts through the trees and brush at the father's side. The father is tripped by the attacking Serpil.

The father cries out as he falls to the ground.

The child goes tumbling and sliding forward.

The mother turns and sees the father going down. She slides to a stop and rushes back.

As the mother is scooping up her child, she sees the Serpil swing his scissors down on the father's back.

She doesn't have time to scream or even to think. She bolts off in the direction that she last saw another Roshuda.

Running frantically, the mother clutches the child close to her body. Tree branches and leaves slash cuts in her face and arms.

She hears a Roshuda's scream snuffed short not far behind her. Intent on getting away, she does not look back.

She hears it before she sees it—a subtle, sustained roar. At first, she thinks of the river as another obstacle.

Within sight of the river to her left, she stops and kneels among some bushes in a clump of trees, trying to get her breath. Movement catches her eye.

There's a raft floating down the river.

Three Roshuda on the raft see her. They wave her over. They begin maneuvering the raft to her side of the river.

She turns toward the river. With a sense of hope and relief, she runs for the raft.

She's halfway down the hill when she sees a Serpil to her right on an intercept course to cut her off. She has no choice but to continue running for the river.

She doubts that she's going to make it. She subconsciously vocalizes a panicked expression of fear.

The Serpil is closing in. It becomes obvious that the Serpil is going to cut her off. She stumbles and falls.

She hits the ground hard and tumbles. She loses her grip on her boy.

He slides down the hill, toward the Serpil.

She struggles to get up. Her right arm is broken, and her left ankle isn't working right. It's probably broken, too.

She ignores the pain and focuses on the change of functionality. With determination, she stumbles forward.

The Serpil moves quickly toward her child.

The boy is oblivious to the approaching Serpil. He's focused on the cuts and scrapes on his arms.

The Serpil is going to get to her little boy first. She lunges forward. Her high-pitched scream is desperate and defiant. "*NO! NAO!*"

The Serpil looks over at her and slows to a walk. The predator stops a few steps from her child and watches her. It seems fascinated.

The mother limps forward. She's mostly dragging her left leg.

The Serpil steps forward and stands over her boy.

The boy's head swivels between the Serpil and his mother.

The mother continues toward her boy with her eyes locked on the Serpil.

She crumbles to the ground at the Serpil's feet. Her breathing is coarse and raspy as she awkwardly tries to grasp her child with her dysfunctional right hand.

She stares up at the large reptile. Her head shakes from side to side.

She maneuvers her boy with her broken right arm. He clings to her side. She crawls backward, dragging her child away from the Serpil.

The Serpil stands there, watching her scramble backward.

She gets out from under the Serpil and tries to stand.

The Serpil quickly lunges forward. The powerful reptile backhandedly swats the mother with the combined force of his great strength and his forward momentum.

The child slips away from her. The mother tumbles through the air before she hits a tree. She bounces off sideways, leaving a large bloodstain dripping on the tree.

The Serpil steps over to the child and picks it up by its arm. It's a small male.

The Serpil pulls his scissors from the scabbard on his waist belt.

The Serpil lifts the child to eye level and raises his scissors to snip off the child's head.

The child locks eyes with the Serpil. The expression on the child's face changes from fear to angry defiance.

The reptile pauses for a moment, surprised by the child's reaction. The Serpil lowers his scissors and studies the young creature.

When the Serpil turns it, the child maintains eye contact and that defiant expression.

The Serpil notices that the child has a discoloration above its right eye.

The Serpil holds the child high and his scissors low. Then the Serpil senses something to his side. To see what's there, the Serpil snaps his head in that direction.

The Serpil is disturbed that someone could have snuck up on him.

It's an adult male Geminy. He's stands firm and expressionless, just out of the reptile's reach.

The Serpil and the Geminy lock eyes.

The Geminy raises his right arm from his side.

The Serpil looks at the Geminy's hand and sees that he's holding a weapon.

The Serpil looks back at the Geminy, who is still expressionless, except for a slight twitching at one side of his upper lip and nose.

The Roshuda fires his weapon.

The Serpil is knocked backward as the discharge rips a large hole through the Serpil's head.

The Roshuda dives forward and catches the falling child.

The Roshuda hits the ground rolling, comes up on his feet, and runs to the raft. Clutching the child with both arms, he jumps onto the raft.

The other two Roshuda push the raft away from the riverbank. The two quickly and enthusiastically get paddling.

The raft disappears around the bend, just as several more Serpils arrive at the spot where the dead mother and the dead Serpil are sprawled in the dirt.

Days later, the Roshuda carries the child up to the medical facility. He's not sure what else to do.

There are two front doors made of clear glass. The large doors somehow open by themselves when people walk up to them.

This place is huge. The front area alone is much larger than a whole medical facility where he comes from.

The medical facilities that the Roshuda has known were small wooden buildings with one wooden front door.

The walls in this facility are white and smooth. Everything is white—and clean.

He's never seen more than a few people at a time inside a medical facility. There must be twenty to thirty people in this front area, and they are not taking up much of the room.

Nobody greets him to ask how they can help.

The Roshuda lowers the boy to his own feet but holds onto his wrist.

The Roshuda is lost in this incredible place.

He feels like he just walked into the future.

He sees the people being helped. He watches the people working. He notices that one woman seems to be in charge.

The Roshuda is hesitant. "Excuse me . . . nurse . . . we could use some help with this child."

The busy nurse turns distractedly. "What's wrong with him?"

The Roshuda is unsure how to answer. "I don't know."

The nurse glances at the child, then pulls out a notebook. "What's his name?"

The Roshuda tries to explain. "We don't know who he is. We rescued him from a Serpil attack. A woman he was with, probably his mother, was killed. We got away on a raft, found a truck, and made it to here."

The nurse nods, grasping the situation. "You did good. Are you dropping him off, or are you going to care for him?"

The Roshuda hasn't thought that far ahead. "Oh, umm, we'll care for him . . . until we can find some family, I guess."

The nurse signals to an assistant. "Would you please take these two into a room? Look over the child and get him cleaned up some."

The young assistant smiles at the boy. She gestures with her arm, then leads the Roshuda toward a small room.

The assistant escorts the two Roshuda into an exam room while the nurse resumes checking on the other people in her admitting room.

A moment later, the assistant emerges from the exam room appearing concerned. She shuffles quickly to the nurse.

The assistant stammers. "Nurse . . . the boy . . ."

The nurse is impatient. "Yes, what is it?"

The assistant pleads. "Could you please take a quick look?"

The nurse is puzzled by the assistant's strange behavior. She follows the assistant, her curiosity growing.

The assistant enters the room. The nurse stops abruptly in the open doorway.

The nurse gasps. "Go get Dr. Donmahy!"

Dr. Donmahy is overworked and exhausted. With all the battle injuries he's been treating lately, it's been a long time since he's had proper sleep or food.

He drops his gown and gloves in the receptacle, walks out of the surgery room, and plops down in the first chair he sees.

It only takes a few breaths before Dr. Donmahy feels like he's going to fall asleep in the chair. He's wearily blinking his eyes when an assistant comes running around a corner and shuffles straight up to him.

The assistant is frantic. "Doctor Donmahy, you need to see this! The admitting nurse sent me to get you."

Donmahy mumbles. "What's the emergency?"

The assistant struggles to avoid an explanation while conveying a sense of urgency. "Well, it's not an emergency, but you need to see this."

Donmahy thinks, *If it's not an emergency, the only thing I need to see is the inside of my eyelids.* When this thought passes, the exhausted doctor realizes that he's already on his feet and following the assistant down a hallway.

The nurse sees the doctor enter the admitting area. She heads for the exam room with the boy and his caretaker.

Dr. Donmahy dutifully follows the nurse.

Dr. Donmahy perks up as he enters the room. "How are we doing today?"

The nurse turns to the boy. "Would you please show Dr. Donmahy your chest?"

The boy looks at the man who's been taking care of him recently. The speechless Roshuda nods and gestures as if to say, "It's good, go ahead."

The boy is uncertain and self-conscious as he opens his shirt.

Written on his chest is, "My name is Rigeus Donmahy."

The boy feels like he might be in trouble. "Is this bad? My mother did it."

The nurse is heartbroken. "No child, this is good. This is very good, Rigeus."

Dr. Donmahy fondly reminisces. "I remember the day that I brought you home from the Care House. Wow, that was five years ago now—five good years."

He watches Rigeus adjust the sail, still impressed with the kid for being able to rig it onto the boat. It's not just that Rigeus had the idea to put a sail on the rowboat, but mostly that he was able to do it and make it work so well.

Donmahy picks up one of the leaves on the bottom of the boat as he continues. "The first thing you did was run straight for this pond. You pulled off your clothes along the way and jumped into the water."

Donmahy laughs about it now. "You gave me a panic until your head popped back up above the water. You swam all the way to the other side of the pond. When you got out of the water and looked back at me, you had such an exuberant smile. It appeared to me that your whole body was smiling."

Rigeus looks from his sail to the pond. "I love the water."

Donmahy casually twirls the leaf. "Yes, it's very Roshuda how you take to the water. I've never heard of anyone so young knowing how to swim, before or since."

Donmahy continues in a caring tone. "Rigeus, for you to know how to swim at such a young age, your parents had to have afforded a significant amount of time to teach you. It's another example—it shows us again, that your parents loved you very much."

Donmahy drops the leaf in the water so they can watch it float away.

Rigeus answers apologetically. "I remember that day, too. I'm sorry that woman didn't like me."

Donmahy glances sideways at Rigeus. "I should probably thank you for that. I'll tell you more about her someday when you are grown up and have a child or two of your own. You know, I would not have met Roda if that hadn't happened."

Rigeus smiles. "I like Roda."

Donmahy approves. "She likes you, too. And Duro loves you very much."

Rigeus drops a handful of leaves in the water. The two watch as the leaves drift away.

Rigeus is grateful. "It's really nice how Duro takes care of me and teaches me a lot."

Donmahy reflects. "Yes, she has been of great help, and Duro assures me that she will continue to be of service to care for you for a long time."

Donmahy considers Rigeus for a moment and comes to a decision. "Actually, Rigeus, that brings me to something important we need to discuss."

Rigeus drops the leaves in his hand. The word "important" always gets his full attention. It usually means something bad.

Donmahy tries to explain. "I'll be starting a new job in a few days. I'll be traveling occasionally. One of the first things I'll be doing is going to an important conference. There are a lot of issues to be addressed. I could be gone for a significant length of time."

Rigeus is familiar with the part about being gone for a while, but he doesn't understand the first part. "Will you still be helping people?"

Donmahy gazes across the pond. "I will only be directly caring for a small number of people, friends who I've been seeing for a long time. Mostly I'll be doing administrative work. Incredible advancements continue to be made in Wellness. With this promotion, I'll be able to help many more people with the emerging technologies. I will call like I always do when I'm working late at the facility."

Rigeus nods sadly. "I hope you're not gone a lot."

Donmahy is touched. "We will still have a lot of time together. I wouldn't have taken the job if I couldn't be home with you and Roda most of the time."

A fatherly instinct strikes Donmahy. "It's good to have a woman in your life, Rigeus. That is something I plan to tell you more about *before* you have kids of your own."

They sit in silence for a moment, lost in their own thoughts. It's good to give the boy some time to process the information.

He's impressed, as always, when Rigeus maneuvers the boat under a tree branch hanging over the water. Donmahy reaches up with the Beel Net and plucks two fruits. He washes them with some drinking water over the side of the boat.

Rigeus is suddenly concerned and hopeful. "Will I be allowed to take the boat out by myself if you're not here?"

Donmahy scratches his chin, contemplating. "You have shown a remarkable ability and responsibility. If you continue to do so, I believe you can be safe on your own."

Dr. Donmahy indulgently considers the future. "When you're a little older, we can move your boat to the lake."

The two enjoy their boat ride together. The fruit tastes great. The breeze feels good. The tranquility is rejuvenating. The occasional conversation is rewarding.

The smiles they share are genuine and heartfelt.

Rimnoy Egasduh wakes up most mornings, eats a meal with his parents, and goes to the Learning Center. As far back as Rimnoy can remember, he has been doing the same thing—sleep, eat, learn, eat, sleep. Well, that's most days. On days when his parents don't go to work, it's—sleep, eat, eat, sleep.

It's a long walk to the Learning Center. Rimnoy has walked this same path on most days for most of his years. He knows this route down to fine details—like bumps in the path, who lives in most of the houses, and what crop is growing in the field.

The route to the Learning Center goes through the neighborhood, over the hill, around the farm field, and up to the Community Buildings.

Rimnoy turns around the last corner of the farmer's field. He's getting close to the Learning Center when he sees a kid emerge from the capnorple field and hurry into the Learning Center.

That was weird. What was that kid doing in the field?

Rimnoy is currently taking three classes. Before the first class and after the third class, Rimnoy goes to the self-study room.

Rimnoy walks into his favorite self-study room to finish the day. Some kids on the other side of the room are arguing about something.

Others begin drifting toward the commotion. He's curious about what's going on. Rimnoy drifts toward the other side.

A bunch of kids are in the way. Rimnoy can't see what's happening.

Many in the crowd are whooping and hollering. Some leave the crowd and hurry away.

Rimnoy drifts closer. He still can't see much—mostly an occasional glimpse of two people's legs shuffling around in a circle of onlookers.

The Attendants arrive, a lot of them. The Attendants move in and break up what seems to have been a fight. The people who were apparently fighting are taken away. It's over.

"Come with me, please!" an Attendant says forcefully.

Rimnoy looks around to see who is being taken. An Attendant places a hand on Rimnoy's shoulder. Startled, Rimnoy looks up at the Attendant.

The Attendant repeats the command. "Come with me, please!"

Rimnoy's frightened. "What? Me? I didn't do anything!"

The Attendant speaks with authority. "Then we just need your Witness Statement. I saw you observing the scene."

The Attendant maneuvers Rimnoy toward the line of people being taken away.

Rimnoy babbles in disbelief. "I didn't see anything! There were too many people in front of me."

The Attendant speaks in a neutral and mechanical tone. "Please include as much information in your statement as possible."

Rimnoy is placed in a room. The room is empty except for the one small table and one small chair. There is one small light in the ceiling. The door is locked from the other side.

After a very long wait, an Attendant enters the room, gives Rimnoy a questionnaire, and exits the room.

Completing the report doesn't take much time. Rimnoy didn't see anything, and he doesn't have much to say about the incident.

A different Attendant enters the room. The Attendant goes straight to the table and scoops up the report.

This Attendant is friendly and cheerful. "Hello. Do you have anything else to add?"

Rimnoy is afraid of this Attendant. "No."

The Attendant smiles. "Thank you for your participation. You may exit through the lobby at the end of the hall."

It sounds to Rimnoy like he can leave. He doesn't wait around for clarification. Unless somebody stops him again, he's leaving. Nobody stops him.

Rimnoy heads for home at a quick pace. This part is slightly downhill until he gets past the Learning Center. Then the ground is mostly level until you get past the farm field—which currently has capnorple plants taller than he is. After the field, the path goes up a steep hill, across the top, and back down the other side. Then you get to the neighborhood.

Rimnoy is almost at the turn around the end of the field. He stops in the shade of a tree to get a pebble out of his shoe. He notices that someone is walking along the edge of the field near the Learning Center.

It's the kid from this morning, the one who came out of the field. The kid looks around suspiciously. Then the kid goes into the field.

Rimnoy doesn't know what to think of it.

Over the next tenth of a year, Rimnoy looks closely every time he walks past that area at the edge of the field. He can never tell where the kid was going into or out of the field.

Rimnoy always thinks, *I wouldn't go in there. You could get lost, or the farmer could see you or something.*

One day after classes, Rimnoy is in the self-study room closest to his exit for the long walk home. Math isn't one of his favorite subjects, and he's struggling with it.

Rimnoy blurts out his frustration. "How many different ways can people come up with to re-arrange a lot of numbers?"

"I can help you with that."

Rimnoy turns and looks for the source of the voice. It's the kid from the capnorple field.

The kid says, "I'm good with math."

Rimnoy is not sure what to do. He shrugs. "If you want."

The kid smiles. "Let me take a look at what you're working on."

The kid leans over and looks at the book. The kid swivels the book to get a better look. He thumbs back through a few pages.

After a moment, the kid speaks. "Yeah, I remember when I took this class. I think the way they try to explain this part is confusing, too."

Rimnoy is more confused. "You took this class before?"

The kid shrugs. "Couple years ago."

Rimnoy is surprised. "But, I think we're the same age."

The kid shrugs again. "I took it early."

The kid tries to help. "They try to get you to understand this whole complicated concept. The way I got *this* math was to think of it like this . . ."

Rimnoy listens and watches. The kid explains the math, shows some examples, and fills in a couple answers.

Rimnoy's brain feels numb. None of this makes any sense.

Rimnoy's thoughts drift. "I saw you going in and out of the capnorple field. What are you doing in there?"

The kid cringes. He leans forward, lifts his shoulders, and waves his hand in a downward motion.

The kid whispers. "Not so loud. It's a secret passage. I'll show you, if you want to see it. But you can't tell anyone."

Rimnoy shifts uncomfortably. "I don't know."

It takes a while, but Rimnoy gets the assignment completed with the kid's help. It's late when the two leave the Learning Center. There isn't much daylight left.

Rimnoy and the kid walk together toward the capnorple field.

Rimnoy is tired. He struggles to think of something to say. "Thank you for all the help with the math."

The kid looks tired, too. "I'm glad I could help. You'll get it. Just keep working at it."

Rimnoy doesn't want to think about math anymore. "My name is Rimnoy."

The kid smiles. "My name is Rigeus."

Rimnoy feels a little more conversational. "My parents work at the mines. Father is always covered in dirt when he gets home from work. Mother looks clean, but they both are always very tired."

Rigeus is uncomfortable with the conversation turning to family. "My, um, dad, is a doctor, sort of. He was a doctor. Now he's more of a manager."

They get to the spot where Rimnoy saw Rigeus disappear into the field before.

Rigeus drifts toward the field. "Do you want to take the quick way with me?"

Rimnoy is frightened by the thought. "Through the field?"

Rigeus seems unafraid. "It takes you straight to the neighborhood. You don't have to go around the field and over the hill."

Rimnoy looks at the thick growth of the crop and shudders. "Aren't you afraid of getting lost in there?"

Rigeus speaks in his teaching voice. "I've been through here many times. Besides, all you have to do is look at where the sun is in the sky. Just keep walking in a direction that keeps the sun in the same spot."

Rimnoy is still afraid of getting lost in the field. "It's already late. What if it gets dark?"

Rigeus laughs. "I have been through the field in the dark, many times. I know some of the stars, so I follow them. Most of the time, I get to the Learning Center early. Sometimes, like today, I leave late."

Rigeus continues casually. "It's not that late, anyway, and it's not that far. It's shorter across the field than it is from here to the end of the field. If you go down the path, I'll be on the other side of the field before you get to the corner down there."

Rimnoy looks into the field. He doesn't like it. The plant stalks are as tall as he can reach over his head.

Rimnoy thinks fast for an excuse. "I don't think my parents would want me to go in there."

Rigeus shrugs. "I'll see you later, then. Glad to meet you, Rimnoy."

Rimnoy is noncommittal. "Yeah. Glad to meet you. Um, thanks again for the help."

Rigeus does a funny side-stepping approach to the edge of the field. He disappears into the capnorple stalks.

Rimnoy thinks, *What a weird kid*. He walks along the edge of the field, on the path toward the corner.

At the corner of the field, Rimnoy stops for a moment. He thinks about how Rigeus is already on the other side and into the neighborhood.

Rimnoy would still rather take the way that he knows, even though it will probably be dark by the time he gets to the other side of the hill.

The sun slips behind the horizon when he's halfway down the hill. When Rimnoy gets to the bottom of the hill, it *is* getting dark.

Rimnoy thinks about Rigeus mentioning the stars. Rimnoy looks up at the sky and ponders as he walks. He's never really looked at the stars before.

In the fading dark blue sky, Rimnoy can already see fifteen or twenty stars.

Rimnoy hasn't seen the kid for several tenths of a year.

Rimnoy continues to take the long way around the farmer's field. Every time he walks past the "secret passage" spot, Rimnoy looks for signs of activity. He can never say for sure if there are any tracks in or out of the field.

The field has been planted and harvested two times since Rimnoy last talked with Rigeus. There's nothing in the farmer's field right now. Rimnoy wonders if Rigeus goes across the field when there's no crop growth.

Rimnoy isn't sure which sounds worse: going through the field when you *can* be seen or going through the field when the plants are so tall that you *can't* be seen. Either way, the thought of going across the field is not appealing to Rimnoy.

Rimnoy is staying late in his usual self-study room at the Learning Center. He's struggling with math again and finding it difficult to stay focused on it.

Rimnoy sees Rigeus walk into the room and look around. Rimnoy thinks it's ironic that he met Rigeus when he was having trouble with a math assignment. Now, he's having trouble again, and he sees Rigeus again.

Rigeus head-nods a hello. He smiles and shows his hand—like they're old friends and they just saw each other yesterday. It's actually been a long time. Rigeus turns and walks away, toward the science section.

Considering how often Rimnoy has problems with the math, it shouldn't be surprising that he would cross paths with Rigeus again in the study room.

Rimnoy drifts over to see what Rigeus is doing.

Rigeus is sitting at a table in the corner with a stack of books on his left side. He has a book open in front of him. He flips back and forth between several pages. Rigeus sets the book down on his right side and opens the top book from the stack on his left side.

Rimnoy has never seen anybody read small parts of a bunch of books before. What a weird kid.

Rimnoy goes back to the math book he's having trouble with. One book at a time is more than enough for him.

Rimnoy waits until Rigeus is leaving. He follows Rigeus out the door. It's full dark outside, except for the lights from the Learning Center.

Rimnoy catches up with Rigeus at the end of the Learning Center walkway. Rimnoy acts like he's a little surprised. "I thought that was you."

Rigeus smiles but looks tired. "Yeah, I saw you earlier. Tried to say hello without disturbing you."

They start walking down the path, lit only by very dim starlight. Rimnoy can barely see his own feet. He has walked this path so many times and knows the path well.

It's strange, though. Everything seems different in the dark.

Rimnoy tries not to think about the eerie darkness. "I haven't seen you in a while."

Rigeus nods. "I haven't been here as much. I also work the Job Boards sometimes."

Rimnoy is surprised that Rigeus works. Occasionally, some older kids will do a little work on the Job Boards, but mostly, the Job Boards are for adults.

They reach the farm field. The field was harvested recently. The leftover stuff was churned back into the ground a few days ago.

Rigeus casually walks over to the edge of the field. He looks around a little. Then Rigeus does his staggered-step thing into the field.

Rimnoy stops on the path. "Why do you walk like that into the field?"

Rigeus explains. "So I don't leave a trail that the farmer will see."

Rigeus walks a few more steps into the field. He looks back at Rimnoy, who is still standing on the path.

Rigeus pauses, surprised at Rimnoy's hesitation. "Are you coming this way?"

Rimnoy has never been out here this late before. He can see some lights from the neighborhood through the trees on the other side of the field.

Rimnoy looks down the path. It's very dark. It's a long way around on the path. He looks back across the field.

The neighborhood lights seem very close in that direction.

Well, there's no way to get lost in the empty field with some neighborhood lights visible. Nobody should be able to see them. He looks at Rigeus. Rimnoy still hesitates, but he walks toward the field.

Even though he can see the neighborhood lights, Rimnoy knows he still wouldn't be going through the field right now if Rigeus wasn't here.

The ground in the field is a little rough and difficult to walk on.

Rimnoy tries to distract himself by talking. "What were you working on so late at the Learning Center?"

Rigeus sounds serious. "I'm thinking about doing a modification to my boat. I was looking for any kind of information that might help."

Rimnoy is surprised. "You have a boat?" He doesn't know anybody their age who has their own boat.

Rigeus cheerfully rambles. "Yeah, it's in the lake, at the southern tip. I take it to a little island not far from the shore. I spend a lot of time there, studying and looking at the stars and thinking."

Rigeus talks about the boat as they walk. Rimnoy is feeling more comfortable with cutting across the field.

They're across already. Wow, that was fast.

After study days, Rimnoy looks for Rigeus so that they can cut through the field together. Sometimes, Rimnoy will stay late at the Learning Center, just so he can catch Rigeus.

On the walk home, Rigeus is talking about the food around them in the field.

Rigeus stops and puts his hand on a stalk, as high up as he can reach. He bends the stalk over gently until he can put his other hand on the capnorple fruit.

Rigeus inspects the fruit. "Food tastes much better right off the plant than when you get it from the store."

Rimnoy doesn't see it as food. When it comes from the store, he knows it's food. While things are still on the plant, they're not ready yet—or something.

Rigeus plucks the fruit. He pulls over another stalk and looks at the fruit. He releases the stalk and it springs back in place. He pulls over a third stalk and looks at the fruit. Rigeus plucks the fruit.

Rigeus pulls out his water bottle. He washes off both pieces of fruit. He bites into one and starts chewing. He looks over at Rimnoy and smiles, with a purple dot of capnorple juice on his chin.

Rigeus extends the other fruit, offering it to Rimnoy. Rimnoy can smell it. It smells good. The fruit looks like it should.

Rigeus takes another bite and chews happily. He's still holding out the other fruit. Rimnoy steps toward the fruit.

Rimnoy takes the capnorple. The fruit feels normal. Looking at Rigeus, Rimnoy takes a small bite.

The fruit is a little firmer and it's sweeter. It tastes very good.

Rigeus walks on, eating his capnorple.

Rimnoy and Rigeus begin meeting at the edge of the field in the morning. It's a much shorter walk, so Rimnoy is happy to meet Rigeus and cut across the field on the way to the Learning Center.

Rigeus stays late at the Learning Center most of the time. Rimnoy is still uncomfortable about going through the field by himself. If Rigeus isn't there, Rimnoy goes around the field. Rimnoy can either wait, study more, or walk home the long way.

Rimnoy usually takes the old path to get home.

The latest capnorple crop grows up around them as they routinely cut across the field in the mornings.

This morning, as the two are cutting across the field, Rigeus is talking about his boat again. Rimnoy doesn't understand much about boats, but Rigeus seems happy to talk about it. Rimnoy just lets Rigeus talk and occasionally grunts an "Mmm" or a "Huh."

Suddenly a booming voice calls out. "Hey! What are you kids doing here?"

The boys jump in surprise at the sound of the voice and the old farmer leaping out of the tall crop.

Rigeus is startled, but he has a plan in case he ever runs into the farmer. "We're just saving a lot of time and effort by going across the field instead of going around it."

The old farmer tries not to smile but can't help it. "Well, I understand about trailin' through."

The farmer makes a late point. ". . . as long as you're respectful!"

The farmer looks at the two boys, still trying not to smile. He does a double-take at Rimnoy.

The farmer barks at Rimnoy. "Have you been eating my capnorple?"

Rimnoy stands stiff, with his hands behind his back. Rimnoy has a mouthful of capnorple, which he hasn't been able to chew or swallow since the farmer suddenly appeared.

Rimnoy stares wide-eyed at the farmer and vigorously shakes his head.

Rigeus follows up on his earlier planned statement. "No. We're just walking through to the Learning Center."

The farmer's demeanor is clearly more friendly. "Well, I don't mind if you have some occasional good food."

The farmer adds quickly, "As long as you're respectful!"

The farmer seems to recite from memory, "That means no damaging the crop. And don't be taking a lot of produce, or selling them or something. Most importantly, don't be wasteful."

Rigeus likes the old farmer. "We just want to travel through. We wouldn't want to cause you any needless stress."

The farmer is enjoying the talk with the kids. "I understand about taking the shorter path through my field."

The farmer thinks about how things have changed, compared to when he was young. Sometimes, it's difficult to comprehend. There are so many people now. Almost all of them are strangers, too.

The farmer gets serious, yet still friendly. "As long as it's just you two. If a lot of people try to come through here, I'll have to prevent everybody from being on the property."

Rigeus is happy to hear this. “We understand. Thank you.”

The farmer shows concern for the boys. “I use some dangerous equipment working the fields. You need to be mindful. If you ever hear the equipment, you need to get out of the field as fast as you can.”

Rigeus smiles. “I know. I’ve watched you harvest many times. It’s very impressive how your machines collect the food.”

The farmer nods. “Yes, it is. Those machines are amazing.” He looks around at his crop. “Well, I’ve got to get back to work. You boys get on to your studies.”

The farmer starts to walk away. He turns back to the boys. He points his hand at them. “Don’t forget about being respectful!”

Rigeus is glad to have met the farmer. It was good to talk with him. It’s good to know that they have permission to cut through the field now.

Rigeus looks over at Rimnoy—he’s standing there, stiff as a tree. He looks terrified, like he’s about to pee his pants. He also has purple capnorple juice all around his mouth.

The farmer moves off to the side to let the boys get on their way. He chuckles to himself. He knows about trailin’ through fields.

Back when he was their age, everybody around had to trail through each other’s fields to get to most places.

The farmer has watched the movement of the kids through his field for a time. A few times, he followed the kids until they left the field. He’s seen these two boys trailin’ through and listened to them talk.

They seem like good kids. He wanted to meet them. He also wanted to lay down some of the ground rules.

Watching the kids scamper off, the old farmer feels a sadness in his heart about the things that have been lost.

Like with the trailin’ through—there was a sense of community about it. Everybody was happy to share a bite of food with the neighbors traveling through a field and everybody got to sample some different foods as they traveled.

That’s not the way it is anymore. It will never be that way again.

Rimnoy hasn't seen Rigeus at the edge of the field in the morning, recently. He seems to disappear every so often.

Rimnoy has had to walk the long way to the Learning Center.

Today is an off day. Rimnoy is hanging around the house. There's nothing to do—or nothing he feels like doing.

Rimnoy's parents are inside resting, as usual. It seems to Rimnoy that all they ever do when they're at home is rest. They plop themselves onto the furniture in whichever room they happen to be in.

It seems like they're playing a game where the object is to move as little as possible. Whoever does the least—wins.

Rimnoy is restless. He goes from sitting in the reclining chair in the shade of the tree to sitting in the swinging chair in the shade of the front porch.

Rimnoy watches the activity on the road. There isn't much. Two cars have gone past. Rimnoy didn't know who they were.

A beat-up car is coming down the street going very slow. It drifts for a bit, then lurches faster again.

What a junker! Rimnoy's surprised the thing moves at all. Rimnoy feels embarrassed for whoever owns *that* car.

The pile-of-junk car suddenly stops in front of Rimnoy's house. Rimnoy is thinking, *Oh great, the scrap pile is going to break down right in front of my house.*

The door opens on the other side. The driver is getting out. It's Rigeus!

Rigeus stands up and shows his hand.

Rimnoy is freaked! Rimnoy springs out of his chair and nearly runs over to the car.

Rimnoy looks around inside the car. It's as trashed on the inside as it looks on the outside.

Rigeus sits down at the driver's console and invites Rimnoy to join him. "Get a sit."

Rimnoy opens the passenger door. The door creaks and thumps as it opens. The passenger chair is worn out. Much of the padding is gone.

Rimnoy gets in the car and sits down. He looks over at Rigeus. *Wow, Rigeus has a car, his own car.*

Rigeus smiles. "I'm going down to the lake. Do you wanna go?"

Rimnoy turns and looks to the house for a moment. When he turns back, a smile grows across his face. He says, "Yeah, let's go."

Rimnoy pulls the restraint straps across and clips the four-point harness. The clip comes loose and the two sides recoil back to Rimnoy's shoulders. He clips it again, making sure that the restraint straps are holding.

Rigeus begins driving the car forward. Rimnoy has traveled in his parent's car his whole life. This is different.

As they roll down the road, Rimnoy stares out the front window in awe. His whole life, he's been traveling this neighborhood. Somehow, things look different.

For one thing, he's up front! He can see out the front of the vehicle, instead of just seeing treetops and rooftops through the small side window in the back of his parent's car.

The view is more like when he's walking, except everything is going past much faster.

Rimnoy exclaims enthusiastically, "Wow, Rigeus. This is great!"

The car jolts from a bump in the road. The clip on Rimnoy's restraint comes loose and the straps recoil back to Rimnoy's shoulders, again.

Rigeus notes offhandedly, "I'm going to fix that."

Rimnoy is impressed. "How did you get a car?"

Rigeus says, "Working the Job Boards."

Rimnoy is depressed. "I thought about that. My parents say I will be working more than I want when I'm older. Right now, I should be focused on my studies."

Rimnoy chuckles. "My parents would *not* let me get a car."

Rimnoy turns thoughtfully. "Your parents let you get a car?"

Rigeus hesitates, and then speaks in a more somber voice. "Actually, both my parents were killed in 12 of 13 when I was little."

Rigeus glances at Rimnoy, then back to the road. "Dr. Donmahy took me in. We both have the same last name. He's like my father. But he's away for work more than he's home."

Rigeus tries to cheer up. "I was mostly raised by my Caretaker, Duro. She's like my mother. Only, she has family of her own—a mate and two kids. Her kids are a lot older than me."

Suddenly, all the power in the car shuts off. Both occupants are thrown forward. Rimnoy is thrust against the straps over his shoulders.

The car coasts for a few lengths.

The power suddenly comes back on. The car lurches a few times. The car accelerates rapidly. The two boys are pinned back in their chairs.

Then the car returns to normal.

Rigeus says matter-of-factly, "It does that sometimes."

The car creeps up the gradual slope into the mountains. Before long, they're heading down the steeper side to the lake.

In places, the road (more like a trail) gets steep and switchbacks. Rimnoy wonders what would happen if the car's power shut off now.

Rimnoy doesn't know anything about cars. He figures Rigeus would know what to do if something went wrong.

The car pulls to a stop on a wide ledge. Rimnoy and Rigeus are just high enough to look across the large body of water. They can see most of the lake from here.

The trail down to the shore is steep in a few places but short and relatively easy. Rigeus walks straight to a craft tied to a pier.

Rimnoy has seen the boats that people get for their ponds. This boat is much larger than Rimnoy expected.

The back half of the boat looks like a large backyard shack. The front half looks like a very large pond boat with a deck over the hull. There is a large sail over the deck, a small sail at the front, and a small sail at the back end.

Rimnoy walks onto the pier cautiously.

He inspects the back half of the boat. On the wall across the middle of the boat is a driver's console. The rest of the back half looks like housing.

Rigeus goes to the controls. He's looking over everything. He looks up at Rimnoy. "You can get on. Get a sit."

Rigeus goes back to the controls.

Rimnoy is a little nervous, but he's also curious. With a focused effort, Rimnoy steps across the gap between the pier and the boat.

It rocks a little—not too bad.

Rimnoy takes short steps over to the wide-chair at the back of the room. He sits down quickly. The boat continues to rock gently and evenly.

Rigeus points to his controls. "You can drive the whole boat from here. Course settings go into here, and the boat makes the adjustments. You can override if you want, just by using the controls. Otherwise, the boat is always on auto-drive."

Rimnoy is impressed with the wide-chair. It's very comfortable. "Wow, Rigeus, this is good. This is really yours?"

Rigeus grins. "Yeah, I bought the original hull. My dad helped me get the boat down here. I've been making improvements for a long time."

Rimnoy shakes his head. "You have a very nice boat but a piece-of-junk car?"

Rigeus laughs. "I've had the boat for years. I just got the car."

Rigeus looks out the forward window and gazes across the water. "Let's go out for a cruise."

Rimnoy is instantly wary. "Is it safe? Aren't you working on it?"

Rigeus contemplates. "Well, I'm usually considering modifications, but I'm not working on anything right now. Haven't in a while."

Rigeus tries to ease Rimnoy's concerns. "I've taken it all around the lake. I've gone past those places where lots of people like to gather."

Rigeus shares in confidence, "When I go past the popular spots, I go to the far side of the lake. There are too many people to have to deal with if they start climbing all over my boat."

Rigeus shrugs. "Mostly, I just go to that little island right over there."

Rimnoy sits up and cranes his neck to look out the window.

It isn't much of an island. There are probably fifteen to twenty trees on it. It looks like you could probably walk completely around it in the time it would take to eat a capnorple.

Rimnoy looks at the water between the boat and the island. The island isn't far away, but what if something happened to the boat?

Rimnoy never learned how to swim. He's seen other people swimming. It doesn't look that difficult.

If the boat sank halfway to the island, it would be a long swim back to the shore. Rimnoy doesn't like the thought of having to try to swim back from halfway.

Rigeus encourages, "Hey Rimnoy, want to go see the island?"

Rimnoy discourages, "Nah, I can see it from here."

Rigeus tries again. "How about we just take the boat halfway?"

Rimnoy is alarmed. "Halfway? Why halfway?!"

Rigeus is ready to get the boat moving. "No reason. We'll only go a fourth of the way, for now."

Rimnoy watches Rigeus push three buttons. The boat lurches a little. Then it begins to move slowly forward.

Rimnoy feels uncomfortable about leaving the shore.

The forward thrust subsides. The boat coasts a short distance. Rimnoy watches Rigeus push the left of two buttons in a set. The boat comes to a stop.

Rigeus steps out of the housing section and onto the front deck. Rimnoy watches Rigeus open a compartment and remove an L-shaped tube.

Rigeus lowers the tube into the water. He looks down the tube. He turns the tube in a circle while looking down the tube. He turns the tube back to a few places.

Rimnoy is still inside the housing. "What are you doing?"

Rigeus explains, "I'm using this scope to look around under the water. Want to get a look?"

Rimnoy looks out at the water.

He looks back to the shore. Weird, it looks different from here compared to standing on the shore. He can see much farther up and down the shoreline. He can also see up the mountainside.

Rimnoy turns and looks past the island, toward the shore on the other side. The other side of the lake seems very far away—farther than it looked from the pier.

Rimnoy thinks about how much water is in the lake. The thought is ominous.

Rigeus looks up at Rimnoy and becomes concerned. "Are you good? Is something wrong?"

Rimnoy is increasingly uneasy. "I've never been on a boat before."

Rigeus is taken aback by the thought. "Wow, really? I've spent much of my life on, in, or near the water."

Rimnoy has had enough. Rimnoy pleads, "Can we go back now?"

Rigeus responds with concern, "Yeah, okay. It's good."

Rigeus puts the scope back in the compartment and moves inside. Rigeus walks past Rimnoy and goes to the controls. Rimnoy watches as Rigeus presses the right of the two buttons in the set.

Then, Rigeus presses one other button.

Rigeus tries to help. "Why don't you sit down? We'll be turning and moving back to the pier."

Rimnoy shuffles over to the wide-chair and rolls down onto it.

Rigeus casually saunters over to the other end of the wide-chair. He plops comfortably into it, with a big smile and an "Aaahhh."

The boat accelerates forward and turns. The course straightens out for a moment. Then, the boat pivots on its central axis, spinning the bow around in the opposite direction.

The boat coasts backward for a moment. Then the boat comes to a complete stop.

Rigeus ponders with satisfaction, "I'm gonna check on something." Rigeus stands up and walks off the boat.

They must be parked back at the pier. Rimnoy takes a good look around before standing up. The boat feels much more secure.

Rimnoy walks to the door of the housing. With a focused effort, Rimnoy steps across the narrow gap between the boat and the pier. He moves quickly onto the shore.

Rigeus has been giving Rimnoy rides to the Learning Center in the mornings. Rigeus always stays late and often doesn't know when he's going to leave, so Rimnoy still walks home most of the time.

Rimnoy does cut through the field sometimes, if the crop is tall enough to hide in. He hurries through the field, constantly looking to avoid the farmer. Rimnoy does not take any of the capnorple fruit or other foods.

The next morning, Rigeus pulls up in his car. Rimnoy jumps in, being careful not to get stabbed by the framework of the chair.

Rimnoy tries the clip on the restraint straps, as he does every time he gets in the car. Rimnoy is surprised! Rigeus fixed the restraint clip.

Rimnoy is still impressed by how fast they get to the Learning Center, even though the distance they travel is probably three or four times longer than if they walked.

Rimnoy likes riding in the car. Sometimes Rigeus takes different routes, too.

Rimnoy has lived here his whole life, and he hasn't seen much of the town. Riding in the car, Rimnoy has been able to see much more of this place.

There is a lot more to this town than he realized.

This morning, Rigeus is driving through another new area.

Rimnoy is struck by all the large, fancy-looking homes. They all seem to have nice cars, too. The people here all look happy.

Then he sees her.

She's beautiful. She's standing in front of a house, talking with a small group of people. She has a heart-warming smile. Those clothes look good on her.

Rimnoy stares at her as the car rolls past. Panic! She's turning to look at them.

Without thinking about it, Rimnoy whips his head away and ducks down in his chair. Rimnoy doesn't want her to see him in this crappy car.

Rimnoy looks up at Rigeus. Rigeus gives him a head nod and a smile. Neither of them says anything.

Rimnoy goes back to observing the unfamiliar parts of town. They continue traveling in silence until they get close to the Learning Center.

Rigeus breaks the silence. "I'm starting a class today in the East Building. I'm going to park between the buildings, and we can both walk from there."

Rimnoy ponders. "The East Building? I've never been in there. I just figured it was the same as the West Building."

Rigeus explains. "It basically is the same. The floor plan is like a mirror image, though. At first, everything seems backward. But it doesn't take long to become familiar with it."

After completing his studies for the day, Rimnoy thinks about the walk home. Riding in the car is much better. Maybe he can wait and catch Rigeus leaving early—well, early for Rigeus, late for everybody else.

Rimnoy decides to walk over to the East Building. It might be interesting to see what it looks like on the inside.

Walking up to the door of the East Building looks the same as walking up to a door on the West Building. Stepping inside the East Building seems familiar, but feels different.

Rimnoy takes short, slow steps as he looks around.

He drifts to the arch of a self-study room. It's weird. The things in the room are the same—tables, chairs, archives, people—but it's all different.

The tables and chairs are arranged differently. The archives look newer and more cleanly organized. There are people sitting, standing, studying, whispering in small groups, and moving around. But they're all different people.

The East Building itself, the rooms, hallways, etc., are all the same shapes and sizes as the West Building, but it's like Rigeus said. It's a reverse image—with everything inside being familiar, yet strange.

It's the same thing—only different.

Then he sees her. The girl from the neighborhood. She's sitting at a table on the far side of the room.

Rimnoy glances around the room as he tries to think of a reason to go over there. Rimnoy looks back at the girl.

Aaahhh! She's looking at him!

He's mortified. He's been standing in the archway for an embarrassingly long time.

Rimnoy turns and walks quickly down the hall. He doesn't know where he's going. Everything is backwards. He forgot why he's even in this weird building.

He sees a door. Rimnoy changes direction and goes out the door.

For a moment, Rimnoy is lost. What he's seeing is completely unfamiliar. He must be on the other side of the East Building.

Rimnoy doesn't know which way to go.

Rationally, if he walks to the end of the building, he should be able to figure out where he is. This way is shorter.

With a feeling of panic awaiting the outcome, Rimnoy hurries to the corner of the building. He peeks around the corner as if there could be a hidden danger.

He knows where he is. That's the West Building. That's the door he always goes out to walk home.

Whew! What a relief.

Rimnoy hurries down the walkway and onto the path. He gets to the farmer's field, already planning to cut across. Good, the capnorple is still tall.

Actually, the capnorple is very tall.

Rimnoy enters the field. As he's walking, he gets a sense that something isn't right. It's darker in here than it should be.

Rimnoy realizes that he's never seen the capnorple grow this tall before. He pulls over a stalk and looks at the fruit.

Eeww! The fruit is rotten.

Rimnoy walks on a short distance. He pulls down several more capnorple stalks. All the fruit is rotting in the field.

Something's wrong. Where's the farmer?

Rimnoy cuts through the capnorple field for the next few days. The field stinks more each day. The stench is getting bad.

After a three-day break, Rimnoy leaves the Learning Center planning to cut through the field on the way home. As Rimnoy approaches the farm field, he hears a lot of truck noise.

Three large trucks are in the field. These are not the farmer's trucks.

The strange trucks are clearing the field. It looks like the trucks are not just removing the rotten plants, they're scraping off the top layer of dirt, too.

These trucks are dumping the plants and dirt into other, larger trucks. The larger trucks are hauling it all away.

Rimnoy can't cut across the field. He has to go the long way.

Today is the last day of the current class schedule and the last day before a long break. Rigeus drives the shortest route to the Learning Center.

Rigeus seems preoccupied. "My last class is right before lunch. I can give you a ride home after that."

Rimnoy doesn't want to miss a ride. His last class is right after lunch. He can go to the class earlier, during his first self-study time.

Rimnoy decides. "Sounds good."

Rigeus elaborates. "I'm going over to Tigicby to see about taking classes at the Learning Annex. I'll also need to look into other things if I go there. I'll have to find a place where I can put my boat. I'll need to find a place to stay, where to get food, and I'll check the local Job Boards—a lot of little things."

Rimnoy's brain is going numb. "Whoa, that seems like too much to do."

Rigeus nods. "It's a lot. But it's like my dad says: 'Sometimes you have to make large tasks into smaller pieces—break it down into steps to take.' I have a plan and a tentative schedule."

Later, Rimnoy finishes his last class and walks back to the car. He leans against the car and waits for Rigeus.

He walks to the end of the car and looks toward the door to see if Rigeus is even out of the building yet.

Rimnoy hears a sweet voice behind him. "Are you lost?"

Rimnoy turns around. It's her, the girl from the neighborhood—and the East Building self-study room.

Rimnoy tries to calm his nerves, unsuccessfully. "Um, no. I'm waiting for a friend. He's giving me a ride home."

That sounds lame. Rimnoy brainstorms for something to say. "My, uh . . . my car needs repairs."

Rimnoy tries to look casual. He steps over and leans against another car—a nice car.

The girl smiles. "My name is Shugyi Donmayer, but everybody calls me *Shoog*."

Rimnoy is excited. "I'm Rimnoy Egasduh. Everybody calls me Rimnoy."

Shoog seems startled. "Rim-noy?"

Rimnoy is confused. "Yeah. Why?"

Shoog deadpans. "Oh. Nothing."

Shoog smiles and shows her hand as she walks away. "Bye, for now."

Rimnoy is thrilled about having talked with her, and relieved that it's over. "Yeah, bye."

Classes are done. Eight or ten days later, not even sure, it's boring.

Rimnoy has watched a lot of videos, played some games, read some stories, but mostly plopped on furniture in and out of the house. All the old stuff doesn't seem like it's as much fun as it was.

Rigeus is fun to be around. He's always doing something.

Rimnoy wishes he would've started cutting across the field sooner. It's no big deal now. Rigeus taught him that.

Rimnoy is still not sure about the boat, though. Thinking about it, he realizes that he is glad to have gone on the boat for a short ride. Now, he wonders what it looked like through that scope Rigeus was using.

When Rigeus gets back, Rimnoy would like to go on the boat again. Maybe even go over to the island.

A few days later, Rimnoy is trying to think of something to do. He decides to walk to the market. Not to buy anything—he doesn't have any money—but it's something to do.

On the way to the market, Rimnoy passes the Job Boards building. There are a lot of people running around—in and out of the building.

He goes inside to see what's happening.

There doesn't seem to be anything in particular that has everybody so excited. Most people here just seem to be in a hurry.

Rimnoy drifts over to some Job Boards.

At first, Rimnoy focuses on what the jobs are. He's not qualified for most of them. He wouldn't want to do any of the others he sees.

Then he starts focusing on what they pay. What a shocker.

The jobs that he *couldn't* do pay a lot more than the jobs he *could* do.

Rimnoy thinks about how great it would be to have his own car. He looks back at the jobs—and the pay.

Rimnoy would have to work for a very long time just to get a junker car like Rigeus. How is he supposed to get to a job without a car, anyway?

Rimnoy steps back from the boards and looks around at the other people in the room. Most of them look hungry.

Rimnoy thinks it's weird how he doesn't recognize any of the people here. Then he sees a familiar face. It's Shoog.

Rimnoy watches her. Shoog seems to be looking for a job. She doesn't look happy.

As Shoog is moving from one Board to the next, she glances around the room. She sees Rimnoy. Shoog instantly gives him a big smile and shows her hand.

Rimnoy smiles back and raises his hand.

Rimnoy is pleased to see Shoog moving toward him. Suddenly, Rimnoy doesn't feel so alone in this crowd.

Shoog flashes a sly smile. "Finding anything good?"

At first, Rimnoy thinks she's talking about him finding her, just now. Shoog turns toward the Job Boards.

Rimnoy realizes that Shoog is talking about the jobs. He lazily shakes his head and pans across the board.

Rimnoy is disappointed with the job possibilities. "None of the jobs I could get look like something I'd want to do. Specially for what they pay."

Shoog is also disappointed. "I can usually get something with the Medical Center or the Animal Shelter. It looks like I missed the recent openings by a few days."

Rimnoy is curious. "What do you do at those places?"

Shoog rolls her head to the side. "Mostly things like stocking supplies and cleaning. Sometimes, at the Med Center, I help move the unwell people from their beds to wherever they need to go."

Rimnoy doesn't like the sound of that.

Shoog gives up looking for a job. "I guess I'll try back in a few days. Maybe I'll go to the lake and get a swim. Do you want to go? There should be a lot of people there."

Whoa, yes, Rimnoy would like to go somewhere with her. He doesn't like the part about a lot of people being there, though.

Rimnoy thinks about Rigeus's boat. It's at the lake, and nobody else is around.

Rimnoy says it out loud before sorting his thoughts. Surprising himself, he blurts out,

"I have a boat—at the lake."

Shoog is surprised, too. "You, have a *boat*, at the lake?"

Rimnoy realizes what he just said. It's kind-of true, in a way, with Rigeus being gone for a while.

Rimnoy digs deeper. "It's not a pond boat, either. It has a small housing space at the back—um, at the stern, I mean."

Shoog laughs. "I accept. I would like to see your boat."

They stand there, smiling at each other. Rimnoy feels warm and happy all over.

Shoog finally asks, "Should we take your car or mine?"

Uh-oh. Rimnoy thinks fast. "It looks like I'm not going to have a car for a while."

Rimnoy looks up at the Job Boards and shakes his head with dissatisfaction.

Shoog nods with understanding. "Yeah, I get it. I had a bearing go out on my car. I couldn't drive for six days. I'd rather take my car, anyway."

Shoog isn't very happy with the road (more of a trail).

Rimnoy says what Rigeus said, during Rimnoy's first travel here. "The road looks worse than it really is. I think it's partly that the vegetation is so close on the sides—makes it feel different."

Shoog appears to think about it for a little while. Then she seems to agree. Shoog relaxes back into her chair.

Rimnoy is amazed that he's even in this situation. How did this happen, anyway?

At the end of the trees, a blue dot of sky appears. Shoog eases the car out of the trees and toward the parking ledge.

Shoog is out of the car first. She takes a long, sweeping look around. She gazes across the lake. She peers intently down the shoreline.

Shoog laughs and jumps up and down. "Wow, Rimnoy. This is great!"

Rimnoy is out of the car, but he doesn't want to get that close to the edge of the cliff. Rimnoy looks up and around, nodding and smiling.

Shoog points down the shoreline. "See that middle beach? That's where I usually go. All my friends go to that one. Most of us have been to some of the others but, that's our *favorite*."

Rimnoy walks a little closer. He stops well back from the edge. He can see some of the beaches along the shoreline. He thinks he can see the one she's talking about.

Shoog ponders. "It's interesting to see it from here. And see what's around it."

Rimnoy wants to get away from the cliff edge. "Well, would you like to see the boat? It's a short walk down this path."

However he got into this, Rimnoy is committed now. Rimnoy smiles and points his hand toward the downward path.

Smiling, Shoog extends her hand in the direction that Rimnoy indicated. Rimnoy leads the way.

The path levels off. Rimnoy and Shoog walk out onto the shoreline. The boat is just a short distance away, at the small pier.

Shoog looks over at the boat as they walk. She looks up and down the shoreline. Then she looks back at the boat. She rises up and skips a few steps ahead.

Shoog is hopeful. "That's your boat?"

Shoog stops and looks back at Rimnoy, appraisingly. Her expression seems to change from impressed to doubtful. She's not going to believe that it's *his* boat.

Rimnoy thinks fast. "Well, it's my family's boat."

That's sort-of true, with Rigeus being his friend. Yeah, that's good. He should probably think about how he's going to explain all this.

Shoog hurries onto the pier. She peeks into the side window of the housing section. Rimnoy steps onto the pier.

Shoog funny-steps over to the door. Grinning, she allows Rimnoy to open the door.

Having anticipated it, Rimnoy steps over the narrow gap between the pier and the boat, as if he's done it a hundred times.

Shoog looks at the gap and looks up at Rimnoy. In an unexpected reflex, Rimnoy holds out his hand to help her across.

Shoog smiles like, "I'm not worried about that little gap." Then her smile changes to, "This is nice." She takes his hand and steps across.

Rimnoy doesn't want to let go of Shoog's hand, and she doesn't pull it away.

He shows her the boat. Or more accurately, Shoog walks around the cabin and Rimnoy follows her. Shoog is looking at everything.

Rimnoy is only looking at her.

Shoog opens a panel on the side wall. She gasps in delight. "The cooler is loaded! Is it good if I get a drink?"

Rimnoy didn't know there was a cooler. "Well, yes! I'd like something to drink, too." Rimnoy peeks into the cooler.

Shoog is correct. The cooler is huge, and it's full of good stuff.

This is going to be fun!

Shoog gets a water and Rimnoy chooses a fruit juice. Their hands come apart as they open their drinks.

Shoog drifts over to the wide-chair and sits down on one end.

Rimnoy wants to sit next to Shoog. He starts drifting over to the other side of the wide-chair.

Shoog glances out the window. "Can you take us out on the water?"

Rimnoy veers away from the wide-chair. He's now heading toward the driver's console.

It's a small room. Rimnoy is across it before he can think of anything to say or do. Rimnoy finds himself at the driver's console.

Rimnoy looks at a bunch of gauges that mean nothing to him. He looks at the controls. He did watch Rigeus use the controls.

He desperately hopes that he can remember what to do. Then he remembers this control pad. Rigeus pressed buttons on this pad.

Rimnoy wasn't trying to learn how the boat works when Rigeus was going over all this. At the time, it just sounded like Rigeus talking about his boat again. Rimnoy was thinking more about the boat sinking.

Rimnoy recognizes the set of two buttons. The left button made the boat stop. The right button made the boat rumble a little—before the boat returned to the pier.

Back to the control pad. Rimnoy doesn't know what buttons Rigeus pushed, but he remembers the pattern. It was three buttons, in a straight line, from top to bottom.

Shoog asks with concern, "Is something wrong?"

Rimnoy tries to be reassuring. "No, nothing wrong. I'm just, uh, checking the gauges and things, to make sure everything is good. Before we go, I mean."

Shoog is reassured. "This is wonderful, Rimnoy."

He has to try something.

Rimnoy is almost sure that it was the three buttons along the right side. He presses them, loosely imitating the way Rigeus did it.

Nothing happens.

Then, Rimnoy feels a little rumbling. He recalls that it did this last time, before they left the pier. At that time, he didn't know enough to even think about it.

Rimnoy wants to sit down before they move. He looks to the back of the boat. Shoog is sitting on one end of the wide-chair. Rimnoy wants to get seated on the other end of the wide-chair, next to Shoog.

Before he can take a step, Shoog jumps up and runs to look out the window.

The boat slowly starts moving forward. Rimnoy is caught at the console.

Rimnoy wants to reach over and grab something to hold on to, but he doesn't want to touch any of the controls. Oh, there are handholds on each side of the driver's console.

The boat is underway!

Rimnoy looks at nothing except Shoog, like he usually does when she's around.

Shoog is bouncing on her feet in excitement as she looks out the window. She giggles.

The boat seems to do what it did last time. It drives out a short distance and coasts.

Shoog looks over at Rimnoy. He's standing there with one hand on the console.

Shoog is still smiling but she sounds serious. "You look good standing there at the controls."

Rimnoy was about to press the left button to stop the boat. He presses the button. The boat stops.

Rimnoy waves his hands open, as if to say, "Here we are."

Early the next day, Rimnoy starts walking back to the boat. It's a very long walk, but Rimnoy feels like he's walking on clouds.

By the time he gets to the boat, it's well past midday. Clouds or not, that was a long walk. He's thirsty, hungry, and tired.

Rimnoy helps himself to some food and drinks.

Rimnoy lounges in the boat for the rest of the day. He looks over all the stuff in the boat. It feels good being on the boat now.

He falls asleep with the gentle rocking of the waves.

The next morning, Rimnoy feels a bit daring.

Rimnoy decides to take the boat out. He presses the three buttons to take the boat out like before. The boat moves out, then coasts.

Instead of pressing the left button to stop, Rimnoy experiments with the controls.

Rimnoy is loving life now that he and Shoog are a couple.

Shoog picks him up in her car and they go places. They take the boat out. They've even been to the island a few times.

Rigeus has a great setup out there. Somehow, he's built a small cabin on the island. He has lights, a cooler, and some weird-looking instruments. It's all powered by a small amount of residential-grade NRG.

Rimnoy doesn't know what the instruments do. He's tried to think of something to say if Shoog asks about them. He's glad that she's never asked.

Shoog has been working a three-day job with the Med Center. Rimnoy and Shoog haven't seen each other for four days.

The job is scheduled for long days, so Shoog has been focused on that. Shoog said that the job pays very well, so it's worth the stress and sleep deprivation for a few days.

On the night of her third and last shift, Shoog stops by Rimnoy's house on her way home. She looks very tired, but happy.

Shoog vents about the stress from the job. Then she laughs about it.

Now that the job is over, she would like to go out on the boat and *decompress.*

Rimnoy promises Shoog that they can take the boat out the next day and stay overnight. That reminds him, the food and supplies on the boat are running low.

He should probably look into finding a job soon.

The next day, Rimnoy wakes up early and is unable to get back to sleep.

He has been waiting impatiently for Shoog to pick him up, and it's past midday.

Rimnoy is restless.

For the thousandth time, Rimnoy stares down the road, looking for Shoog's car. Finally, her car appears and approaches.

What a relief.

Rimnoy hopes that she's not going to change the plans. Shoog does that sometimes. As long as they're together, Rimnoy usually doesn't mind.

Today, Rimnoy just wants to get down to the boat and be alone with Shoog.

Shoog's car stops in front of Rimnoy. The passenger window goes down. Shoog leans over from the driver's console.

Shoog smiles. "Are we still on for the lake?"

Rimnoy's heart swells. Shoog looks very good. She's already wearing a swimsuit. The plans have not changed. Whew!

Rimnoy beams. "I love the water. Let's go."

On the drive out to the boat, Shoog talks about her last few days at work.

Rimnoy would not want to do most of the tasks that she did. Dealing with all those people isn't for him.

Shoog says that she likes the work and helping the people. Rimnoy can see how she would like it—and that she'd be good at it, too.

Anticipation increases when they get to the parking ledge. As usual, Shoog takes a moment to look up the shoreline at "her" beach. They go down the trail, across the shoreline, onto the pier and into the boat.

Rimnoy gets the boat underway.

Shoog goes straight to the wide-chair and plops across it with an "Aaahhh," followed by a giggle of relief.

Shoog's little giggles just melt Rimnoy's heart. He is so happy to be here with her.

Rimnoy sets a course to take the boat to the other side of the island. They found a spot where all you can see is the side of the island, water, and the distant shore on the other side of the lake. It's very secluded.

The boat begins to move away from the pier.

Rimnoy walks over to the cooler and opens it. Whoa, there's not as much in here as Rimnoy thought. There should be enough to get them through the night, though.

Rimnoy is gracious. "Would you like something to drink?"

Shoog purrs. "Get whatever you like and we'll share it."

Shoog sits up to allow Rimnoy to join her on the wide-chair.

Just as Rimnoy is sitting down, they hear a distant voice. They can't tell what the voice is saying, but they can hear the shouting.

Shoog is up first. She goes to the port-side door and steps out. Rimnoy follows her to the door. They stand there listening.

There's the voice again.

Shoog stares toward the shore. "It's coming from the pier."

Shoog's expression tells Rimnoy to go first. Rimnoy obligingly shuffles to the back of the boat. Shoog is right behind him.

Even though Rimnoy is going first, Shoog sees him first. "Somebody is standing on the pier. He's shouting at us."

Panic strikes Rimnoy. It's Rigeus!

Rimnoy stammers. "Yeah. I know him from the Learning Center. We're friends."

Shoog is relieved, but curious. "Why is he waving at us?"

Rimnoy thinks fast. "Whatever it is, it can wait. I'll get with him later."

Rimnoy smiles nervously. "Let's get back inside the boat."

Rimnoy is very tense.

They turn and walk back toward the door. Shoog stops at the doorway, turns around, and glances back at the pier.

The guy is jumping up and down and waving. They can barely hear his distant shouts.

Now he's calling Rimnoy's name.

Rimnoy feels panic spreading through him. Shoog stands in the doorway, frowning at him.

Rimnoy has to do something. He turns back toward the pier. Rigeus is unrecognizable at this distance.

Rimnoy waves one arm over his head and shouts (but not very loud), "I'll get with you soon, Rigeus."

Rimnoy instantly wishes that he hadn't said the name "Rigeus."

Shoog still looks uneasy.

The boat tacks around the island and comes to a stop in their little secluded spot.

Rimnoy is unsettled. Rigeus is back. Rimnoy forgot that Rigeus would be back soon. That, and Rimnoy has been in a dream world with Shoog.

Shoog is uncomfortable. She's standing in front of the wide-chair, but she is not sitting down. "I don't know, Rimnoy. Your friend, Rigeus, was frantic. He wasn't just waving hello. Whatever it is, it seems important."

Rimnoy wants to say something that will both dismiss Shoog's concerns and get back to the good mood again. He can't think of anything to say.

He gestures and kind-of opens his mouth, but no words come out.

Shoog gives him the "determined" look. "Let's go back. You have to find out what's going on."

Rimnoy knows they have to go back. He's seen *that* look before.

Rimnoy begins to feel sick to his stomach.

He really wanted to share time with Shoog tonight. What's going to happen now? He doesn't know what to do. Now he's getting a headache, too.

Rimnoy is dreading the near future.

Rimnoy pushes the one button that takes the boat back to the pier. It doesn't matter where the boat happens to be, that one button will always run it back and dock the boat.

When they reach the pier, Rigeus is gone.

Rimnoy and Shoog climb up to the parking ledge. Shoog's car is the only one there. They see tracks in the dirt of a different car, recently pulling in, parking, and leaving.

Shoog runs to her car. "Hurry! We might be able to catch him."

They scramble into the car and get on the road (more of a trail). Shoog is definitely driving faster than usual.

They don't really expect to see Rigeus's car on the winding drive up from the lake, but they still look for a dust trail.

Shoog and Rimnoy crest the top of the hill. The road stretches ahead in a straight line for a good distance. There are no cars on the road.

Rigeus isn't there.

Shoog stops her car. She looks at Rimnoy with a puzzled expression. Shoog slowly shakes her head. "He couldn't have gone this way."

Rimnoy shrugs.

Shoog searches for an answer to the disappearance of Rigeus. "Do you know of another road?"

Rimnoy is as puzzled as she is. "No. If there's a turnoff somewhere, I've never seen it."

Shoog concurs. "I've never seen anything that looked like it might be another road. There must be some other way, though."

Actually, Rimnoy doesn't want to find Rigeus right now. He would prefer, very much, to talk with Rigeus alone first.

Rimnoy feels that he needs to get good with Rigeus before Shoog talks with him.

Rimnoy sees a possible way out of this mess. "If we haven't seen another road by now, it's unlikely that we'll be able to find it. We don't have much time before it gets dark."

Rimnoy tries to sound confident. "I'm sure I'll see him tomorrow."

Shoog looks back down the road. She thinks for a moment. Then she slowly drives toward the town.

It's been three days since they saw Rigeus at the lake.

Rimnoy hasn't seen or talked with Shoog since then. He's worried about Shoog and her absence lately.

Classes are starting at the Learning Center today. Maybe Shoog has just been getting ready for her next classes.

Rimnoy is waiting to get a ride to the Learning Center with Rigeus. This will give Rimnoy a chance to talk with Rigeus before Shoog does.

Rimnoy waits a long time. Rigeus doesn't show up.

Rimnoy starts walking. He was hoping for the chance to talk with Rigeus—and the ride. Rimnoy gets to the end of the neighborhood, planning to cut across the field.

The field is gone!

They're building a wall around what *was* the field. They're building houses.

As Rimnoy walks the long path around, he observes the development. Properties are sectioned off and some housing frames are starting to go up.

These lots are huge. They're about three times the size of properties in Rimnoy's neighborhood. From what he can tell, the houses will be about three times larger than the houses in his neighborhood, too.

Rimnoy finally gets to the Learning Center. He walks into the West Building from habit. He looks around at the familiar people and surroundings.

Rimnoy doesn't feel like studying. He feels miserable.

He looks for Rigeus or Shoog. He would like to see Rigeus first.

Rimnoy walks through the entire West Building, looking for Rigeus or Shoog. He doesn't see them. They're probably both in the East Building.

Angst builds in Rimnoy as he thinks about Rigeus and Shoog being in the same building. What if they see each other—and talk?

Rimnoy enters the East Building with trepidation. Now, he's looking to find Rigeus and avoid Shoog. He has to talk with Rigeus first.

What should he say when he finds Rigeus? He will just have to explain the situation with Shoog and everything that's happened.

They're friends. Rigeus should understand.

Rimnoy approaches the self-study room. He stands at the side of the entrance, trying to be invisible. He gazes around the room.

He's planning to pounce on Rigeus or disappear if he sees Shoog.

"Rimnoy!"

It's Shoog, and she's right behind him!

Rimnoy turns to face Shoog. He tries to smile, as if to say, "It's good to see you."

Shoog is *not* happy. "I talked with Rigeus before he left. He moved to Tigicby, to study at the Annex. He said that the boat is his and I believe him."

Shoog squints pitifully at Rimnoy. "Why did you tell me the boat belonged to your family?"

Rimnoy shrinks with guilt. "I just wanted to be with you. Would you have shared time with me if you knew the boat wasn't mine?"

Shoog's mood changes back to anger. "I might have. Probably. I definitely won't *now*. When I think about Rigeus calling to us from the shore... You turned your back on him, and we drove away."

Shoog's mood seems to change back to pity. "How could you do such a thing, Rimnoy?"

Rimnoy stands there frozen. He can't think of anything to say.

Shoog says, "Bye, Rimnoy," and she walks away.

Rimnoy has a passing thought to ask her for a ride home. Then it hits him.

It's over.

They're not a couple anymore.

Rimnoy looks around in the Learning Center East Building. People are staring at him. He starts walking toward the door.

Even before he gets out the door, Rimnoy knows that this is the last time he will ever be in the East Building.

Actually, Rimnoy didn't plan to take any classes in the West Building. He was just going to do some self-study.

Rimnoy walks past the West Building. He steps off the Learning Center walkway and onto the dirt path that takes him home. He knows that he will never come back to the Learning Center again.

He thinks about Shoog and feels a tightness in his chest. The realization that Rigeus is gone begins to sink in.

Rimnoy feels the crush of his life imploding.

Rimnoy walks the old path home—down to the corner of the new development, over the hill, toward the old neighborhood.

Rimnoy glances at the partially built wall surrounding the new neighborhood. He remembers how cutting across the field was such an adventure at first. It was fun when Rigeus was there.

That's not the way it is anymore. It will never be that way again.

Dughom Yeasirn wakes up every morning with a smile. His first thoughts are always of his mate and their two young kids. He's got it good, and he's happy.

Well, he's mostly happy. It pains Dughom when he has to leave his family, almost every day, to go to his job.

Dughom doesn't like his job much, although he's glad to have it. The job provides a good home and living for his family.

Thinking about his family, and all the fun they have together, is what gets Dughom through the long days at the job.

Dughom is a press operator. He stands at the press. A unit comes down the line and stops at his press. Dughom manually lowers a lever and presses a button. Then the unit moves down the line.

Dughom's main priority is to ensure that no foreign objects are in the press chamber. He has to make sure that nothing else is under the press as he lowers the press head onto the unit. Then, he presses the button for the machine to compress and sonic-weld the unit.

Dughom does this a thousand times a day.

Dughom has been doing this job for long enough that his lever-arm is bigger than his button-arm.

The shapes and sizes of the units change. Usually, the press heads are changed every few days. However, the actions that Dughom takes are always the same. Watch the unit enter the press chamber, make sure it's good, lower the lever, and press the button.

Ugh! Working the press is *so* monotonous. Although, it's not as bad as the position ahead of him.

Quality Control 9 is a fancy-sounding title for someone who watches a thousand units go down the line every day, while looking for any improperly combined parts of a unit.

The QC9 operator uses a hook to pull defective units off the line and dump the parts into a recovery bin.

Some days, QC9 will pull five to ten defective units off the line. Most of the time, there are no defective units for many long days. Then suddenly, there will be a defective unit and QC9 has to instantly be on it with the stick!

Monotony interspersed with panic.

QC9 goes through a lot of people. Most people will only do that job for a few days. Some people last for a tenth.

Dughom is happy with the latest QC9 worker. He's good and he's been there for nearly three tenths of a year, now. They have been able to talk some and are becoming friends.

It's a different kind of talking though, while working. Some conversations are very long, consisting of two or four words at a time, in between focusing on the job. Many conversations are very brief and lack details.

Some conversations are touched on numerous times over a lengthy period of time. Many conversations are started and never finished.

Even with all that chaos, you can get to know each other, over time. Dughom knows that this not-so-young adult is good-hearted.

He's smart, too. He changed the position from pulling defectives off the line with a hook, to pushing defectives off with a Y-shaped stick. Pushing looks much easier.

Another day begins.

Dughom ambles up to his press. The press operator and QC9 nod to each other that they're ready. Units begin running down the line.

Dughom lets his mind go numb. He thinks about his family and dreams about things. Dughom pulls the lever and pushes the button, while he stares blankly at the press chamber.

Another day begins.

Once a tenth, Dughom and family get together with friends and relatives for an outdoor afternoon meal. There's a lot of talking and some activities.

It's always a lot of fun.

Everybody enjoys the get-togethers and Dughom feels good about it. It's one of the things that helps him get through the workdays.

Dughom is anxiously anticipating the end of this shift. He has a four-day break and he's hosting the next get-together at his house in two days.

Dughom invited his QC9 partner to the get-together and he gratefully agreed.

Having an occasional outside attendee usually adds to the fun. It will also be an opportunity to engage in some normal conversation, as opposed to the "work-talk conversation."

Finally, the shift crawls to an end.

With a quick confirmation that his QC9 partner and his mate will be at the get-together, Dughom is out of the building and heading home.

The get-together day has been fun from the moment everybody woke up this morning. The kids are running around, giggling and screaming. Dughom's mate is enjoying her "having a hundred things to do."

People begin to arrive and scatter in and out of the house. Some drift into their comfortable roles of helping with the food preparation or attending to an activity.

Dughom's young daughter scampers into the back yard. She looks and points at him.

His daughter squirms as she delivers the message. "There's somebody here for you. He says he's your friend from work."

She is so adorable.

Dughom declares to his daughter, "You are so wonderful. Thank you, precious girl."

Dughom glides to the front door. He's gratified to be able to share his home life with his new friend. "Welcome! So glad you could make it."

Dughom glances past his friend with concern. "Where's your mate?"

His friend explains. "Her coworker had something come up. She went into work, to cover part of the shift. She's planning to be here, just a bit late. She has been happily anticipating this event, as have I."

Dughom beams with relief. "Great! Great. Well, we're having a good start. There's good people and some fun stuff to do. Know that you are welcome and be comfortable."Dughom leads his friend through the house. "You can get to know your way around the house. Let's start with the backyard."

As is customary, Dughom presents his guest at the door to the backyard.

Dughom makes a gracious presentation. "Everybody, this is my friend and work partner. He also studies at the Annex. Please welcome, Rigeus Donmahy."

Six or eight people smile, nod, or show their hands in greeting.

Only about a quarter of the people are even aware of the introduction. Most people are occupied with other conversations and activities.

An older couple approaches with big smiles and open hands. They introduce themselves to Rigeus and begin chatting.

Rigeus smiles, looking genuinely interested in what they have to say.

Dughom leaves Rigeus to mingle and drifts over to the food preparation station. The food looks like it's going good.

Dughom feels a little silly-happy as he sets out the table with the plates and eating accessories.

Dughom gazes around his backyard and soaks in the positive energy.

Later, after they've eaten, Dughom and Rigeus finally get a chance to relax and talk.

They both are pleased that their mates have been getting along so well.

Dughom watches their mates enjoying the "trouble" of cleaning up after the meal. He knows that they enjoy the talking, as they go about their busy-ness.

Dughom is content. "I really enjoy these get-togethers."

Rigeus relaxes. "I can see why. We have been enjoying this day very much. Thank you Dughom, for inviting us."

Dughom is gratified. "It's great having you two here. I hope you'll attend others, too."

Rigeus answers sincerely. "Sounds great."

They both enjoy a comfortable pause in the conversation. They sip their drinks and watch the activity going on.

Dughom wonders, "Are you still studying—space stuff—at the Annex?"

Rigeus chuckles. "Yeah. I need to do a project for an engineering class. I've been thinking about a modification to the QC9 position."

Dughom chuckles, too. "I'm impressed that you've been able to do that boring job for so long. How do you get through it?"

Rigeus groans. "It's very bad, sometimes. Usually, I'm giving the job a very minimal amount of attention. I kind-of reduce it to a subconscious level."

Rigeus shrugs. "The pattern is so consistent as the units come down the line. I simply face that way and don't think about it. If there's an inconsistency in the pattern, I notice it."

Rigeus leans toward Dughom to speak in confidence. "Most of the time, I'm working on other things—thinking about them."

Dughom laughs loud and slaps his hand on his chair. He leans toward Rigeus and talks low to extend the conspiracy. "Most of the time, *I'm* thinking about other things, too."

Dughom sits back and observes his backyard. "I like to think about times like this."

Work has been a little more interesting lately. Rigeus installed a machine he designed at his QC9 position.

The machine sits on a frame over the line. Sensors track units going down the line.

If a unit's profile is outside the programmed tolerances, a bar swings diagonally across the line. The defective unit runs down the diverter, off the line, and into a recovery bin.

At first, Rigeus was frequently checking the machine to see if it was working correctly. For a while now, he's only been checking the machine rarely, to see if it's not working correctly.

Dughom walks in to work this morning to find that Rigeus is already there, working on his QC9 machine.

Rigeus gives a distracted head-nod greeting. He begins closing access panels and cleaning up the area.

Dughom notices a small desk nearby. He figures the desk is for Rigeus to use.

Dughom laughs as he watches Rigeus gather a tall armful of books, notebooks, tools, parts, and miscellaneous.

Rigeus deftly juggles everything out of his arms and onto the desk. The jumbled load transforms into a fairly organized distribution of items.

Rigeus shares the latest news. "I'm working on an agreement to have the QC9 Monitor installed on all the lines. Well, four more lines. After they test out, then the rest of the lines."

Dughom is surprised and impressed. "You can do all that?"

Rigeus nods. "The hard part is the designing. It's easier to put all the parts together, once you know what the parts are. You can get any parts you want, fabricated by somebody."

Dughom is awed by the thought. "That makes me feel . . . very impressed with the Roshuda Geminy, that we're so advanced and we have the ability to do things like that."

Dughom and Rigeus look at each other and give each other a slight nod. This is a moment of understanding and agreement.

They are proud of their Species.

Dughom is enjoying another get-together. This one is at his mate's sister's house. Dughom always feels comfortable here.

Rigeus and his attractive mate have been attending most of the get-togethers since the first one.

Dughom and Rigeus are enjoying their usual time relaxing and talking, just before the get-together is over.

They watch Dughom's uncle and his friend get into another heated debate. It's a regular activity for them at the get-togethers. It can be mildly entertaining.

Everybody knows that those two are longtime friends. Sometimes they can appear to be vehement adversaries, but everybody knows better.

Over the years, those two have called on each other in times of trouble. They've helped each other often. They have a strong friendship and trust in each other. Yet, they argue enthusiastically over numerous topics.

Rigeus views their squabbles with a different perspective. "Dughom? Why do you think that we are so divided, so much of the time? Our Species, I mean—as a Species. The other Species don't seem to have the kinds of internal conflicts that the Geminy always have."

Dughom considers the question for a moment. "I don't talk with many people about this kind of stuff, Rigeus. I will talk with you about it, though."

Dughom confides in his friend. "I have thought about it and discussed it with a few people, over the years."

Dughom holds up two fingers. "The Roshuda Geminy have always been of two minds."

Dughom lowers his hand. "Also, people generally like to be around other people who are like themselves. Most people have numerous overlapping interests, whether it's Roshuda or Geminy, socioeconomic, favorite hobbies, or many other things."

Dughom gets to the point. "However, we seem to have a talent for disagreeing. The increasing problem is that the more complex life gets, the more there is for people to disagree about. A group can agree on two or three issues easier than twenty or thirty."

Dughom ruminates philosophically. "The Geminy civilization is like a beautiful, multi-faceted jewel."

Dughom continues ironically, "Unfortunately, it seems that the more facets of Roshuda Geminy there are, the more fractures occur within the gem of society."

Dughom feels depressed about the divisive nature of his Species and worries about the future. He looks at Rigeus.

Rigeus looks like he's depressed and worrying about the future.

Dughom tries to shake it off and get back to a good mood. "Everybody seems to like all this space travel stuff that's been going on. Even *I* like it, and I don't know anything about space or other worlds."

Dughom gestures at the crowded backyard. "My whole world is right here—my mate and kids, and this town. But I still like the thought of Geminy living in those other places, someday."

Rigeus seems lost in thought. "Maybe space exploration can help unite people—something in common. Like an achievement that we all share, as a Species."

Dughom listens to Rigeus talk at length about his theory of space travel to unite the Roshuda Geminy. It sounds like a nice idea.

Not long after Rigeus got QC9 Monitors installed on every line, he quit. Rigeus went to work at the Space Information Center. He and his mate moved there.

Rigeus has started a great new life.

Dughom feels like his life has lost something. Sure, it's partly that the kids are getting older, but it's other things, too.

Dughom and his family have been skipping a few get-togethers recently, too. They are not the only ones. Others have been increasingly skipping the get-togethers in recent years.

Dughom walks up to his press. He nods at the QC9 Monitor out of habit. He notes the modification of the sensors on the recovery bin, to indicate when the bin is getting full.

Dughom also looks at the stack of indicator lights on a pole that can be seen from nearly anywhere on the processing floor. More good work by Rigeus.

Dughom feels an oppressive weight in his chest. His job is grinding him down.

Dughom is impressed by what his friend was able to do with the whole QC9 Monitor thing. He's proud of Rigeus.

However, Dughom's job is even more crushing now. He doesn't even have a QC9 partner to talk with.

Dughom is alone at his press, all day long.

Another day begins.

R8

The Tubell Shuttle banks wide over the ocean and levels off. They're fast approaching the far north island.

The copilot listens to the comms unit strapped above an eye. "We're getting a communication from Island 5. They say they're under attack!"

The pilot looks one eye at the copilot, one eye at the passenger, one eye at the control panel, and one eye at the monitor.

The pilot says the obvious. "We'll get there as soon as we are able."

Moments later, on the approach, they can see the Tubells down on the frozen ground. The situation looks dire. A vehicle is chasing them—a vehicle with a lot of fire power.

The copilot looks three eyes at the vehicle. "It looks like the Serpils."

The passenger, one of the Tubellstacene Organizers, lifts a tentacle in the Tubell version of shouting. "We have to save them!"

The pilot shifts the eye away from the copilot and focuses more on the monitor. "The way I see it, there are two options. One: the Tubells down there get killed and we get away with our shuttle, or two: they get killed, *we* get killed, and those Serpil get away with our shuttle."

After a short pause, the pilot shifts the eye back to the copilot. "Does anybody see it differently?"

Everybody on the shuttle is silent. They know the pilot is correct.

The pilot shifts the eye from the copilot, then the eye from the control panel to the monitor. "However, it looks like we can still get the NRG. Their work will not be in vain—or worse, end up in the claws of the Serpilgeneret."

The pilot raises a tentacle. "Wrap a tentacle around something! We're going in fast and we're not staying to look around."

The passenger goes into Organizer mode. "They were able to get the last piece needed for the prototype Shields system. If it works, those people down there will have died to make it happen."

The moment the shuttle touches the ground, the copilot is out the door. The pilot uses the moment to confer with the Organizer. "Our people are in great danger. The Serpils are a serious existential threat."

The Organizer looks three eyes at the pilot. "I hear about it all. I share your concerns, my friend. This is an uncertain time for our Species." The Organizer's two side-eyes look downward in despair.

The copilot enters the shuttle, presses a button to close the hatch, and heads back toward the Shields console. "We got the NRG!"

The copilot doesn't slow down until reaching the console. The Organizer is already hurrying toward the back of the Shuttle to check the Shields systems.

The hatch seals. The pilot lifts off, smooth and soft.

The pilot mumbles needlessly, "Let's get that NRG hooked up to the Shields."

Purstenpodler is old enough to understand that there is a competition for land between her people, the Drels, and the Geminy. The Geminy are friends, but the Drels still want to win and Claim the land.

Purstenpodler lives in the Drel Capitol, Region 7 of Continent 7. Both of her parents have Primary Occupations in the Housing Committee. Her Primary Occupation will likely be in the Committees.

Drel parents have a strong instinct to teach their children whatever it is that they know. Young Drels eagerly absorb the knowledge and influence of the culture around them as they learn and grow. There are exceptions, but most of the time, Drels will have the same or a similar Primary Occupation as a parent.

The land competition is on Continent 3. Even though the new land is far away, it still involves the Committees. Purstenpodler's parents will be involved in making housing available in the new lands.

Even though Purstenpodler knows the competition is serious, people are generally enjoying the race against the Geminy.

Then the mood changes. People are concerned. Purstenpodler doesn't know all the reasons why, but she knows that it's bad.

The Serpils have attacked the Tubells.

Since the Serpil attack on the Tubells' remote island, things have been hectic. Many Drel Committee Members have been reassigned to the Species Relations Committee and the Security Committee.

Purstenpodler has been studying intensely to become a Housing Committee Apprentice. With the Serpilgeneret making openly hostile acts, everybody is being advanced quickly—including students and Apprentices.

The Drelstenprupo are very concerned about the long-term ramifications of the Serpil attack. Any conflict among the four Higher Species is a threat to World Stability.

The G.R.I.D. System Agreements (initiated by the Drels) were a good first step. However, the Agreements are all academic. The Agreements do not approach things like Species Relations or treaties to help stabilize the world.

The Drelstenprupo continue making their clandestine efforts regarding World Stability. A few favors here and some deals there is preferable to destructive hostilities.

The Drels have been making deals with the Serpils and Geminy throughout history, but for some reason, the Tubells remain aloof. Purstenpodler thinks it's curious, considering that Drels and Tubells are more alike than either is like the other two Species.

Yet, the Drels have never been able to establish any Inside contacts with the Tubells.

Purstenpodler and many others have been graduated early. So far, she likes being an Apprentice in the Housing Committee.

Today, Purstenpodler is sitting in the Apprentices Wing. Her main task is to continually watch the Committee Members. If one of the Members looks at her, she has to see it quickly and move to provide assistance. Most of the time, she runs errands, like checking a fact or getting drinks brought in.

Purstenpodler likes hearing all the Inside info discussed in the Housing Committee.

Before, she rarely attended Committee meetings. She didn't understand much of what was going on, and too many other things occupied her time.

The Committee meetings are held in auditoriums so that a large number of people are able to attend.

Historically, Community Meetings were held outside with unlimited capacity. Most people would attend the rare meetings and contribute.

Now, numerous Committee Meetings are held nearly every day and are attended by very few people not directly involved in the Committees.

Attendee seating rarely has more than a small number of people. There are some "regulars," but usually the people attending vary by the topics scheduled to be discussed.

Otherwise, most people are busy with their own Occupations and immediate lives.

Committee Member 1: "As you can see in The Plan, we have people and supplies in 2 of 3, staged and ready to move into 1 of 3."

Committee Member 2: "The Race has been looking good. I think we will be able to Claim 1 of 3 before the Geminy do, easily."

Committee Member 3: "I still think it's too close. I have an aide monitoring communications, with instructions to let me know immediately, even during meetings, if there's any new information regarding 1 of 3."

Committee Member 1: "This discussion about 1 of 3 has been interesting, as always. Does anybody have more about 1 of 3?"

Committee Member 1—after a pause: "The matter is shelved. Next on the agenda is New Burrows on the Islands."

In studies, Purstenpodler learned about a lot of this. Then, it was theories and examples. Now, it's real!

The Housing Committee meeting has been droning on—mostly Continuing Reports.

Purstenpodler has seen enough to know that the information being heard will be discussed many more times before any decisions are made. All the talk now is a long way from anything important happening.

The usual monotony is interrupted by an aide who enters the auditorium and approaches the Members table. This is highly unusual.

Committee Member 3 has a whispered exchange with his aide. The aide hurries away. Committee Member 3 stands and holds a note in the air.

Committee Member 3: "My aide has brought me some information. This is an early report and will need to be verified."

People adjust forward in their chairs with curiosity.

Committee Member 3—proclaiming: "The *Geminy* have Claimed Region 1 of 3."

First, there is silence. Then a murmur grows in the auditorium.

This is bad.

With the Race for 1 of 3 over, the Housing Committee meetings have become dull and tedious. There is no more Meeting Discussion about 1 of 3.

However, outside the meetings, people continue to talk about the surprise loss of 1 of 3. Some people are asking a lot of questions.

The Housing Committee meetings become a regular routine of Study, Plan, and Organize.

There are many topics to be addressed. The usual tasks still need to get done.

Committee Member 1: "I suggest that we all take some time to know the whole report and re-address next tenth. The matter is shelved."

A few Housing Committee Members and Apprentices have been transferred. Species Relations and Security need more people.

Purstenpodler has been getting more important tasks, lately. She's been doing some of the things that Committee Members usually do.

Actually, it's not just her. There are four others who seem to be increasingly asked to do more and take on more responsibility. Purstenpodler and the others have also noticed who else is in the clique.

As everybody takes their seats in the meeting auditorium, the "in the clique" Apprentices discreetly acknowledge each other. They sit in their usual seats and give no outward indication that they're aware of "something" going on.

Committee Member 1 opens the meeting and introduces the first topic. The Committee Clerk begins recapping the previous discussion.

Purstenpodler notices that several of the Committee Members appear to be distracted. They seem to be uncomfortable about something and are trying to hide their discomfort.

An aide enters the auditorium and approaches the Members table. The aide hands a note to Committee Member 3 and they whisper a brief discussion. The aide walks away.

Everybody in the auditorium adjusts forward in their chairs.

Committee Member 3: "My aide has brought me some information. This is an early report and will need to be verified."

Committee Member 3—standing from his chair: "The Serpils have taken Island 5."

First, there is silence. Then a murmur grows in the auditorium.

Many of the people attending the meeting are outwardly agitated. Most of the Apprentices are unsure about how to react, other than displaying anxiety.

Purstenpodler casually glances at a few of the others in the clique. They remain calm and exchange Inside eye-blinks.

Purstenpodler is one of two from the clique to be advanced early to Housing Committee Member. She's a little unsure about contributing to the Committee as a Member.

She wasn't an Apprentice for long. She is apprehensive about being directly involved in the decision-making.

Things look different from this side of the Members table.

One of the first things Purstenpodler is going to do is get her own Burrow. She is a Committee Member now, and she's still living with her parents.

Purstenpodler has been interested in a particular place. The Burrow land is part of a new batch of Housing that the Committee's been discussing.

New Housing has mostly been developed in large sections of valley land.

Typical Drel housing is a two-story Burrow with the living area mostly underground. The above-ground level of the structure is utilitarian—used as a garage, office space, storage, etc. The Drels use gently sloped ramps to get between levels.

Every Burrow has land around it to grow food. The usual development of a new Burrow includes a surrounding crop system.

The new batch of Housing includes areas around the Capitol that have not been previously developed. There are many places that are higher up on the mountains.

Some places near the top are only large enough for one Burrow. Purstenpodler would like one of these homes.

Purstenpodler should be able to get the exact homesite that she wants. One of the Inside perks of being a Member of the Housing Committee is having first choice of Housing.

Committee Member 1, who was Committee Member 3 before the recent re-alignment, opens the meeting and introduces the first topic.

The Committee Clerk recaps the previous discussion of the topic.

Committee Member 1 still does his play of having an aide bring important news to him during a meeting. This play has become so familiar that many people in the auditorium respond like it's part of the usual proceedings—except that it's a more interesting part.

Committee Member 1: "My aide has brought me some information. This is an early report and will need to be verified."

Committee Member 1 stands up from his chair to deliver the news. He takes a big breath, probably for dramatic purposes. The crowd responds accordingly.

Committee Member 1: "The Serpils have attacked the Tubells again. This time it's at Island 1."

First, there is silence. Then a murmur grows in the auditorium.

Purstenpodler now sits in the middle of the Housing Committee table. They have been losing their Member 1 and advancing someone new about every tenth of a year.

Purstenpodler hasn't been a Committee Member for very long. At this rate, she may be Committee Member 1 soon.

She's good with that. Most of the Housing tasks are routine, anyway.

The other three from the old Apprentices clique were advanced to other Committees.

Two were sent to be Apprentices for the Species Relations Committee, and both are now Members. One went straight to Member of the Infrastructure Committee.

They all maintain their Apprentices clique—discreetly. They know that they might be able to help each other, or get help, at some point in the future.

Committee Member 1 opens the meeting and prepares to introduce the first topic. It's not on the schedule.

Committee Member 1—between happy and relieved: "Multiple confirmed reports state that the Tubells have repelled the Serpil shuttle attack at Island 1."

Committee Member 4: "My sources say that the Tubells invented a type of mobile shield that reflects NRG weapon discharges. It deflects the blasts back in the direction from which they were fired. Apparently, it was effective against the Serpils."

Purstenpodler contributes a thought. "For the Tubells, that almost sounds like a weapon."

Committee Member 8: "It's still defensive. If they don't get shot at, their shield won't send anything back."

The Tubells are known to be pacifists. The Tubells are not timid, though. They have been the first Species to make numerous advancements.

The Drels are *not* pacifists. The Drelstenprupo prefer not to fight, but if backed into a corner, Drels will get as scrappy as necessary.

Purstenpodler thinks Serpils may perceive the peaceful nature of Tubells as a weakness and the Serpils are drawn to attack the Tubellstacene by some primal instinct.

It could just be that Serpils consider the Tubells to be "good eatin'."

Today is a Support Occupation day. Purstenpodler is contributing in Food Supply.

Purstenpodler has done shifts in the Food Exchange Building, but she usually helps with harvesting, including at her own Burrow.

It seemed strange the first few times that she was on a harvest crew at her own home.

Purstenpodler's crew truck pulls into the Processing Building with their second harvest of the day. She's expecting to take a good break and get a great lunch. One of the Inside perks of Food Supply is first choice of the incoming foods.

Purstenpodler gets out of the truck, returns her Beel Net to the tool shed, and heads for the lunchroom. Someone runs up to her with a message.

The messenger hands her a note as he tells her what's on it. "The Serpils have attacked the Tubell Mainland, Continent 5. As Housing Committee Member 1, your presence is required at the auditorium for a Special Joint Committee meeting."

The messenger is certainly from the Security Committee. He escorts her to a waiting car. They drive off fast and are soon at the auditorium.

Three representatives from each of the higher Committees are supposed to be in attendance at Special Joint Committee meetings. Not everybody can be collected in time, so you never know who or how many will make it.

The auditorium is already packed with people. This building is about four times larger than the Housing Committee auditorium, which is always mostly empty.

So far, Purstenpodler is the only one from the Housing Committee, Member or otherwise. She feels outnumbered.

While the assembled people are taking seats and getting organized, she scans the auditorium for anybody from Housing. She would like to see another Member, but even an Apprentice or an aide would be nice.

Purstenpodler recognizes some of the Committee Members in the auditorium. She knows the former Housing Members who are now in, or leading, other Committees. It's an important circle of friends.

Executive Committee Member 1: "The Serpilgeneret has attacked the Tubells at 3 of 5. Obviously, this level of attack is unprecedented."

Species Relations Committee Member 1: "This will have potentially serious ramifications for long-term World Stability."

She's been advanced again.

Purstenpodler is now in the Executive Committee.

She doesn't know of anyone else who went directly from Housing to Executive. Three other Members from her former Housing circles are already in the Executive, but they were in other Committees first.

Purstenpodler is confident. She's been playing this game her whole life.

She's got her Inside sources across Drel society and all over the planet—except for the Tubells. Nobody has sources within the Tubellstacene.

Most importantly, Purstenpodler has her many circles of friends throughout the Committees. The whole Committee system is circles within circles.

Executive Committee Member 1 opens the meeting and introduces the first topic. It's not on the schedule.

Executive Committee Member 1: "The Serpilgeneret has been repelled from 3 of 5. Their shuttle is returning to Continent 13."

As a newer Member, Purstenpodler is observing and learning the scope of the Committee. The meeting touches on a large number of various topics. This is where the important issues get decided.

Naturally, it requires a lot of time to *make* a decision.

After the meeting, everybody files out of the auditorium and into the back corridors. It was a good meeting. Much was discussed, and a decision was actually reached.

Purstenpodler navigates her way through the corridors packed with people. There are about ten times more Members in the Executive than there were in Housing. Every Member has their inner circle orbiting around them, too.

One of the things she learned in Executive is that the Geminy have been steadily Claiming land in Continent 6. Other than that, the Geminy have been quiet.

Some say too quiet.

Quiet sounds good to Purstenpodler. Now that the Serpil–Tubell conflict is over, it would be good if things were quiet for a while!

The Speaker rubs her Donma patch above her right eye, to center herself. She steps up to the podium. She looks out at the large crowd in the outdoor staging area.

The large industrial complex is at her back. She adjusts her microphone. The wind ruffles her papers. The seated audience is silent in anticipation.

She begins with a greeting smile. "As we open this spaceport and begin launching shuttles and starships, we would like to acknowledge the one who made it all possible. His revolutionary accomplishments forever changed our understanding of science and our understanding of the solar system that we live in. His enormous volume of work shaped many of the fields necessary for the endeavor that we now undertake."

She continues enthusiastically, "As we look to colonize the neighboring worlds, we seek to secure for our Species . . . a place in the future."

The audience is captivated.

"We *wish* to make this effort so that the Roshuda Geminy may continue to learn and grow."

"We *must* make this effort so that the Roshuda Geminy will *not* be subject to extinction by a single global catastrophe."

She stands tall and proud. "We built this spaceport, we launch this starship, and we strive for a great Roshuda Geminy future—in your honor, Rigeus Donmahy!"

The Serpil guard bursts into the Serpil Analyst's office. "Your Drel spy is here. He says he has more information regarding the new Geminy Spaceport."

The Analyst snaps to attention. She has been waiting and hoping to get more of this high-value information. "Bring him in."

The Drel enters the doorway. He pauses briefly, stands up straight, and puts on a greeting smile. He extends a folder of documents.

The Serpil guard behind him disrespectfully pushes the Drel into the room.

The Analyst laughs, then gets impatient. "Good to see you. What do you have?"

The Drel ingratiates himself to her. "I obtained the information you wanted."

The Analyst scans the contents of the folder. She pauses at a few places. She references a checklist.

She is pleased with the information, but she doesn't want to show it. "This is good. Be assured, we will not attack your home Region."

The Drel snivels. "You said that if we got this information for you, that you wouldn't attack the Drelstenprupo. I understood that to mean anywhere, not just my Region."

The Serpil Analyst waves dismissively. "We won't attack the Drels, as long as your people don't interfere with us."

The veiled threat is not lost on the Drel operative. He will emphasize this threat in his report to the Species Relations Committee Member who secretly gave him the information and sent him on this mission.

A COMET TALE

The Comet floats in eternity through the silence of space. It's a silence so deep, so deafening, that patterns emerge to rebel against the silence.

The vibration of an impact. An ice crystal forming and growing. Water evaporating away.

These things create sound waves. The sounds are not heard in open space, from the outside, but the sounds reverberate within the Comet itself.

One can appreciate the Comet's defiance of the silence in space.

"You may not hear me but, *I make sound!*"

Over a span of Time incomprehensible, the Comet experiences vibrations of sound. An impact with a dust particle—*bang!* A collision with a water molecule—*boom!* An ice crystal growing—*crackle!* The eternal sound of silence.

A star distinguishes itself from the others.

The star becomes slightly brighter. It becomes bigger. The star becomes a focal point in the Comet's sky. As the Comet drifts, the star gets closer.

Time drifts along with the Comet.

The star grows from a point of light to an instrument of heat. The solar wind melts ice on the Comet's surface. At first, a few notes like a whispered prophecy—then a drum roll like an intro to a Symphony.

Time marches on.

A sphere adds itself to the Comet's sky. It's a living world that gives the Comet an audience. As it passes the world, so near, the people look up and behold the Comet.

The Comet grows larger in their sky. The people point to it, as if they're reaching for the Comet itself.

The Comet plays its Symphony. It's a performance that will not be heard or forgotten.

The audience send messages to each other through satellites in orbit, messages that applaud the Comet, applause that makes no sound.

The sphere recedes.

The instrument of light and heat dims.

The echoes fade.

Drops of water, so recently composed, drift back to the Comet's surface.

The star becomes just another point of light. The Symphony is over. The silence grows. Again, the time has come to talk in silence with the darkness.

The Comet measures time not by cycles, not by lifetimes, not by civilizations, not by Species.

The Comet measures time by the music it makes.

R9

Dorpenlestrup has received numerous commendations for his work in the Transportation Committee. He's happy about it and proud of his accomplishments.

The massively large Drel towns may give the impression that it would take a long time to get to places. However, Drels can get in their personal vehicles and usually be anywhere they want to go in a very short time with little or no stress.

Even going from town to town is relatively quick and very efficient.

Most of this is due to the efforts of the Transportation Committee. Dorpenlestrup contributed to many of the successful projects.

One of Dorpenlestrup's favorite projects is the Automated System. Even though he likes it, he always has a moment of hesitation before switching to the Auto-System.

Most people have this same reaction. For a short time after switching, there's a period of adjustment where people need to allow themselves to trust the Auto-System.

People know about the rare incidents when there are injuries or fatalities while on the Auto-System. This is usually due to extremely unpredictable circumstances.

The possibility of being injured while on the Auto-System is minuscule. The probability of being killed while on the Auto-System is almost a statistical impossibility, but it does happen on rare occasions.

The risk is acceptable, considering the benefits of the Auto-System.

Time and stress are two of the most important considerations of those benefits. The Auto-System is time-tested and reliable. Traveling on the Auto-System is fast and easy.

Dorpenlestrup appreciates the option to drive his vehicle if he likes, or not drive if he prefers, and still be able to get to where he wants, quickly.

The Auto-System also improves Transportation Stability, courtesy of the Transportation Committee.

The two old Roshuda friends are sitting on an island beach in the shade of a tree, sipping drinks, relaxing, and watching the waves.

Friend One reminisces, "Remember the Comet that passed by a while back?"

Friend Two lazily answers, "Yeah, we got some NRG from it."

Friend One confides, "Yes, but what isn't widely known is that we also took some rock and ice samples. Our scientists have been studying the samples since then."

Friend Two is surprised. "It doesn't seem like there would be much to study for that long of a time."

Friend One exclaims, "For that Comet, there is. It wasn't like other Comets for a few reasons."

Friend One explains. "All other comets we know about travel in a circular orbit around our sun, along with the planets, moons, and everything else. That Comet entered our solar system at a steep right angle to the plane of the ecliptic."

Friend One pauses while a wave crashes on the shore. "It came from above us, from our north side, and continued on in a direction to our south . . . and it passed through in a straight line. Though, in passing through our system, the Comet's trajectory *was* slightly altered."

Friend Two begins to understand. "So, you're saying that the Comet wasn't part of our solar system? It came from a different solar system?"

Friend One nods. "That's a possibility, even likely. We really don't know where it came from."

Friend One delights in sharing the fun part. "What we do know is that it contained two elements of which we were previously unaware."

Friend Two is intrigued. "New elements?"

Friend One concludes, "Yeah, the Comet samples contain hydrogen, helium, iron . . . many known elements. There are also two elements that we have never discovered before. They still haven't been officially named yet."

Friend Two muses, "I wonder how old that Comet is. Has it seen other civilizations in other solar systems, in the ancient past? Will it see other people in another part of the galaxy, in the distant future?"

Friend One loves the tack in the conversation. "Those are all good questions and only a few of the questions that our scientists have been asking. It is really an amazing coincidence that we happened to have recently launched a spacecraft and were able to get those samples at precisely the time that this special Comet passed by."

Friend Two exclaims, "Talk about timing!"

Friend One marvels at an irony. "Most of our people admired the Comet for a short time, celebrated its appearance in our sky, then they mostly went on about their daily lives. For some of us, the Comet *became* part of our daily lives and still is."

Friend Two is still pondering the Comet. "It occurs to me that this Comet will still be out there, traveling through space, when all that we know and will ever learn, no longer exists."

Friend One chuckles, then shares the juiciest part. "Our people walked on it. We left Geminy footprints and equipment on that Comet! Those footprints may exist for a very, *very* long time."

It feels strange to Dorpenlestrup to be sitting in the Apprentices Wing again, after having been a Member in the Transportation Committee for so many years.

Everything changed when the Roshuda Geminy built a spaceport and sent a starship to the asteroids. Everything changed again when the Serpilgeneret built a spaceport and launched their own starship.

Dorpenlestrup knows that it's still a promotion to be in this new Space Committee, even as an Apprentice. More than half of the Apprentices here are former Members of other Committees. It's likely that most of the rest of the Space Committee Apprentices were close to being advanced to Members of their various Committees.

Dorpenlestrup expects to be advanced to Member soon.

A few of the current Space Committee Members were in the Species Relations Committee during the "Serpil Spaceport scandal." Some of them will likely be removed, and Space Committee Apprentices will be advanced to Members.

Investigations continue regarding the Serpil Spaceport scandal. The Serpils were not supposed to be able to get a spaceport before the Drels had their own built and operational.

Dorpenlestrup knows what the outcome will be when all the investigations conclude. The Executive Committee will find that there were too many circles-within-circles working the Serpilgeneret, and the Serpils played the Drels.

A number of lower-level Drels will be reprimanded and demoted. Several higher-level Drels will be praised and promoted. Then, everybody will move on.

Space Committee Member 1: "The Roshuda Geminy appear to be acquiring a substantial amount of high-grade NRG from the asteroids."

Space Committee Member 2: "My aide has brought me some information. This is an early report and will need to be verified. The Serpilgeneret starship is approaching the asteroids."

Rand Meyousigh knows that he could be a wealthy Roshuda. He's sitting on a fortune of NRG. He's also stuck on an asteroid.

Even when he's ridiculously busy, he thinks a lot about all the good that could come from the NRG. His angst intensifies while he languishes on the lonely asteroid and an excruciating amount of time slips away.

His situation and the uncertain fate of his treasure are tormenting.

A shadow moves across the asteroid. It's a starship.

The Serpil sits at the control panel, observing the incoming information. He likes this—being on a starship. It's good that he's part of the action sometimes.

He reports the progress as it happens. "We are in the area of the objective asteroid."

It's something very special to be on this first mission, too. The Serpilgeneret are now a spacefaring Species and expanding into the asteroids.

"We are in position over the asteroid."

He waits for the tactical to be completed.

"The Geminy target has been eliminated."

Everything is going as planned.

"The Advancing Force is dropping to the surface."

If he had stayed on the planet, he would probably be involved with Boat Patrol. This is much better.

"The NRG is secured."

As he concludes, he grins a big, reptilian, teeth-filled Serpil smile.

"NRG transport complete. We have the NRG."

Yes, being in space is good.

"The Asteroid Wars have begun!"

Dorpenlestrup is so tired of hearing that!

Dorpenlestrup gets into his car. He activates the Auto-System and takes a moment to catch his breath. He begins to relax as the vehicle gets underway.

Dorpenlestrup is now Space Committee Member 14, and the Committee has grown considerably since its founding. Soon, Space Committee will be the second-largest Committee.

Of course, Executive needs to always be the largest Committee.

Dorpenlestrup's car parallels the ridge and begins to drop down into the valley. It's always an impressive sight. The Drel Housing developments spread across the entire valley for as far as you can see in every direction.

Dorpenlestrup's Burrow is near the summit on the other side of the valley.

When Dorpenlestrup was in the Transportation Committee, he was able to work a deal with a friend in Housing. They both got nice roads to their exclusive homes, with full access to the Auto-System.

Dorpenlestrup marvels at the sight of the development below. The Drel Sprawl is largely possible due to a lot of great work by his Transportation Committee. Drels are proud of their elaborate and efficient road systems.

Other Species have tried to emulate Drel transportation systems, but it doesn't work as well for them. Consultants have tried working with the Serpilgeneret and the Roshuda Geminy, but the problems are not with the Drel systems.

The Drels make their transportation work efficiently because of the way Drels use them. Things are clearly understood by all, and Drels are gracious toward each other.

The others don't always implement, and sometimes don't follow, designed protocols. The Serpils and Geminy can be too timid or too pushy, which causes confusion and chaos.

Much of Drel traffic is short-distance travel or otherwise not on the Auto-System. Drels can travel much faster and safer, partly because of their consideration for other drivers.

There's no such thing as a "Drel jam car" or a "reckless Drel driver." These are the reasons why the others are unable to have the efficiency of travel that the Drels enjoy.

The Drelstenprupo may not be the most aggressive Species, the boldest Species, or the most creative Species, but Drels are the most amicable.

Drels benefit the most because of this.

Of course, well-designed transportation systems are helpful, too.

The vehicle powers down, breaking Dorpenlestrup's train of thought. A quick glance out the window confirms. He's home.

Isregy Donmahu is excited to be joining the Geminy Diplomatic Team.

Already, at his first conference, he's met and become friends with a Tubell Initiate, Nable Stelectu.

Isregy and Nable meet frequently at the cafeteria for dinner and conversation.

Isregy and Nable both talk in their own languages. They wear translation devices, which the Drels invented. The Geminy and Serpils wear the devices over an ear. The Tubells strap the devices against their bodies somewhere, usually between their eyes and tentacles, but sometimes above an eye.

Nable speaks proudly of his Species. "The Tubellstacene have accomplished much and made some great contributions to the world. A Tubell was the first to travel through the air. The great Beel Tectalnus invented the first aircraft."

Isregy acknowledges as much. "Our history tells of seeing that aircraft, a giant balloon with a boat attached at the bottom. It was the first time that the Geminy had seen anything besides clouds and meteors in the air. The sighting inspired us to consider air travel and eventually build our own aircraft."

Nable expounds on his ancestral hero. "Beel adapted the concept of the boat rudder to make advanced aircraft possible. Beel's work has been the basis of many great accomplishments. Beel had a lot of great ideas."

Isregy contemplates tangentially, "Our scientists have discovered the remains of a creature that is likely to have been able to travel through the air."

Nable bloviates, "The Serpils sometimes claim that they were the first to invent an aircraft, which is humorous to the Tubells, Blurpy, blurpy. They had a craft, blurpy, but they could not get theirs off the ground. Everyone knows that the Serpils were actually the last to achieve air travel."

Isregy answers sadly, "And the first thing the Serpils did was attack the Tubells."

Nable acknowledges this fact. "Yes, we have always thought that it was curious and suspicious how the Serpils attacked us instead of the Drels. It would have been much more convenient and logical for the Serpils to attack the Drels at that time."

Nable explains, "We have noticed many suspicious curiosities regarding the Drels. Another was how they achieved air travel almost immediately after the Geminy and with designs that were essentially identical to yours."

Isregy agrees. "Yes, we did notice that, too."

Nable postulates. "The Serpils could never get their aircraft to work. Isn't it curiously suspicious that when they were poised to attack the Drels by boat, the Serpils were suddenly able to travel by air? Then, instead of attacking the Drels with their new air power, why did the Serpils go out of their way to *not* attack the Drels?"

The new Drel starship will be run by three Starship Committee Members and an Apprentice. The three Members will rotate being Member 1 on a shift basis, with a majority vote option.

The main priority is to avoid any asteroid battles.

The Drel starship approaches the subject asteroid. It appears to be abandoned. There's evidence of previous mining activity. Nobody is here now, though.

They send down a team to investigate.

Asteroid Team Member 1 reports the findings to the Starship Committee assembled on the starship.

Team Member 1: "The Geminy were here. It doesn't take much time to know that. It's easy to tell by the trash they leave behind."

The Drels would not leave their trash behind when they leave—especially some of the more personal items.

Team Member 1: "The Geminy started a small mining operation here. It looks like they didn't do much. All indications are that nobody has been here for an acceptable length of time."

Team Member 1: "The Geminy left behind a lot of equipment, too. It looks like they left in a hurry. Probly had something to do with the Serpils, though there's no evidence that the Serpils have been here. You can tell that very easily."

The Serpils are even worse about their trash. At least the Geminy try to bury most of their trash, though not very deep.

Team Member 1: "The mining equipment looks like it's in good condition. We'll give it a closer look and hopefully do a test run for some NRG soon."

The Drelstenprupo will work this asteroid.

The people on the surface have an interesting side project, too. They will be able to document, photograph, multi-scan, categorize, and catalog every scrap of the Geminy trash. The Drels learn a lot about other Species by doing this kind of project—including some of the more disturbing things.

The Drelstenprupo are now a spacefaring Species. They have an asteroid to Claim, and all the resources contained therein.

The Drels must go to space, mine the asteroids, and keep up with the other Species, for World Stability.

The three Tubell delegates are standing in Reeg Slinreept's office. They're making disgusting sounds out of the one orifice between their legs.

Reeg can't decide which is worse: the natural Tubell speech or the Serpil translation spoken in a Drel voice.

Reeg feels that it's beneath him to have to listen to them.

Reeg also doesn't like how they never turn to face you. Tubells don't even have a face! With an eye on all four sides of their bodies, they can be looking in any direction. Reeg is never sure if a Tubell is looking at him or looking at something else with a different eye.

The Tubells are pleading for the Serpilgeneret to stop the attacks. It's pointless. The Serpils need to expand.

Also, there is just something about the Tubells that drives Serpils to instinctively want to kill them.

One of the Tubells is trying to make a point. "You have your land. We have our land. We must ask you to refrain from trying to take our land."

Reeg finds it difficult to maintain his attention on what the Tubells are saying.

He can't stand the sound of them any longer. Rolling his head, Reeg signals to the other member of the Serpilgeneret delegation.

The Tubell continues, "There is no reason that we—"

Reeg interrupts the Tubell delegate. "Have them prepared."

The other Serpil delegate is relieved. "I have been thinking the same!"

The other Serpil delegate begins to push the Tubells toward the door. Four large Serpil guards appear.

The Tubells are confused. "Prepared? I don't understand."

Reeg is more interested now. "I want three eyes and a large midsection. You can share the rest among yourselves."

The other Serpil delegate is quick to inform the guard. "I want a whole tentacle and a couple of the eyes."

The Tubells are beginning to understand. "What? We are official representatives of—"

The guard happily acknowledges. "Yes! I'll have it sent over as soon as it's ready."

The Tubells make a few last utterances as they're dragged out of the room.

Reeg exhales and relaxes. "I'm glad that's over."

Isregy Donmahu and his assistant stride down the corridor to the Serpil delegate's office. It's not a meeting Isregy wants to have, but it must be done.

Isregy notices some small bugs crawling around on the dirty floor. He can never get accustomed to how the Serpils seem comfortable living in filth. A small creature bolts from a pile of trash, scurries down the corridor, and stops near the next corner.

Someone needs to come through here with a Beel Net.

As Isregy approaches the entrance to the office, he smells cooked fish. His stomach churns as the stench gets stronger. He suppresses an urge to vomit.

Isregy turns to his assistant and whispers, "Fish, uuhhgg."

Yomni scrunches up her nose in agreement.

Isregy pauses near the doorway for a moment to prepare himself before entering the Serpil delegate's office.

Reeg sits comfortably reclined at his desk. As the Geminy delegation enters through the front entrance, empty food plates are being removed and carried out a side entrance.

Isregy assumes the posture of the diplomat with a smile. "Reeg Slinreept, I'm Isregy Donmahu. This is my colleague, Yomni Geshurda. Thank you for agreeing to see us before my scheduled appointment with the Tubellstacene delegation."

Isregy and Yomni nod to both Reeg and the other Serpil delegate in the room.

Reeg looks over the two Geminy.

The male, Isregy, is taller, larger, and more muscular than the average Geminy. He's one of those with a dark spot above the right eye.

Reeg still isn't impressed.

The female, whatever her name was, doesn't interest Reeg.

He watches as the two Geminy sit down on the other side of his desk.

Reeg belches along with the first two words. "*That appointment* . . . with the Tubells will no longer take place."

Isregy pauses, taking in Reeg's comment. Isregy and Yomni glance at each other.

Isregy inquires with apprehension, "Why would you say that?"

Reeg smacks his lips, grins, and rubs his belly.

Isregy fishes for information. "I know you don't like the Tubells. However—"

Reeg interrupts casually. "I like Tubells. I think they're delicious."

Reeg pauses for a moment. He rolls his shoulders a few times.

Reeg grins a big, reptilian, teeth-filled Serpil smile. "Their delegation was not an exception."

The realization sinks in. Isregy tries to calm his fear and anger about the disturbing loss of his Tubell friends.

Isregy is incredulous. "You . . . killed the Tubell delegation?"

Reeg remains silent.

Isregy's anger surpasses his fear. "The Tubells are *not* food! They're—"

"Everything is food to the Serpilgeneret," Reeg interjects.

Reeg examines Isregy, then Yomni, in an appraising manner, as if looking at a menu.

Isregy's fear increases but doesn't quite tip the balance over his anger.

Isregy maintains his composure and speaks pointedly. "The Geminy are not food to you or anyone or anything."

Isregy and Reeg lock eyes. A long, tense moment passes between them.

Isregy rises to his full height. "Let's set aside any agreement between our peoples for a moment, Reeg. Let's make a deal between you and me—right now."

Looking put off by Isregy's aggressiveness, Reeg rolls his shoulders forward in that irritating manner Serpils have.

Isregy lays it down. "If you're even slightly considering having me or any of my delegation as a meal, hunt it yourself. Starting with me!"

Reeg looks at the female. She's sitting there calmly, looking back at him. She doesn't seem surprised or concerned at all. Is she just backing his play, or is there something else?

Reeg locks eyes with Isregy again.

Isregy maintains a demeanor of confidence. The look in his eyes conveys an unspoken, yet unmistakable, message. *Do it, so I can kill you.*

Reeg knows about some Geminy customs, like raising their arms in victory after defeating an opponent. He gets the message, though he has no fear and no doubt that he could kill this little Geminy.

It might not be easy, though—and besides, he's not hungry right now.

Reeg waves dismissively. "You may leave."

Isregy stands his ground, unblinking. His muscles are twitching slightly.

He would very much like to attack and kill this repulsive reptile. Isregy has no doubt that he could do it, and quickly. He might have already if he wasn't responsible for Yomni and the rest of the Geminy delegation.

Reeg is losing patience. "Leave *now!*"

Isregy stands firm for two long, deep breaths.

Yomni calmly stands and looks at Isregy, waiting to follow his lead. She's not sure if Isregy will leave, or if he will kill the Serpil.

Isregy gestures for her to depart, or maybe to cover the door. Yomni moves slowly toward the exit while watching Isregy's back.

Isregy is still trying to decide what he's going to do. With great internal conflict, he slowly backs off. Isregy does not turn his back to Reeg as he and Yomni gradually make their way out of the room.

After the Geminy are gone, the other Serpil delegate turns to Reeg and says, "I didn't think you were going to let them leave."

Reeg thinks for a moment. "I believe to do otherwise would be . . . trouble that is better avoided at this time."

Reeg's stomach is feeling queasy.

He's angry that the primates ruined his lunch. "The Geminy. If that irritating food had waited much longer, I could have changed my belief—easily."

The Drels have acquired Inside information that requires a Special Joint Committee meeting. The Committee representatives assemble.

Space Committee Member 1: "Both the Geminy and the Serpils are planning to go to the neighboring planet. They will likely Claim land on the planet and mine the nearby asteroids."

Species Relations Committee Member 1: "The Drelstenprupo must keep up with the others—for Interplanetary Stability."

Executive Committee Member 1: "The Drels will also establish a colony on the other world, and mine the asteroids. But first, we need to review all the reports and discuss all the implications. We'll schedule another meeting in a few tenths."

Isregy affectionately greets his old friend. "Nable Stelectu, you old driftwood. It is good to see you, my friend."

Nable utters "Blurpys" and bounces on three tentacles. "You are a good friend, Isregy Donmahu."

Isregy teases, "Wow, Nable, your blue skin is looking a lot more gray than the last time I saw you. If it keeps going like that, you will end up looking like a Geminy."

Nable cheerfully plays along. "I would be appalled if I looked like a Geminy. Blurpy."

They have known each other for a long time, and they have been through a lot together. They both take a moment to just enjoy each other's presence.

It's a brief moment.

Nable gets to the point. "I wanted to talk with you directly and suggest that you be wary of the Drels."

Isregy feigns ignorance. "The Drels? The Serpils have always been adversaries of the Geminy. We've never had any problems with the Drels."

Nable doesn't catch the sarcasm. "Are you sure? I believe that one of the things our two Species have in common is curiosity."

Isregy smiles. "I agree, Nable. I would add to that, a desire to take the initiative."

Nable chuckles at the praise. "Blurpy, blurpy. I agree with that."

Nable makes his pitch. "The Geminy have had a curiosity about space travel for a long time, and your people have obviously demonstrated the initiative to accomplish it. The Geminy, living on other worlds, and on ships in space. It's amazing to think about."

Isregy is gracious. "The Tubells were the first to accomplish air travel. Without your example, we might never have thought of space travel."

Nable dismisses the compliment. "The Serpils and the Drels have never shown any interest in space travel. Yet, they accomplished it almost immediately after the Geminy."

Isregy gets back to the point. "Yes, and with spaceport technology that is almost identical to ours."

Nable is relieved that his friend sees it. "I'm glad you realize this, Isregy."

Nable moves on. "For this reason and many others, we wish to warn your people about the Drels."

Isregy adds to the equation, "You know, of course, a large faction of Geminy believe that the Serpils are too powerful and an alliance with the Drels is necessary."

Nable is adamant. "The Tubells believe that the Drels are not to be trusted!"

Isregy does trust his old friend. "I respect your concern, Nable. I also appreciate your friendship and the effort you made to tell me this."

Nable understands the diplomatic language. "I appreciate your friendship, too. That is why I had to speak with you."

Isregy drops the diplomatic airs. "Our talks are always good. I suggest that we have more conversations on subjects that are more pleasant."

Nable slumps. "It is with much regret that I must tell you that this will be our last meeting."

Nable lowers the two eyes that are looking at Isregy. "The Tubells are facing extinction."

Isregy is already aware of the possibility. "Nable, if we work together, we still might be able to save your Species."

Nable looks one eye back at Isregy. "You mean, if we fight together. This is not our way . . . and you know it."

Isregy pleads. “You have to fight if you’re going to survive.”

Nable has difficulty believing the fate of his Species. “You don’t understand.”

Nable pauses for a moment, trying to find a way to say it.

Isregy tries to think of another way to convince Nable and the Tubells to fight without belaboring the point.

Nable hints at it. “Have you seen any younger Tubells?”

Nable backtracks. “We have watched the Serpils grow in numbers. We have seen them become very powerful with the resources that they bring back from the asteroids.”

Nable explains. “We know that the Serpils will not stop taking our land and hunting Tubells for food. For a long time, we have been unwilling to bring offspring into the world, knowing what their fate would be.”

Nable looks all eyes to the horizon. “The Tubells still alive are unwilling or unable to reproduce now. When the last of the Tubells dies, there will be no more. We will soon be extinct.”

Nable is filled with sadness. “It is too late for us to venture from this world. We will not be a Species that lives on other worlds or on ships in space.”

Nable reluctantly accepts it. “The things that we have accomplished will have to be enough for my Species. Our time in the light has passed. For the Tubellstacene Species, this is the end.”

ACKNOWLEDGMENTS

Special acknowledgement goes to Dnar, for bringing these chronicles to the Humans of Earth. Dnar has been doing an excellent job with everything from the big-picture concept to the seemingly endless minutia. Dnar is a credit to his Species. It is my great pleasure (and burden) to be Dnar's Human assistant and representative on Earth.

Dnar refers to everyone at Brown Books Publishing Group as a credit to the Species. Thank you for your help and contributions Milli Brown, Tom Reale, Brittany Griffiths, Tony Daniel, Ben Davidoff, Mary Winzer, Danny Whitworth, Jonathan Alcott, and Abby Gregory.

Others who have been helpful and who are considered to be a credit to the Species include Tone Hoover and Lori Hoover.

One who might not necessarily be considered a credit to the Species, yet has still been helpful, is Milo Goob.

AUTHOR BIO

Rand Paulsen hails from the American Southwest, having lived mostly in Nevada.

Rand's early years consisted of on-again, off-again construction work and a variety of temp jobs while attending college. He was rewarded with wide-ranging exposures and some amazing experiences. During his backpacking period, Rand "bagged some peaks" and traveled as far as Guam.

With interests ranging from history to space travel, and drawing on his adventurous background, Rand humorously shares the individual life stories of four very different, intelligent species in the fast-paced journey of the Ascending Species series.

In Rand's distinctive and fun way, he hopes to encourage consideration of time, perspective, and Species.